The First Church of Siren

Book Two: Mission to Earth

A Novel By

Wig Nelson

ISBN-10 0983314454
ISBN-13 9780983314455

Printed in the United States of America

Front Cover Photograph © Jean Schweitzer/Dreamstime.com

Back Cover Author Photograph by Jennifer Breiling

Also By Wig Nelson

Sirens

The Psychic

The Conga Player's Dues

Jacks and Hands

Starry Night

Tall Tales Long & Short

Tall Tales Long & Short II

The Little Shop of Lyrics

A Feeling of Power
The Musical

Xeries Press

Indialantic, Florida

xeriespress.com

C D's By Wig Nelson

On The Simple Side

Wigged Out

Fire and Life

Get There

Soundscapes

Fools You Bet On

A Feeling of Power
The Musical

Some of the creator's work falls into a class all of its own with cell and synapse shining forth and shouting perfection from the rooftops. It blazingly dares you to find a flaw in its design and intention. It beckons you not to join its ranks, but rather celebrate the possibility of the existence of such glory. We are all the richer for it by merely occupying the same universe, and we are reduced to tears by such impossible beauty.

A thousand ships and starlit trips will plead to deify a face and place it in our quarter. We do well to pray for breath enough to focus a clear mind and eyes to capture a word for which there is no word. There is only purity until we corrupt it with the shortcomings of our senses. Yet, we have no choice but to try to make it part of ourselves. After all, some of us are only human.

This book is dedicated to the sirens.
They knew they couldn't stay away.

Acknowledgments

I'd like to thank my favorite pilot, Nigel *Cap'* Walker.
And he'd like to thank Carla Dugan for returning from the dead.

We must slow down to a human tempo and we'll begin to have time to listen.

- *Thomas Merton*

Be very careful what you wish for.

- Master Phodan of Preculis

The First Church of Siren

Book Two:

Mission to Earth

Prologue

Capt. Walker found love late in life. Carla Dugan captured his heart at the age of sixty and left him a widower at sixty-three. No wonder his heart failed him when he saw her walk up their driveway a year after he left a bouquet of flowers at the site of her interment. He clutched his chest and began to cough as hard as he could, remembering the advice of how to save your own life when having a heart attack. As it turned out, that wasn't necessary because he wasn't really alone. Aside from his golden retriever, Isabelle, who was always dutifully glued to his side, and Carla, who couldn't possibly be real, could she, there was a man in a sky blue robe with a smiling face, looking down at him peacefully when he regained consciousness. He looked up into the man's soft blue eyes and found comfort there. He felt a great weight born of exhaustion rather than any cardiac malady. His dry lips formed the words, "My heart . . ."

"Is fine, now," said the tall man known as Grand Master *Phodan* of the planet *Preculis*. "You had some plaque lining the walls of your pulmonary and coronary arteries, and some of it broke loose and lodged in the right ventricle of your heart. I have removed any danger of that happening again."

"What?" asked a sleepy Nigel Walker. "Removed the danger? But how?"

"I reached into your chest with this," said The Grand Master holding up a small cylinder with a three tined tuning fork at either end. "I also used it to remove the arthritic tissue insulting the tendons in both of your knees. I'd say that, physically, you are about ten years younger than you were when you woke up this morning."

"What would you have me say? Thank you?" asked Cap' Walker bitterly. "You are also responsible for delivering that . . . monster to my door. Would you have me thank you for that as well?"

"Say whatever pleases you or doesn't, Cap' Walker. All we ask is that you consider the proposition we presented you with three days ago."

"Yes, I remember now," said Walker. "You walked across the field from out by the lake and were upon us in an instant. Isabelle never gave a peep, which is a first. She's the best watchdog that God ever put on this green Earth."

"I'm sure she is," said The Grand Master. "Your furry friend there has a kind heart and would lay down her life for yours in the blink of an eye were she ever called upon to do so. But she knew that you were never in any danger and didn't see the need to rise and tax her painful hip for no good reason. We have become good friends since then, and I was able to give her some medical relief as well. Her hip no longer bothers her, and since your knees are feeling much better of late, she expects to resume your abandoned regimen of morning walks to the reservoir. She may not ever catch the ducks, but she still would like to startle them into the water. It's a game she relishes and has sorely missed for the past few years."

"How do you know where I used to walk my dog?"

"She told me, of course. And that's not all she had to say. She is glad that I have come here to St. Cloud in search of a pilot. She has been concerned about your sedentary lifestyle for some time. The way she tells it, you have been wasting away, marking time, waiting for her to pass like your beloved, Carla."

"Don't you mention her name to me, you bastard. Do you mean to toy with my pain? Pick at the scab for your own pleasure?"

"I wish you only peace, Cap' Walker. Isabelle told me where your Carla was placed to rest. I was truly saddened to hear that she suffered painfully from her condition. I am sorry that I had not arrived here in time to return her health to her. But she is healthy now."

"She is dead now."

"She sits on your bed in the other room. She awaits a long overdue reunion with you and Isabelle."

"What? A clone? Is that what you've done? Dug up her poor body and made a God-forsaken copy of her?"

"There has been no digging, Cap'. She is not a copy of your dear wife. She *is* your dear wife."

"Nonsense. What you are saying is impossible. You can't raise the dead, or are you Jesus Christ or something?"

"No one has raised the dead. The dead are meant to enjoy the rest that is their reward. I have merely revisited one who once was your beloved wife, Carla."

"I never asked you for a clone," said Walker miserably.

"I suggest you talk to her before you reserve any absolute opinions about the matter of her legitimacy. You may find yourself pleasantly surprised."

"But why? What is all this for?"

"As I have said, I am in need of your services. I have need of a pilot."

"I'm retired," said Walker.

"I need you to come out of retirement for a short while. Your training and services will take less than two months of your time. Then you and Carla and Isabelle will have your peaceful life and many years to enjoy it. You won't even retain any memory of my having been here at all."

"You intend to brainwash us, is that it?"

"Nothing of the sort," said Master *Phodan*. "You and your wife have no need to retain the memory of our encounter, Cap', while Isabelle, on the other hand, would like to remember me as we have become quite close."

"You leave my dog alone, Mister . . . er"

"I am Master *Phodan* of the planet *Preculis*."

"Oh, goody. I'm Batman, pleased to meet you."

"No, I'd say you're about to become more like a middle-aged Luke Skywalker," said The Grand Master.

Chapter One

Nigel Walker had always been referred to as *Cap' Walker* for as long as he could remember. The strange thing about that circumstance is the fact that he had never in his forty years of maritime service been the captain of a ship. At first, he was a boatswain or "warrant officer" in the Merchant Marines, his principal duties being responsible for the rigging, anchors and cables aboard ship. Then upon returning to seaman's school, he received his commercial captain's license and served for thirty years as a pilot for Carnival Cruise Lines.

Since cruise ship captains are forbidden to enter any port city for fear of huge insurance liabilities and varying characteristics of the charted waters, a "pilot" is always sent out to the ship to negotiate the passage to the mooring. Cap' Walker's pilot vessel had a captain of its own, but he never enjoyed that official title for himself. Those who knew he lacked the designation called him Cap' as a harmless pet name, and those who didn't always assumed he held the rank. The only person who didn't call him Cap' Walker or simply "Cap'" was his lovely wife of three short years. She always called him Nigel.

Grand Master *Phodan* made his case clearly and left him to mull over the decision for a short while with his wife, Carla, and his four-legged companion, Isabelle. He cautiously made his way to the bedroom and slowly opened the door. Carla looked up at him shyly and her eyes smiled at him beneath the bangs of her short auburn locks. Her lips curled up into a slight grin as well, and she said, "Nigel, I've missed you, dear."

"Don't call me Nigel, Miss . . ."

"It's Mrs. My name is Mrs. Carla Walker."

"Then you must be something straight out of hell," said Cap' trying to punish her for bringing up the feelings that he had missed for so long. He had lost Carla over a year ago to ovarian cancer and the end days were nothing short of a torture session for both of them."

"I'm pain free, Nige . . . err, Cap'. That's what they did for me. I feel wonderful. My body feels like it did when we were first dating. Do you remember back then? You made me wait ten long years before you finally bought me a ring."

"Those devils did a fine job of it, I'll say that. You don't look a day older than the time we first met. They've done a good job of briefing you about your past as well."

"No one had to brief me, Cap'. I remember every moment we've ever had together."

"They can't clone a memory, Mrs. Carla Walker."

"Please don't call me that, Cap'. I'm not just some cheap piece of meat that they threw together. I'm your wife."

Isabelle chose that moment to enter the bedroom and jump up on the bed to join Carla. She gave her as thorough a face-licking as she had ever gotten before. She wagged her tail and turned to Cap' Walker and said, "ROOOOF!"

"Well, it looks like you've got her fooled," said Cap' Walker."

"There's no fooling Isabelle," said Carla. "You know that she is the smartest dog that ever lived."

Isabelle adamantly agreed with her assertion, "ROOOF!"

"She's always been a good judge of character," said Walker.

"Thanks for the testimonial, Belle," said Carla. She scratched the top of the dog's head just behind the eyes. "Such a pretty baby," she cooed.

Cap' Walker couldn't shake how eerily familiar the whole setting was. It was like he could close his eyes and open them to life as it was six or eight years ago; what was undoubtedly the best of times for all three of them. He looked over at Carla and noticed the tears rolling down her cheeks. It was a sight he had seldom seen as their life together had never facilitated the need for tears. *A woman's greatest weapon,* he reflected once having said the words out loud to Carla on the rare occasion he was careless with her feelings. The sight of *whomever this woman was* crying was once again clearly his undoing. He addressed the issue pointedly, "Don't do that, Mrs. Walker. You can't just walk into my life out of the grave and sit on my bed and cry." *My God, what am I saying?*

"I haven't walked out of any grave. I don't exactly know how I'm here, but the important thing is that I am. I am here, and I am a real woman with real feelings whether or not you want to give me the benefit of the doubt." Her tears were free flowing now, and she unconsciously reached over to the bedside table for a tissue to blow her nose. The backhanded movement served as evidence that she knew the location of the box without looking at it. Again Cap' Walker was getting the eerie feeling – this time with accompanying gooseflesh as well. *Damn, she looks so perfect. Perfect in every way . . .* and then he noticed, "You don't have a scar on your leg."

"Sorry to disappoint you," she said through her tears.

"My wife had a scar on her leg."

"Well, I don't know what to tell you," she said sobbing through the tissue.

"Well, where did it go?" he asked accusingly.

"How the hell am *I* supposed to know?" she pleaded.

"My *wife* had a nasty scar on her right leg from her knee to her ankle. But you don't have any scar, do you?"

"I guess not."

"Well, can you tell me how it got there? On my wife's leg?"

"You mean on your other wife's leg?" she said angrily. "Yes, of course, I can."

"Then tell it," he demanded.

"Well, I don't exactly remember the precise moment; all I remember is you running into the barn in response to my scream. You saw the blood and said, 'Oh, my dear God in heaven, what happened?' I told you that I didn't really know. I think I was in shock for a moment there. Then you said, 'Oh, honey I'm so sorry. It was the nail. I've been meaning to replace it.' "

Cap' Walker looked at her questioningly and asked, "So you were cut by a nail, is that what you're telling me?"

"Apparently, I wasn't cut by anything at all as you can plainly see. But your other Carla, your first Carla, was cut by an ax. The rusty nail was holding the ax to the wall until it let go."

"You *do* remember," said Cap' Walker.

"Of course, I do, Cap'. You felt so guilty for putting me in harm's way by not replacing that stupid nail that you started to cry. Then I felt guilty for making you feel so bad when actually it didn't hurt all that much. My leg went numb, as I remember it, and I don't even remember feeling the twelve stitches they used to close me up."

"They shot you with a local, remember?"

"If you say so," said Carla still weeping.

"Don't you remember complaining to the doctor about it?"

"Yes, I guess I do. I told him that I hate needles."

"And what did I say to you at that point?"

"You said, 'Oh, be quiet, woman. You're leaking all over the gurney.' "

"That's right, I did. Now, stop your crying, woman. You're leaking all over the bed."

"Oh, Cap', can you feel my heart? Is there any way I can get you back?"

"Call me, Nigel," said Cap' Walker.

Chapter Two

The North Monopole Valley
Of The Planet Siren

Brad Early weighed in at barely one-hundred and thirty pounds. His skin was a sickly yellow hue, and his cheeks had sunken in so far, you could make out the suggestion of a temporal mandibular joint in his skeletal skull. His eyes were bloodshot, and he was leaning weakly on a cane. His lovely siren companion was crying while holding onto his free hand, "Bradley, you have to stop."

"I don't have a choice anymore, Sarah. It's become what I am at this point."

"What? Are you some kind of strange animal now? Like a condor with two arms and two legs?"

"I'm not sure what I am now. I only know what I have to do."

"You have to go over the edge, right? You can't remain standing here on this cliff, can you?"

"No, Sarah. I can't."

"What about us, Bradley? What do we have now? *Is there an us,* now?"

"There is a me, and there is the sky, and there is an edge to this cliff. That's all I know; all I *want* to know."

"But it's so empty. So tragic. Have you looked at yourself in the mirror lately?"

"As a matter of fact, I haven't. Physical appearance isn't as important to me as it once was."

"What about my appearance? Do you still find me beautiful?"

"You're as beautiful as anything else that is tied to this cliff. You are the grass and the flowers and the animals in the field."

"Oh, so now I'm a sheep." She started to cry more fiercely. "I've lost you, now. I see it. I've lost you to a damnable sport, for Creator's sake."

"It's not a sport, Sarah. The Creator made this valley and the monopole beneath it."

"The Creator also made the deep serpents on *Preculis,* but I'm sure they don't have any desire to jump in and swim with them."

"You wouldn't understand. You're too tied to the soil. It's a way of life, a way of finally living. Something that was denied me on Earth. Call it freedom."

"I call it madness, Bradley, and I long for Earth. It was such a mistake to come here to Siren."

"It was the best decision of your life."

"If Master *Phodan* will hear the appeal, I'll be on the first transfer."

"Yes, I'm sure you will. You and all the other *priests* of your *Church of Siren.* The Creator doesn't hear *my* prayers, at least he doesn't dole out any miracles where they are concerned, but somehow you have the ear of Him, why it that, Sarah?"

"You're delusional, Bradley. You're imagining things that aren't really happening. It fuels your anger against me and sends you off the cliff into your non-life. I want you back here."

"Or what, Sarah? How are you going to scold me now? I passed *their* test to get here, and now I can't be a member of your Church. Well, have a nice trip back to Earth if you can swing it," said Brad. Clearly his path was laid out before him, and there was no turning back now. He didn't even turn to witness her retreating form, but he clearly heard her sobs as he stumbled shakily forward to the edge of the cliff. His muscles in his arms and legs had atrophied to the point of near palsy, but what he was evolving into had little use for them now. He tightened the bracelets and anklets that were charged with the positive magnetic force. His shoulder harness and wide belts were equally charged with the positive magnetism that would repel the positive iron mono-core. The strange geophysical anomaly was peculiar to the planet Siren and could be found nowhere else in the entire solar system. It was called a "monopole."

As he inched ever closer to the edge of the cliff, a huge *Sirenian* condor burst forth up the precipice, his lethal beak missing Bradley's vulnerable neck by mere inches. The bird had a wingspan of twenty-two feet and very sharp talons at the end of his three-toed feet. Bradley checked the gauges showing the charge of his tasing pistol. He could fire half a dozen shots and still deliver the 18,000 volts needed to knock out the dangerous predators. A seventh shot would just make them mad. In that unfortunate circumstance, the great condors were known to *play with their food.* With a final prayer that the Creator would hold him safely on this passage, he jumped.

Instead of falling down from the edge of the cliff, he began to rise slowly in the air. The bracelets and anklets held neutral buoyancy above the valley while he activated the small jets on the sides of his wide sash-like belt. He rose quickly through the thermals and reached a height that even the condors rarely attained. The world of Siren grew smaller at such an altitude, and his lack of oxygen would facilitate a light-headed ballet of soaring euphoria that was unequaled by any of the many privileges enjoyed by the celebrated sirens of Earth. The fact that Brad Early was a true human rather than a siren had little to do with his addiction. Both were equally afflicted. But there was another human from their group of newcomers who was as severely afflicted as well. His name was Alex Janzen. He was persuaded to return with the sirens to their home world by the beautiful Durbah Purness. Now Durbah suffered the same fate as her fellow siren Sarah Poole. They had both lost their men to a horrible self-destructive addiction. The most insidious addiction of them all - the addiction to soaring over the monopole valley. Their only hope was to spirit their loved ones away from the valley, by force if necessary, to hopefully bring them back to the core values of reality and thus save their lives. Love would give them the strength to do so. Even if it meant going back on a promise not to use their intense powers of electrum in their eyes and pheromones to drive their human companions mad with desire.

And the *Preculians* were just now listening to the appeal of the Earth sirens that might give them the passage back to Earth. Theirs was said to be a one-way trip from Earth to Siren, but who knew of the dangerous elements of the strange new world that awaited them. They were devoid of the mindset that was essential and possibly took many thousands of years to acquire. They had to learn the hard way that you can't just reach up and embrace paradise without paying your dues and learning the ropes. As Milton tells us time and again: "It is better to rule in hell than to serve in paradise." Unfortunately, the only master being served on Siren was a hideous addiction for Brad Early and Alex Janzen. The sirens had a much nobler path to take. They had a world to rule and save from its own cruel devices. They had a church to build and a mission to engage. A mission to what was once their world - a desperate mission back to Earth.

~

Alex checked the double-straps of his mag-belts. Naturally, the bracelets were worn more than the anklets given the fact that he moved his arms much more than his legs as they were both buoyed against the forces of wind and gravity. He determined that, although it would be wise to replace them soon, the belts would hold fast for the three-hour session he intended to embark upon. Durbah Purness drove him to the summit of the steep *Sirenian* range peak, but was too overcome with emotion to witness his pathetic trek with the help of a wheeled walker to the edge of the precipice. The drop to the bottom of the valley floor was nearly twelve-hundred feet, but that number was inconsequential. His intention was for a direction decidedly up instead of down. The mag-belts would enable him to easily accomplish that task. Once he pushed off from the edge of the cliff, he would engage the small jets to propel him forward. He would steer the attitude nozzles with his thighs and forearms into either a straight forward ascent or a rolling climb that had become a recent milestone of his abilities. He was a rocket man.

He was defined by his time breaking the law of gravity. The hours he logged were a measure of his evolution into something otherworldly, something more than human and undoubtedly greater than mere *sirenity*. The sirens were a beautiful people beyond a doubt, but the humans who embraced the monopole valley understood a concept of greatness that surely escaped them. Sirens were content to live in harmony with nature and each other, whereas the monopole rocket men were destined to be nature's master.

Alex remembered his dreams of flying during his life back on Earth. He would wake with the dim recollection that he had done something special for the sake of doing it, not for the notoriety or reward for accomplishing the feat. Indeed, in his dreams, he often felt that he had to hide his ability from those ordinary men and women who were forever bonded to the ground. He would look furtively around him before pushing off from the ground and landing on the nearest treetop or roofline. In his dream, he would crouch down hundreds of feet in the air and cautiously look to see whether anyone had witnessed his extraordinary feat.

But that was then and this was now. Now he was oblivious to any onlookers and felt he had the right to crow from the bottom of his posi-grain-impacted lungs that he was the *master of flight* and a force to be reckoned with. No one would dare to try to keep pace with the *rocket man* from Earth as he blasted off into a world of flight in a waking state. It was no dream this time, and he was determined not to blink lest he miss a single glorious moment of it. But this flight, this day, would end in tragedy.

After ascending to nearly two-thousand feet, the euphoria brought about by the thinning air and hypoxia was interrupted by pain. It was a rude, cruel searing pain at first on both of his shoulder blades, and then he felt the piercing talons of the *Sirenian* condor puncture his pectoral muscles as she crouched into a ball of considerable dead weight intending to ride him to the ground. The bird was massive. Her body was an oily reeking stench of death. Although they were hideous to contemplate, the condors were revered by one of the valley tribes called the *Condoros*. They knew the importance of the huge creatures to rid the valley of rotting diseased meat. They were the scavengers, an all important link in the chain of decomposers along with the maggots and the flies. As such, their appearance and odor were something straight out of hell.

The bird closed its talons more tightly around Alex's shoulders, perhaps to foreshadow what the near-future had in store for him. She twisted her long neck around in front of his face and looked into his eyes. The reddish fire that surrounded her pupils was filled with contempt if not hate itself. She opened her mouth and expelled a maelstrom of smells from hell. Alex couldn't help but think that his own rotting flesh would soon join those smells in a tragic conclusion of his pitiful existence. *Perhaps this is the fitting end of all fliers,* he thought. He opened his mouth and screamed, "Oh, Durbah, I'm so sorry. How could I ever have let this God-forsaken valley take you from me? Please forgive me . . ."

Suddenly Alex felt a searing pain on the left-hand side of his neck. He thought that one of the toe talons of the great bird had punctured his carotid artery right blow his ear. He reached up and his hand closed around a hideous vermin that was biting his neck. It was a flea. He grasped it firmly and pulled it away. Looking down at his hand, he could see that the flea was at least an inch in diameter and still had tatters of his ruined flesh at the end of its needle-sharp teeth. He cast it aside and was relieved to see that it fell to Siren at a faster pace than he and the mammoth bird.

Although the condor would weigh over five hundred pounds in the city of Creston, above the Monopole Valley she weighed only half of that. Still it was plenty to overcome the buoyancy of the mag-belts, and he found himself picking up speed as they fell to the ground. Alex thought briefly about using the jets on his waist mag-belt for a weapon. If he were able to remove his belt and point the jets up into the belly of the bird, she might let go and enable him to fire a shot from his tasing pistol. But there was always the danger of losing the belt if not clasped firmly to his body. To lose a mag-belt was sure death for a flier. His body would settle into the valley on its own and become easy prey for any of the rulers of the valley. There were three of them. Aside from the condoros, there were the viperos and the valegatos, fifty-foot snakes and fifteen-foot cats. Both had poisonous fangs and promised a horrible death. He decided not to separate himself from the mag-belt at all costs.

His only hope was the tasing pistol, but since the creature was clearly holding tightly to his shoulders, any shot would serve to tase him as well. The electric jolt would pass through the huge bird by way of its talons and surge into his chest. He would lose consciousness as would the bird as well, and if they were separated, if the giant bird let go, they would go their separate ways because the buoyancy of his mag-belts would once again send him aloft. It was too much to hope for, and yet his only hope. He fired the gun.

Chapter Three

When Durbah had learned that Alex was lost in the valley, she went to *Phodan* for help. He told her that he would not be able to enter the valley of the tribes because they had a powerful hold over his will. He might lose a priceless artifact of *Preculian* technology to them and that had to be avoided at all costs. But *Phodan* knew Durbah would be immune to the powers of the tribesmen and suggested that she employ the help of one of the sirens who have studied the valley. Christos Somah, the son of Councilman Christos of the Council of Regents, was just such a siren.

Normally, the sirens were very careful not to find themselves in the Monopole Valley. They passed down the story that it was inhabited by three savage tribes who could gain control over your emotions with witchcraft and sorcery. Some thought it was only legend, but others were steadfastly cautious to avoid the valley at all times. After shaping the will of Christos Somah with pheromones and electrum in her eyes, Durbah enlisted his help. *Phodan* met with each of them privately before they left for the valley. There was little he could do for them except wish them well and pray for the return of her friend, Alex. He told Durbah he had given a precious artifact to Christos Somah for their protection and was entrusting her for its safe return. *Phodan* insisted that she keep constant control of his will during the entire duration of their journey.

Durbah and Christos Somah set out for the valley by descending the steep hill from Creston on a dirt path that was adjacent to a series of waterfalls. The falls flattened out into sections of the Creston River that would wind back and forth in a serpentine shape until coming upon the next fall. This was repeated until they found themselves nearly three thousand feet below what would be sea level at the shores of Creston.

In a clearing of the Monopole Valley, there was a light brown haze that hung closely to the ground. It rose up about ten feet in the air and then quickly thinned out to the clarity of a star-filled night sky. High above, in the canopy of the surrounding trees, Durbah heard the low pitched cries of the condor chicks. Their wingspans were only six or seven feet wide, and they hadn't yet learned how to fly. Their mother would gradually help them break the gravitational bond of Siren by loosening posi-charged pebbles and mixing them with a sticky enzyme she produced in a pair of ducts on either side of her long throat. She would regurgitate the enzyme into her chicks, and it would adhere to their stomach linings. This effectively reduced their relative weight while over the Monopole Valley.

When entered the clearing, Durbah and Christos Somah heard the *Valegato* tribe chanting, **"Ah do e na –**

Des oo eh jo ma –

Ah do e na –

Des oo eh jo ma."

The women were lined up on one side of the fire, and the men stood on the other side rocking back and forth from one foot to the other. The men's eyes were closed as they chanted the answer line, **"Des oo eh jo ma"** in response to the call line of the women whose eyes were wide open, **"Ah do e na."**

Back and forth it went until it became a part of their breathing. After chanting their respective lines, they would draw breath precisely in time with the chant on the other side of the fire. They continued the chant and teetered on the brink of hyperventilation until their heads were spinning in a self-hypnotic state of euphoria. To Durbah it seemed very much like a pagan sexual rite given the fact the women wore no clothes above the waist, and they all wore little more than small rags of fur in the front and rear of their belts, which were made of braided light-gray leather.

"It's all very sensual," she said to Christos Somah, who was her guide for the remainder of the excursion.

"Sensual, yes, however, the dance is not the least bit sexual. Quite the opposite, in fact."

"But I just assumed . . . with the way they are dressed."

"The way they are dressed is for *your* benefit, Durbah. And for *mine* as well. The *Valegatos* are not accustomed to wearing any clothes at all. They have no need of protection from the cold because they are a nomadic *tent people* who travel north or south as the need arises to find their desired temperature. Since the sun, what little actually penetrates the posi-grains, is constant all-year-round, the only thing that affects their weather is the sea wind that curls over the crest of the *Sirenian* Mountains and down into the valley. There are no seasons here on Siren."

"What did you call this fog that surrounds us? Posigrains?"

"That's right. This, fog as you call it, is really solid matter. Very fine grains of sand, which are positively charged and have broken away from the bedrock of the river. They float in the air up to about a dozen feet and then their weight brings them back down again to the surface."

"And that is the substance used to form the mag-belts, right?"

"That's right. In the valleys above the equator, the charges are positive. Below, on the opposite side of Siren, the charges are negative. But the monopoles in the southern hemispheres are also negative so the same effect occurs."

"And these tribal people harvest the grains?" asked Durbah.

"They do. They sort of metabolize it when it collects in their lungs. Then during the rituals like this one, they breathe very forcefully into a tightly woven cloth and expel the positively charged grains from their lungs. If they didn't, it could become quite painful for them because the magnetic pole beneath us would be repelling a part of their internal organs."

"And is it dangerous for us to breathe the air down here?" she asked.

"Not really. Short-term exposure is not really a problem. You could stay down here for over a month before you would feel the effects. What little posi-grains you collect will be absorbed by your body and eventually eliminated."

"And then I can finally say my shit doesn't sink?" she offered playfully.

Christos Somah laughed so heartily that tears came to his eyes. Apparently he was familiar enough with the crude Earth expression to be thoroughly entertained by the joke. Durbah brought her attention back to the dancers around the fire. "You say this is not a sexual rite, but it looks very sexual to me," she stated shaking her head.

"Quite the contrary, Durbah. The males have wrapped their organs with woven hide of the *valegatos* or *valley cats*. The animal is where the tribe gets its name. If they became sexually excited, I'm afraid it would be quite painful for them. They have to concentrate very carefully to maintain the demeanor of the chant."

"What are they saying," asked Durbah.

"The women are the *Spirits of the Cat*. Notice the face paint, the whiskers and the eye makeup."

"They are very beautiful," said Durbah.

Christos Somah continued, "The ivory colored fangs that are painted on their chins are made of a paste that is actually the ground-up teeth of the *valley cats*. They taunt the men across the fire and state: **Ah do e na** (ahh-doe-ee-nah), which means. 'I have you now, or now you are in my grasp.' To which the men answer: **Des oo eh jo ma** (days-oo-ay-zjo-mah), which means, 'The Creator begs you to let me go.' Soon the women will act out the ritual by walking around the fire and approaching their dance *partner* from behind. Then, they will lean forward and bite the men on the right side of their necks."

"You're kidding?" said Durbah.

"Just watch," said Christos Somah. "It's a very charming dance. I find it fascinating."

As Durbah watched, the women performed the ritual just as Christos Somah had described, latching onto the necks of the men standing in front of them. She could tell it was merely ceremonial and that the bite wasn't fierce enough to break the skin. Then when they broke away, the fangs were no longer painted on the chins of the women, but were planted upon the necks of the men. She was very moved by the experience.

"It's beautiful," she told Christos Somah.

"And it's very important as well. It is a rite of protection from the *valegatos* or *valley cats* that lie in wait up in the trees along the river during their travels. Since they are guiding us into the valley tomorrow, it is very important they perform this ceremony. They feel it is a matter of life and death."

"I see," said Durbah. "Well, perhaps it is for us as well." She rose from her sitting position by the fire and approached the seated *Shamana,* or *female priest.* She was called Bantahasa, which meant *the wife of Bantah,* and she brandished a large wooden bowl in her lap. Seated next to her sat the tribal elder who wore only the *bonesgatos* or *string of teeth* around his neck. The teeth were from the *valegatos* and were needle sharp. They were sharply curved and measured roughly three inches long aside from the two fangs that hung nearly from his breasts to his navel. The *Shamana* understood Durbah's intention and held the bowl out to her. Durbah then placed her index and middle fingers of her right hand into the bowl and gathered up the white paste. She placed her two fingers on either side of her mouth and drew them downward. The result was two fangs painted down each side of her chin ending with points that thinned out and disappeared on her neck. She slowly walked back to Christos Somah and beckoned him, "Will you be my *dance* partner, Christos Somah?"

"You are a remarkable woman, Durbah," he answered rising to his feet.

"I am a woman on a quest. My man is lost in the *valley of the cats*. Ridden down by a condor and placed in her nest to feed her young when they hatch from their Creator-forsaken eggs. I will do anything to spare him that fate."

After delivering Alex to the summit of the mountain, Durbah had returned to her home in Creston Harbour where, after a period of roughly four hours, she was paid a visit by a man known as a *catcher*. The catcher's job was to fly the valley at a low altitude and scoop up any large stones that were floating in the air. The stones, positively charged by once being a part of the monopole bedrock, were typically loosed and sent up into the air by landslides and small *Sirenquakes*. The catcher's job was very important because the loose stones posed a great risk to the airships used to traverse the valley. The ships traveled at over a thousand miles-per-hour and could be critically damaged by a collision with a large enough stone. Unfortunately, many of the stones hovered within a hundred feet of the ground. That was well within the vertical leap of the *valley cats*. But aside from the perilous collection of loose stones, another grim task of the *catcher* was to retrieve a loose, floating mag-belt of a flier.

The catcher stood on Durbah's front porch and lowered his eyes to the wooden floor. There was not a lot to say as he held out the belt, which bore the name of Alex Janzen, other than, "I am sorry." The implication was absolute. If a flier lost a belt, his flight was compromised and he had undoubtedly descended to the valley floor below. The animals that occupied the valley floor were any number of atrocities. The *valegatos* or *valley cats* were over twelve feet long. They had two large fangs on either side of their mouths that were hollow and injected paralyzing venom into their victims. The bite brought about respiratory failure within minutes.

The only natural predator of the *valegatos* were the coil-vipers. These fifty-foot-long *walking snakes* could instantly wrap themselves around the neck of the *cats* and sink their claws through the fur and into the skin. Their bite was lethal as well, but the poison was much slower acting. The hours of agony from a coil-viper's bite was legendary. But aside from the *valegatos* and the *coil-vipers*, the menace Durbah was sure had overcome Alex was the Sirenian condor. These hideous birds were known to latch onto fliers from a blind spot out of the sun and ride them to the valley floor below. Then a quick peck to the head would render their victim unconscious to be picked up and flown to their nest. Before regaining consciousness, the victim was typically glued in place by the regurgitations of a cement-like substance, which bonded his arms and legs to the structure of the nest. Then the mag-belts were snapped by their huge beaks and allowed to float away to eventually be collected by a *catcher*. A quick death would be a blessing because the Sirenian condor did not hunt the fliers for herself. She hunted for her young. Durbah had no doubt Alex Janzen had been subdued by a condor and was now awaiting the cruel beaks of the hatchlings.

She walked over to the fire and pulled her robe over her head letting it fall to the dusty ground. She stood naked before the fire and chanted, *"Ah do e na."* at which point Christos Somah removed his robe as well and stood on the other side of the fire. He chanted in return, *"Des oo eh jo ma."*

They continued the chant back and forth, rhythmically breathing in while their counterparts sent forth the words. A precise syncopation was soon established, and Durbah began to feel the light-headedness of the near-hyperventilation teetering on the brink of consciousness. The Earth expression "runner's high" briefly came to mind, which referred to the euphoric state achieved by marathoners back on Earth. The *Valegatos* tribe quickly became aware of their sense of abandon and immersion into the rite, swaying back and forth, uttering the chant and raising their eyes to the heavens. When Durbah finally rounded the fire and approached Christos Somah from behind, all eyes of the *Valegatos* were upon them. The sexual suggestion of their nudity was not lost on the tribal people of the valley even though they usually performed the ceremony devoid of all clothing as well. There was nothing Durbah could do to downplay the spectacular beauty that was her body, and she seemed to notice a few pained expressions on the faces of the male members of the tribe.

She placed her ceremonial *bite* on the neck of Christos Somah, and when she pulled away, he noticed the *fangs* she had painted on her chin were gone. Apparently, he was well aware of where they had traveled, as he took in her beautiful form that had become a glistening reflection of the fire. He looked into her eyes and, for a moment, thought he noticed the suggestion of gold and silver flecks for which the *Valegatos* were known. The gold and silver quickly faded almost as if she held them in check. *Could there be some ancient connection between these beautiful tribal people and the sirens of Earth?* he wondered. Referring to the white marks that he knew were on his neck, he simply uttered, "I may never wash them off."

Chapter Four

Durbah got back into her robe and sandals and walked over to where the tribal elder was seated. She motioned to him that she would like to join them and ask a few questions. She extended her hand and said, "I am Durbah."

"Welcome Durbah. I am Bantah," said the elder, greeting her warmly with a huge grin that seemed in contrast to the fearsome teeth that hung from his neck. She wondered how much suffering and death of souls was deposited in those bits of calcium. It made her shiver, which the elder mistook for her being cold. He motioned for her to sit between him and the *Shamana,* who then moved in close to her until their sides were touching. She determined that body heat was one way the *Valegatos* regulated the comfort of their present climate. When she looked back at Christos Somah still standing by the fire, she noticed that before he climbed back into his robe, he placed a small silver-colored belt around his waist. She reflected on the strange customs of the people of Siren and supposed wearing a belt *under your clothes* was probably one of them. Christos Somah sat back down by the fire and chose not to join Durbah, seated with the priestess and the tribal elder. She asked the old man, "Who are you sending with us to travel into the valley?"

"My son, Bantah Somah. He is a strong boy and knows the valley well."

"Aren't you afraid for him?"

"He is a smart boy. He can be afraid for himself."

"What should we expect?" she asked him.

The *Shamana* then spoke for the first time, "*Valegatos* du-mala. Valley cats are very bad."

"*Vipos* du-mala neh," said the old man. "The snakes are bad, too."

"It all sounds like a bad nightmare," said Durbah.

"No, child. A nightmare is when you sleep. Sleep in the valley is a very bad idea." He reached into a small furry pouch that hung on the side of his waist and said, "When you walk in the valley, you chew some of these leaves." He handed her a small bundle wrapped in string. "You don't need many to chase away sleep. Maybe two or three a day. For us it takes much more. We are used to them."

Durbah pulled one of the leaves free and held it to her nose. The fragrance was minty and somewhat strong. When she opened her mouth, the elder cautioned, "Not for tonight, child," reaching out to stop her hand. "Tonight you sleep. Tomorrow you chew the leaves."

She slipped the leaf back into the bundle and asked, "Can you give us food enough for two or three days in the valley?"

The *Shamana* laughed briefly and said, "Be careful not to fall over it." The elder raised an eyebrow in her direction as if to mildly scold her for being rude to their guest. He then said, "There is much to eat in the valley. Many kinds of fruit that grow close to the ground. They get their nutrients from the hanging dust that follows the river. There are stalks of wild corn as well. Very sweet and no need to be cooked. A fire is unwise in any case because it may attract the *condoros*."

"You mean they fly at night, too."

"The *condoros* rule the valley. They do whatever they please. A word of caution my child – when you are in the valley, don't take any meat with you. Both the *condoros* and the *valegatos* can find the scent and follow it to the source."

"What else should I be aware of?" asked Durbah.

"Bantah Somah is very wise in the ways of the valley. It was his playground when he was young. Just stay close to him and listen to his words very closely." Just then, a beautiful *Valegatos* maiden walked up and sat facing them. Her long black hair flowed down on either side of her small, shapely breasts and almost reached her tiny waist. Her smooth copper colored skin glistened in the humid, night air, and the firelight was reflected by all of her graceful curves. Gold and silver flecks danced on the edge of the corneas of her green eyes, and Durbah imagined just how much more beautiful the girl's electrum would appear on a world that had a moon. The elder said to her, "You are beautiful tonight Bantah Samah. The *call of the gatos* ceremony agrees with you."

"But where are my fangs, father?" the girl asked slyly.

"On the neck of your young man."

The girls laugh was a soft song. Then she became suddenly serious and looked down at her hands in her lap.

"Speak, child," said the elder.

"I will curse my brother's travels if I do."

"Nonsense, mi samah. You have nothing but protection for your brother. Didn't you join in the dance?"

"I fear it will take more than the dance this time, father."

"Tell me what you know, child," said the elder sternly.

"It is not me, but the vision of the one who sees."

"The young one."

"Yes, father. There has come a vision from John."

"John Poole?" asked Durbah.

"Yes, that is his name," said the elder.

"He's here?"

"He has come to live with us my child," said the *Shamana*. "He has the great power to see."

"I know John Poole," said Durbah. "He's from Earth."

"I am not familiar with that city," said the elder.

"What did he say, Bantah Samah," asked Durbah.

"He saw my brother in the *batcha do condoros*, the *nest of the bird*."

"Perhaps it was merely a dream," said the elder. "The young ones have a vivid imagination."

"If John had a vision, you would do well to believe it will happen. We've learned that the hard way."

"We?" asked the elder.

"My tribe from . . . Earth," said Durbah searching for an explanation that would appease the old man.

"Then I shall believe it," said the elder. "My son will be in the *batcha do condoros*. The bird will be dead and he will be eating the eggs," he boasted, but Durbah noticed a tear escape his eye. His bravado would serve to shore up his determination to release his son into the valley, but the old priestess could see he couldn't lie to his heart. "Come," she said. "Take these old bones to your bed."

~

Chapter Five

C arla Walker woke up with a smile on her face. She thought she must have had a pleasant dream during the night, but she couldn't remember it. She began to softly sing a tune to a rock opera she had attended in her teens, *"Captain Walker didn't come home – his unborn child's never going to' know him."*

Cap', who always loved to hear her sing, began to smile as well. She had sung that tune many times before, which had always given him a warm feeling even though the words were a far cry from the actual description of their life together. First of all, he wasn't really a captain, and second of all, they had never attempted to have a child having found each other well beyond the time when either of them had any interest in becoming parents.

"Believe him missing with a number of men – don't expect to see him again."

Then Cap' joined her on the chorus, *"It's a boy, Mrs. Walker, it's a boy. It's a boy, Mrs. Walker it's a boy. A son! A son! A son!"* He walked over to her as she was just getting up from their bed and handed her a hot cup of coffee. He lightly kissed her on the lips and said, "I've always loved The Who, as you know." It was the first time he had alluded to her memory of their past since she walked back into his life a short time ago. It made her smile. She took the coffee, "Thanks, Nigel. Tell me honestly, babe. Have you ever regretted that I never gave you a son?"

"What? Are you kidding? At my age? Phffft."

"You know it's possible."

"What are you talking about?"

"Well, I never really gave it much thought because at first we used to travel so much, and I was in my fifties when we finally got hitched, but . . ."

"But what?"

"Well, you know that man in the blue robe? The one who calls himself Master *Phodan?*"

"What about him?" asked Cap'.

"He said it's entirely possible."

"Yeah, we could have a mongoloid baby, I guess."

Don't say that, Nigel. They call them Down Syndrome Babies now."

"In either case, no thank you," said Cap'.

"Master *Phodan* said that wouldn't happen, Nigel."

"And just how the hell does he know that?"

"I don't know, but he said he could just about guarantee it if I was interested. I don't think I'm really as old as I used to be, if you know what I mean."

"You sure don't look it. In fact, you look beautiful. As far as having a child goes, just be very careful what you wish for. It just may happen."

"It's funny, but that's exactly what Master *Phodan* said."

~

Durbah sat with Christos Somah watching the embers of the ceremonial fire burn down to glowing red and black jewels that offered warmth to their sleepy forms. She was leaning against his shoulder and telling him the sorrowful tale of how she lost Alex to the lure of the valley.

"A lot of people lose their sanity there," said Christos Somah. "There is a society here on Siren devoted to rescuing them from their addiction and bringing them back to their loved ones."

"I never would have believed it. If you told me back on Earth I would lose Alex on Siren because he preferred flying over loving me, I would have said you're crazy. But that's what it is. It's crazy. I'm not sure I'll ever really get him back even if we can find him."

"You need to be prepared for the worst, Durbah."

"I know."

"If we find any trace of him, and he isn't there . . ."

"I know. I said I know, Christos Somah. I don't want to talk about it right now, okay?"

"As you wish, Durbah. I just wanted you to . . ."

A scream suddenly was a knife through the silence that was in the clearing a moment before. A woman came rushing forth, toward the dying fire, and stopped. She put both her hands on her knees and took a deep breath. She was heavy with perspiration, and Durbah could see that her eyes were filled with tears.

"What is it, mother," said Durbah, using the familiar title of respect the Valegatos use to refer to an older generation.

"Mi samah," she said miserably through tears. "The condoro was very fast." She sank to her knees and an anguished cry burst forth from her lips and rose in volume until it was once again a scream. Durbah knew the implication. The woman's daughter had been taken by one of the hellish birds. It was the very thing she and Christos Somah were here in the valley trying to undo in the case of her lost lover, Alex. The mother knew there would be no rescue attempt made for her daughter even though they would soon know which nest she was taken to. They would soon hear her cries up in the canopy where the huge bird has deposited her to feed her soon-to-hatch young. The girl could try to leave the nest and climb down the tree, but she had been taught never to climb trees since she was old enough to walk. The trees were the domain of the valley cats. The cats would never disturb the eggs, not because they feared the condors, but because they had little taste for the eggs themselves. Some believed the valegatos were allergic to the point of becoming deathly ill if they were to eat an uncooked egg of the condor. However, cooked egg was a rare delicacy and often would entice them to risk an approach to an encampment of the *Valegatos* tribe where they were certainly outnumbered. The cats preferred a one-on-one encounter where the odds were decidedly in their favor.

A full-grown valegato was nearly twelve feet long and had paws the size of man-hole covers. The scratch radius was easily three inches between claws as could be witnessed on the backs of the lucky *Valegatos* tribe members who encountered them and lived to tell about it. Their claws were permanently fixed in place, unlike many species of cat that could retract them. As a result, their tracks had four distinct holes in the hard-packed, dusty ground of the valley just in front of the pad marks. Their coat was orange and gold with dark brown spots evenly spaced along their flanks, and their tails were horizontally striped in black at one-foot intervals with the tip ending in two feet of solid brown. They issued a low-pitched growl that would strike fear in the hearts of the tribal hunters although they knew the sound would never preclude an attack. The cats were mostly pack hunters who used their growl to herd their prey into a dense number of potential victims and pick off the weakest member as they fled the attack. If a single cat were on the hunt or perched on a high branch beneath a condor's nest, it was very rare to hear them before the strike. Unfortunately for the girl imprisoned in the nest, the *Valegatos* tribe knew the odds of retrieving her were slim and none. When Durbah learned of the resignation by the tribe and their intention to abandon her to a horrible end, she was livid. "You what!" she screamed. "Don't you people attach any value to life in this Creator-forsaken valley?"

The elder took her hand and said, "The Creator has designs for all of us, my child. It is best not to change the laws of fate."

"The laws of fate?" she challenged angrily. "What the hell kinds of laws allow you to abandon a small child to unfathomable torture?"

"The valegatos lie in wait under the nests, Durbah. It is all a dance by a grand design," said Bantah. "The condoros don't disturb the cats because they protect the nests from invasion. Gatos don't disturb the condoros because they often take the small ones to their nests. Then the people who don't know any better try to bring the young ones back. This makes an easy meal for the arborediabo, *the devil that waits in the trees.*"

"Well, I'm not going to sit around on my hands while I hear some child screaming at the top of some tree," declared Durbah. Christos Somah took hold of her hand at the elbow and said, "Calm down, Durbah."

"Don't tell me what to do, Christos Somah. I'm getting a little tired of this whole damned planet, and I think your attitude is a little bit cold if you want to know the truth."

"You don't understand," he started to tell her.

"Go to hell, Christos Somah. All of you . . . just go to hell. Or are we already there? Is this hell? I get it now: we all died, and we were bad, and this is hell."

Christos Somah looked at the elder, Bantah, and there was an apology behind his eyes. His expression said to please forgive this beautiful outsider, for she doesn't know the ways of the valley. He reached in and whispered into Durbah's ear, "Can I talk to you in private, Durbah."

"Go away, Christos Somah," she was crying now.

"Durbah, I need to tell you something right now. I don't want anyone else to hear it, but I need to say it to you." He raised his eyebrows and held her eyes with his, "Now, Durbah."

"Oh, alright," she said angrily. She stormed off to the edge of the clearing right where the great "Redwood Giganticas do Sirenas" marked the beginning of the canopy. They were the largest trees she had ever seen in her life. She had seen redwoods in California back on Earth that were fifteen feet in diameter and rose to 300 feet in the air, but the trees in the monopole valley of Siren were at least twice that size. When she reached the trunk of one of the biggest trees, she turned around and leaned back against it, crossing her arms in front of her chest. There was fire in her eyes that had nothing to do with the electrum she was careful not to show Christos Somah. She knew she could shape his will with her powers as well as the will of any of the tribal members, but she was not going to compromise her values and go back on a promise she made to herself. "What is it?" she asked Christos Somah. She hated herself. She hated Siren and what she was becoming.

"Please, Durbah," said Christos Somah closing the distance between them and wrapping his arms around her.

"Stop!" she scolded him pushing his arms away.

"Durbah, this is not like you," said Christos Somah. "You are a great spirit, but you are acting like you are possessed by the diabio."

"Save it, Christos Somah. Just tell me what you want to say before I head off into these trees until I hear the cries of the girl. Then I'm going to climb the tree and get her down, and I don't care if I die doing it. I don't particularly care to live with a bunch of cowards," she fumed once again.

"I will save the girl."

"Oh, great," she said facetiously. Now I have you to add to my guilt."

"What guilt, Durbah? Are you feeling responsible for your lover being lost in the valley? Tell me what is in your heart."

"Oh, I don't know, Christos Somah. Maybe I was too involved in the Church. Maybe I didn't give Alex as much attention as I did when we were back on Earth. There, he was everything to me. I rose each day to find the sun in his hair, and now . . ."

"Now you have found celebrity. Now many people follow your every word. That is a huge responsibility. No one would blame you for the changes of your behavior."

"What do you know about it? Your life is just one big vanilla sundae."

"I am sorry" he said. "What is a sundae?"

"It's not important. Just tell me what you're talking about. How can you save the girl?"

"You have to have faith, Durbah. Have you lost that?"

"That's a fine song and dance, Christos Somah, but did you see the look in that mother's eyes? Have you ever been there? Of course, you haven't."

"I said I will save the girl. I know that I can do this. Now, what you must do is get us two sacks of water and just remain calm. We will head off into the forest tonight and listen for the cries of the girl."

"But what about the cats?" she asked him.

"Let me worry about the cats, Durbah."

"Just what I need," she quipped. "A traveling companion with delusions of grandeur."

"Go," said Christos Somah, "the water."

Durbah left him and sought out Bantah, the tribal elder. He was comforting the woman who was lamenting the loss of her child. Durbah broke through their embrace to give them one last hope. "Bantah, I am sorry to interrupt your conversation, but please introduce me to mother here."

The old man looked quizzically toward Durbah, and she felt that he thought she was being very rude."

"Very well," he began, "this is the wife of our medicine man Mantah, so she is called Mantah Jomah." He tuned to the woman absorbed in her sobbing and said, "Mantah Jomah, this is Durbah from the tribe called Earth."

Durbah didn't bother to correct the misconception that the elder had about her origin and intentions. She was on a task and had to remain directed or else she might doubt herself. In that case, she would be lost. Her emotions were more raw and vivid than she ever had experienced before. Her whole life had been scripted for her, it seemed. She was always in the right place at the right time on Earth. She never knew conflict. Never once had she lost a loved one or knew anyone else who endured that tragedy. For the first time in her life, she looked into the eyes of the mother, Mantah Jomah, and saw pure misery. It brought tears to her eyes as well. She took the woman's hands in hers and made an impossible promise, "Mother, I want you to have faith that your daughter will be well."

Bantah, the tribal elder, looked at her with scorn. He knew that she was only adding to the heartache of the medicine man's woman. He was about to say as much when Durbah continued, "I know that you think your daughter is lost, but I am here to give you hope. You have to have hope. Can you do that?"

The woman couldn't bring words to her lips. Her shoulders began to shake and quake, and she fell to her knees. Durbah knew in her deepest heart that if she gave this woman false hope and was unable to deliver on her empty promise, she would never be able to live with herself. After losing Alex and second guessing her decision to come to Siren in the first place, she felt that her life was starting to lose the grip on all meaning, but she stayed the course, squeezing the woman's hands and said, "Your daughter is not lost, mother. I will lead her back to your fire. Place more wood on it and let it burn through the night. Have faith, Mantah Jomah."

The elder and Shamana felt sorry for Durbah, knowing that her empty words would come back and haunt her when the woman's daughter was eventually lost, but they kept their thoughts to themselves. Bantah said to her, "What do you need for your quest, Durbah?"

"I need two water sacks, please."

"Certainly," he said and walked off to get them for her. Durbah turned to the woman encased in her sorrow, "Mantah Jomah, I would never lie to you, dear. I am not sure how I know this, but I have to have faith. I have faith in a man named, Christos Somah who has said that he will save your daughter. I have faith in Christos Somah, so you should have faith in me. That is all we have, mother. And if we are strong, that will be enough. Will you pray with me?"

The woman coughed and told Durbah, "I don't understand what you are saying, child."

"I am talking about prayer. You may ask the Creator to shine brightly on you and your daughter. And that you will be well and live long and happy lives."

"But the condoro," said the woman, "and the gatos," she said miserably.

"They are also from the Creator, mother. You have to have faith. Just because you know of their victims doesn't mean that you have to become one of them. I'm not sure I understand it myself, but I have to have faith. I have to *pray*."

"Show me," said the woman.

Durbah knelt down on the warm, brown dusty soil and clasped her hands together. She began, *"Ohm Des oo in the cradle that is the stars – your name is above all names. Give us your blessing to live this day and give us the strength to do your will. Help us to forgive those who do not understand your plan – and give them new life that they may know you after their bones rest in the soil – you are the power that moves blood through our bodies - may it always take the path of your design — we ask you now to make the girl safe who was taken tonight. We call her by name, Mantah Samah return to us this night. Mantah Samah return to us this night. Mantah Samah return to us this night."*

The woman began to pray along with Durbah wiping tears from her eyes as she did so, *"Mantah Samah, return to us this night — Mantah Samah, return to us this night."*   The Shamana was dubious. Durbah could tell by her expression, but she joined them as well. The three women were kneeling and rocking back and forth, and their voices blended into one droning monotone, resonating off the embers in the fire when Bantah returned with the water sacs. "Here are your provisions, Durbah. May they serve you well on your quest."

Durbah rose to her feet, "Thank you, Bantah. Don't give up hope for Mantah Samah. I will walk her back to this fire tonight. Gather more wood and keep the flame going. Make the flame fuel your hope. Love will not abandon you. Do you believe what I am saying?"

The old man surprised himself when he told her, "Yes, Durbah. I'm not sure why, but I do believe in what you are saying. I know that you believe it and that is enough for me to have what you call . . . faith."

"Thank you, Bantah. Hold mother Mantah until I return with Christos Somah. He has made me a promise that I believe in. It's all I have left this night."

"I feel that it may be what all of us have this night."

"Yes, Bantah," said Durbah. "It is all that we have."

Chapter Six

Old Ben Mason had been Nigel Walker's neighbor for over thirty years. Nigel didn't really like the man, but he was always respectful and nodded his head when driving by the Mason house in his Ford F-150 truck coming back from his day's work at Port Canaveral. He always took offense when Ben made fun of his seemingly erratic work schedule. When they occasionally met at Carson's Food and Feed, Mason would always chime in, "You get a job yet, Walker?"

Cap' never gave him any never-mind and just said to himself, *"asshole."* The fact that Nigel Walker had a six figure income and worked only four days a week would have sent Ben Mason over the edge, but Cap' would never give him that information. He always just humored him and answered, "Not, yet, Ben. But I've got my resumes in the mail as we speak."

"Well, good luck," Ben Mason would say. "You can't make a living renting out your pasture for the cows of real working men."

"Pays pretty well, Ben," Cap' would often say when he was just too tired of the abuse. "Probably more than you make on that little postage stamp of a farm a' yours."

"Get bent, Walker," Mason would always say never having the imagination to come up with a better line. If Cap' had his way, he would never have to deal with the caustic man who lived next door, which was actually more like a half-mile next door. But the visit from Master *Phodan* changed all that in a New York minute, even though St. Cloud, Florida, was over fourteen hundred miles away from the Big Apple. Ben Mason had seen the man in the blue robe walk out of the lake that joined both of their properties. He immediately did the only thing that his eleven-hundred-cubic-centimeter brain could think of: he got his double barreled shotgun off the peg above the hearth and headed out to confront him. "Just what part of hell did you shake your sorry ass away from?" he demanded.

"I wish you peace," said *Phodan*.

"How would you like a piece of this?" asked Mason brandishing his shotgun. He pulled back both hammers into the fully cocked position.

"Your intention is aggression if I am not mistaken," said *Phodan*.

"Oh, you're mistaken alright. Your biggest mistake was to show yourself to a God fear'n Christian who don't take ta' the cut a' your metal, son."

"I know of Christos, and I know of his son, Christos Somah," said *Phodan*. "The councilman is very wise."

"You're the wise guy, mister blue robe. I've got some double-ought shot right here that's gonna' show you what for," screamed Mason. His fear had taken over him and the mere fact that the peaceful man standing before his shotgun was showing none drove him to shaking. Whether or not he intended to shoot was never really determined, but both barrels let go. The blue robe on *Phodan* was rendered to mere shreds across his mid-section. The dozen lead balls somehow fell to his feet. He picked each one up and, despite their heat, held them out in his hand. "These belong to you, Mr. Mason."

"How do you know my name, you devil. Just what the hell are you anyway?"

"I am a man of peace. And I am the son of man," said *Phodan.*

Mason was reduced to tears. He knelt down on the ground and threw his useless weapon aside. The barrels made a hissing noise because the gun landed on the edge of the lake. Old Ben was sorry that he had ever gotten out of bed on that morning because his world was unraveling right before his eyes. *Phodan* understood the scenario that old Ben Mason couldn't come to terms with. He wanted to help. He reached out his left hand and said, "Give me your hands, Ben. I can help you now."

Mason wasn't sure what was up or down or who he even was at that point. He was crying miserably and just held out his hands to the man in the tattered blue robe.

"This will all pass you by, Ben. This will all go away. The birds will fill your ears on this day, and you will be happy. You will not miss your son who was taken from you in a far-off land fighting a senseless conflict. It will all make sense to you now. You will know that he waits for you with your wife in a better place. A place where you shall all be together again, and you will be happy. Go now and be of peace."

Ben Mason stood up and wiped the tears from his eyes with his palms. He then wiped them on his shirt and looked around at the clouds gathering on the western horizon, "We may get some rain out of that bunch," he said to *Phodan*.

"We will get what the Creator wills."

"Yes, I suppose you're right," said Mason. "Best you not get caught in that blow."

"I shall try not to," said *Phodan*. With that remark, he turned his back on the old man and headed to the nearest house where he had some pressing business with a pilot called Nigel Walker.

~

Chapter Seven

When Durbah rejoined Christos Somah, he asked her, "Did you get the water?"

"Two sacks," she told him.

"Good," he said, "one is for the girl. She is very frightened now and will need to hydrate herself."

"You're a very curious man, Christos Somah. I have no idea how you expect to find the girl, let alone rescue her, and yet I believe you. I believe *in you*."

"That is because you are a wise woman, Durbah. I feel that your wisdom is the reason you are the leader of your Church. The Creator has your ear."

"I'm not sure about that. I'm not sure that we even have tomorrow, Christos Somah. The cats and the condors may have something to say about it."

"They will not touch us tonight."

"I wish I could be as sure as you are."

"You will be when you sleep tonight," he told her.

"Can you see tomorrow when the Earth lines up?"

"Excuse me," said Christos Somah. "I'm not sure what you mean."

"Forget it," said Durbah. A smile was on her lips.

Christos Somah led Durbah into the redwoods for about a half-hour when they heard footfalls on the path behind them.

Bantah Somah had been running to catch up to them. "Where are you off to?" he asked them.

"You have to go back, somah. You will only slow us down tonight."

"I am not your somah," he said indignantly. He was posturing for Durbah, trying to show her he was a great warrior who had no fear of the forest.

"Please, Bantah Somah," began Christos Somah giving him the praise of his title being the son of the elder, "we need you to be rested and strong for the journey that we will make into the valley. Durbah is very afraid for her man who has become lost there. She feels that a condoro has encased him in her batcha, and soon he will feed the hellions."

"There is talk that you intend to find Mantah's woman-child."

"There is always talk," said Christos.

"I want to come with you," said the somah.

"You cannot."

"I can do anything that the Creator wills, Christos."

"And the Creator wills that you return home," said Durbah.

"What does a waheen know?"

"Mind your tongue young one," said Christos Somah.

"What is a waheen?" asked Durbah.

"It doesn't matter," said Christos Somah.

"It matters to me," she said hotly. "If I've just been insulted, I want to know about it."

"I am sorry," said Bantah Samah. "I meant no disrespect to you madam Durbah. It's just that if I return now to the encampment, the young men will think that I was overcome by fear. I have no fear of anything. The valegatos and the condoros are the ones who should fear me," he said proudly filling his lungs with air and puffing out his chest.

Durbah would not back down and she insisted, "What is a waheen, Bantah Samah?"

The young man blushed with shame and looked at the ground.

"Come on," said Durbah. "You said it a minute ago, say it again. Call me a waheen."

"I said I was sorry, madam. It was rude of me to make that statement."

"Well, are you going to tell me what it means or not?"

Christos Somah told her, "It means one who has breasts enough to suckle the young ones."

Durbah's face began to fill with color for the first time in her life. She had never blushed before that she could ever remember. She wasn't quite sure what to say. Christos Somah raised his eyebrows and gestured with his hands that she should say something.

"Thank you?" she offered questioningly.

"It is I who should thank you, madam Durbah. When I saw you earlier tonight, I have to say that your beauty was very painful to me."

Durbah understood what the young man was referring to and then blushed for the second time in her life. Christos

Somah told the young man, again, that he had to return to the *Valegatos,* but he was still reluctant to go. Durbah finally said, "Give me your hands, Bantah Somah."

He held his hands out in front of him, and Durbah took them in hers. She brought the electrum to her eyes shining gold and silver flecks in her corneas holding the young *Valegato* in her gaze. She spoke very softly, "Bantah Somah, you want to please me. You only want what will make me happy on this night and every other one. To think that I am displeased brings you great pain. You want to know how you can serve me the most. You want to know how you can make me happy, and now I will tell you. It will make me happy if you go now and return to the encampment. I will be back soon to join you and when I come, I will have Mantah Samah along with me. Now tell me what you want to do now."

Bantah Somah blinked his eyes a few times and said, "Forgive me madam Durbah, but I have to leave you now. I am going back to my people and will wait for you there."

"Thank you," said Durbah.

"You are welcome," said the young man.

"One more thing before you go," said Durbah. She held her hand to her heart and said, "Desu mah a mi sol." *The Creator wants us to go alone.*

The young man repeated, "Desu mah a mi sol," and then he turned and walked away. Durbah looked at Christos Somah who was shaking his head with one raised eyebrow. He was thinking that this remarkable woman was full of surprises when she said to him, "How's *that* for a waheen?"

Chapter Eight

When Cap' and Carla Walker were just rinsing off their breakfast dishes, Ben Mason knocked on their screen door. "Come in, Ben," said Carla although Cap' was thinking that he should have walked out to the porch and headed him off. It wasn't that he wanted to be rude to the man, but he just felt better about keeping his distance. Ben took off his old fedora and held it in his hand, "Miss Carla," he began, "you're looking pretty this morning."

"That's what you came to say?" asked Cap'.

"Nigel, please mind your manners," said Carla softly. She wasn't really scolding Cap', but she wanted Ben to feel welcome in their house.

"No, that's not what I came to say, but it's the truth, that's all," said Mason.

"Thank you, Ben. See Nigel, some men have a kind tongue when they speak to a lady."

"Aw, I didn't mean anything, Ben, you know that."

"Yes, Cap', I do. Don't give it any mind."

"Well, speaking of mind, what's on yours?" asked Cap'.

"Well, it's probably nothing, but I had a dream last night."

"You came over here to tell me about your dream?"

"Well, sort of. I mean, that's not the whole of it. I have a lot to do today with the rain coming and need'n to hay fore it gets rot."

"Just say it, Ben. Spill the dream."

"Give the man a chance, Nigel. You can be so cold sometimes."

"Naw, he's right Miss Carla. Sometimes I can be a flapjaw."

"So, tell us your dream, Ben. It must have made a big impression on you for you to want to share it. I can never even remember mine most of the time."

"There was this man that rose out of old Alligator Lake out there. Just up and walked like Jesus on the water."

"Go on," said Carla almost knowing where this tale was going.

"I don't mind telling you I was scared. In my dream, that is, not in real life. Cap' will tell you not much scares me anymore now that little Paulie's gone, bless his soul. Damned Afghanistan. Well, as I was saying, I was scared of this man even though he wasn't really scary to look at. He was dressed in a blue robe and had some sandals on his feet."

"Yeah, so you were scared in your dream. It's called a nightmare, Ben. Happens all the time . . ."

"I shot him."

"What?" asked Carla.

"I shot the man. Just like that, both barrels right in the chest."

"That's not very neighborly, Ben," said Cap'.

"He weren't my neighbor, Cap'. It's not like I'd ever shoot you."

"So what about it?" asked Cap'. "Was that all there was to your dream?"

"Sort of, but after I shot the man, he didn't go down. He wasn't even mad at me. He acted like he wanted to help me. Even talked about Paulie bein' in heaven, and how we's gonna' be together sometime in the future."

"That sounds pretty good, Ben. It must have made you feel better about losing him," said Carla.

"Then he holds out his hand and pours out a dozen shot right into mine. They was still hot, too."

"That's a pretty strange dream, Ben," said Cap'.

"Yeah, well, that's not all. When I woke up today guess what was a sittin' on my kitchen table?"

"Surprise me," said Cap'.

"Well it sure as hell surprised me," said Mason. He put his hand in his pocket and pulled out the dozen shotgun pellets and poured them into Cap's hand.

""Now, would you look at that," said Cap'.

"Yeah, go figure," said Mason turning around and walking out the screen door. Carla just smiled at Cap' and said, "Master *Phodan* strikes again."

~

Christos Somah and Durbah started walking through the black night of the redwood forest. The stars were very bright and looked close enough to touch. Durbah wished there was a moon on Siren to help them light the way, but her eyes adjusted to the darkness, and she seemed to see fairly well. She was very glad to have Christos Somah there with her and, for the first time, she felt that Siren was not a benign blue ball of carbon and stone, but rather a force to be reckoned with. There was power in the woods and danger as well. She wondered what would happen to them if they stumbled on a viper lying in the tall grass sleeping. She imagined that the snake would wake up rather quickly and have something to say about it. *How would Christos Somah react to danger?* she wondered. He was such a mild mannered man. She had never even seen him raise his voice, which was always used in a sea of pure calm. Suddenly, he surprised her for the first time, "Durbah, quickly wrap your arms around my waist and hold very tightly to me."

Durbah was confused as to what had come over Christos Somah. She told him, "Really, Christos Somah, do you think this is the proper time to . . ."

"Quickly, Durbah. Hold on to me now!"

Durbah grabbed a hold of Christos Somah and put her arms around him. She squeezed him tightly when she felt him squeezing her in kind. Then she saw the great cat. He was every inch of thirteen feet long and he growled as he came near to them. She had been told that they attacked in dead silence, but this cat wasn't being silent at all. It was an un-Godly noise that issued forth from his snarling lip. She saw his pencil-thick whiskers quiver in anticipation of a lethal bite that was soon to befall them. The cat opened its maw, and Durbah could see the scaly tongue that was long enough and rough enough to actually lick the flesh from their bones. The fangs were daggers. Huge sharp implements that looked like the devil's pitchfork. She closed her eyes and was too afraid to even scream. She knew the bite was imminent and closing fast. Christos Somah screamed for both of them, "Eh jo mah, valegato!"

She expected to feel the searing pain at any second when the evil snarl of the great cat, all at once, turned to a blood curdling scream. It was a screech from hell as Durbah looked down and saw the huge animal's teeth lying at her feet. They had become separated from the animal, broken off and bloody at their roots and no longer a part of the valley cat's jaw. Durbah was astonished. *How could this have happened?* She wondered. When she looked at Christos Somah, she could see his calm face smiling as though he were out for a nice evening stroll, not just released from the jaws of death. She noticed the green viscous venom oozing out of the middle of the fangs on the ground before them. She knew that if she were to prick herself and be exposed to a single drop, she would suffocate in minutes. Respiratory failure was a sure result of a cat bite in the valley. But they weren't going to suffer the bite of the cat on this night. Somehow they were spared and would be of the very few who lived to tell the tale of a cat attack. She looked at Christos Somah and finally asked him, "But how?"

"We had help, Durbah."

"What do you mean?" she asked him.

"Look at my hands, Durbah. What do you see?"

She was holding onto Christos Somah so tightly that her knuckles were white. Christos Somah told her, "I think you can let go of me now." She loosened her grip and backed away from him. When she looked down at his hands, she saw a silver rope that he had wrapped around both of them. He asked her, "Do you get it now?"

"A shield?" she asked.

"Yes, a shield. On loan from *Phodan*. It's what will protect us when we find the girl and climb the tree."

"You could have told me, Christos Somah. I could have died of fright."

"There wasn't time, Durbah. Those cats are really fast."

"He broke his teeth off."

Christos Somah knelt down on the ground and pulled a handkerchief from the pocket of his robe. He carefully wrapped up the broken teeth making sure to stay well clear of the green fluid and needle-sharp tips. He said to Durbah, "Yes, I know. *She* broke *her* teeth off. They may come in handy."

"How do you know it was female?" asked Durbah.

"Her size. The males are a bit smaller, but just as fierce."

"Do you think those loose teeth could kill a condor or a viper?"

"Let's hope that we never find out," said Christos Somah.

Chapter Nine

Carla kissed Cap' Walker on the lips. "What was that for," he asked her.

"Oh, I just wanted to taste my man," she told him.

"No, really. What's on your mind? Is it what that *Phodan* fellow told you about having a child?"

"No, Nigel. I just wanted to say that I'm proud of you for helping out those kids."

"What kids might that be, Carla?"

"The ones who will be stuck up there in that way station."

"What do you know about it?" he asked.

"I was there, Nige."

"You're kidding?"

"Not hardly," she said.

"So now you're an astronaut," he chided.

"Got my wings to prove it."

"What was it like?"

"Unbelievable. It really is a blue marble that we live on. And mostly, there aren't even any clouds. Just water and land. Carbon and stone."

"What does that mean, carbon and stone," asked Cap'.

"Think about it, Nigel. Think about everything everywhere. It's all either carbon or stone."

"Now you're talking like a spacewoman, Carla," he chuckled. "I need you down here with me on Earth."

"Do you know how that sounds to me, Nigel?"

"How what sounds?"

"That you need me."

"I would guess that you like it. The sound, that is."

"You would be right."

"Now, what were we talking about?"

"About you being a pilot."

"What about it."

"I mean you coming out of retirement."

"Now, hold on, woman."

"Oh, Nigel. I can read you like a book. I know that you have already decided to do what *Phodan* has asked of you."

"Oh, you do, do you?"

"Absolutely. And that's why you got a kiss on the lips."

"What do I have to do to get another one?"

"Coming right up," she said crossing the room.

~

Christos Somah held Durbah's hands. They were shaking badly. "She's gone now."

"I don't care, Christos Somah. I feel like I need eyes in the back of my head."

"That's why there are two of us."

"You are a good man, Christos Somah."

"I am not a man. I am a spirit of Siren."

"Oh, you know what I mean."

"Yes, I do. I was only being difficult to break the tension. I think you are a very powerful spirit as well. Siren is richer having you here."

"I think I love you, Christos Somah."

"It was the danger, Durbah. Think about me in the morning and then tell me how you feel."

"I will tell you that I love you in the morning."

"And that will make me smile. What of your man, Alex?"

"I'm not sure how I feel about Alex anymore. I loved him, and I suppose I still do, but . . ."

"But what?"

"He has changed, Christos Somah. He is not the same man who I grew to love back on Earth."

"None of you are the same, Durbah. You have fallen into great celebrity, and no one would expect you to be the same."

"You can have it," she said.

"I do not wish it," said Christos Somah. "I have been thrust into the spotlight as well. My father is one of the Grand Masters of the Council. When I go to Creston, I am not Christos as I called myself when we first met on Earth. I am always referred to as Christos Somah. I don't even have my own identity. That is what celebrity has done for me."

"I should think that anyone would be proud to be the son of Christos," said Durbah.

"Proud, yes. Contented, not on your life. I want to make a big splash in the ocean that is my world, but how can I?"

"You make a big splash for me. Back in the encampment, earlier tonight . . ."

"Yes?"

"Do I have to say it?" asked Durbah.

"I would like to hear it," said Christos Somah.

"I wanted to share your tent if Mantah Jomah hadn't broken the moment."

"I would have liked that as well, Durbah. So what now? What would you have me do now with your heart?"

"Do what you please, Christos Somah. And after we find the girl, I would like to share your tent before we go after Alex."

"Sharing my tent will give me the pleasure of your body. As far as your heart is concerned, I feel I will have little use for it once you release me. I made a promise to you about the girl, Durbah. I will make the same promise about your man. I will find him."

"You may find him, Christos. But he may no longer be my man. Maybe you will be my man."

"The orb will turn as He wills it," said Christos.

"And so I will turn with it," said Durbah, completing the ancient phrase.

~

Just as Carla had promised, she crossed the room and planted a big kiss on the lips of Nigel Walker. He then told her, "Earth girls are easy."

"Shuuud up, you old goat."

He laughed loud and full grabbing her waist and wrestling her down into his recliner. Then their kiss became something more than just love play. There was a force behind Cap' Walker's passion on that day. Two-hundred and seventy days later he would swear that he knew the very hour that his only son was conceived. Carla glowed for the next nine months when she was seen about town. She was a very happy woman, but it pained her to have to hide the grave marker that bore her name. After all, how could she make people understand? She loved the other Carla with all of her heart and prayed by the place where the marker had stood nearly every day. She was grateful for the DNA that Carla had provided for her. And Cap' Walker had the rest. The memories of the life they shared together were enough to piece together the whole package. The entire enchilada. A life with a man she loved.

Chapter Ten

The sirens from Earth were awaiting the decision from *Preculis* as to whether or not they could arrange for travel back to what they now considered their true home. They knew they didn't belong on Siren and were miserable for the most part. Celebrity didn't agree with them, and they found themselves sorely tempted to use their powers of persuasion to manipulate the sirens. They rejected the fact that they were sirens as well. They thought it was a cruel trick on the part of the *Preculians* to bring them to Siren in the first place. They became more reclusive every day and found themselves running away from all the attention that was being thrust upon them. They just wanted to be left alone, but that was impossible. Every being on the planet Siren was fascinated by them. They had lived on another world and so were actually alien beings even though their ancestors were from Siren over five-thousand years ago.

Originally, *Preculis* transported twelve sirens to Earth along with one director or *sensor*. The sensor's job was to gather the sirens together twice a year and impart unconscious directives for the purpose of keeping the existence of Siren a precious secret. One of the ways this was accomplished was to stimulate tension among the humans so that their spiritual evolution was stalled. Technology could hide Siren with the use of a *Great Shield* and a ring of iron gas canisters called *The*

Great Belt orbiting the planet to mask her magnetic signature, but the presence of millions of brother and sister souls were sure to be discovered psychically if nothing else. The evolution of man would come to sense them and seek out their company and any way they could exploit them or acquire ownership of their resources.

Over time, the sirens on Earth were able to accumulate wealth and put themselves in a position to shape the will of humanity. They were the driving force behind every great conflict between nations that could be traced all the way back to Cain and Abel. Now they were a source of conflict on their home world as well. They brought to Siren the one thing that the *Preculians* were very careful not to show them – religion. The *Preculians* suffered a deadly and very long lasting conflict with a planet called *Xeries*. Just like every conflict throughout time, the root of the problem was religion. Religion came into being shortly after the discovery of fire on most worlds, and *Preculis* and *Xeries* caught the infection in a big way. A thirst for ownership was sown into the personality development of every *Preculian* and *Xerian*.

At first there was slavery – ownership of fellow beings. Then, when their slaves did their bidding through armed conflict, armies of slaves were used to take possession of everything from precious metals to loved ones. When they were a primitive people, isolation saved them from the conflict. Before space travel, both races developed their separate religions in peace. Though if there were a way to travel to each other's world, those primitive cultures would have begun waging the *Preculis/Xeries* war with sticks and stones. It was only a matter of time before the unthinkable was possible. The *Preculians* collapsed their enemy planet's star.

The fusion chain from helium to hydrogen – hydrogen to carbon – carbon to iron was accelerated by an accident of exponential speed. One plus one didn't equal two in the sense that physics was changed artificially. Before they knew what was going to happen, their experiment went horribly awry. They only wanted to get the attention of *Xeries* and demonstrate the fact that weaponry had the potential to become a runaway progression of forces. The collapse of the star known as *Xeries* took place in less than a day.

The *Preculians* could actually feel the *procession of souls*. Sorrow became the most prevalent emotion on *Preculis*. Depression was widespread, and for a period of seven years, rampant suicide was the order of the day. Half of the planet's population found ways to do away with themselves. Disease and famine were all that they had to look forward to until they discovered that there was a higher purpose for the people of *Preculis*. They had the responsibility to become *guardians*. When the star *Xeries* collapsed, it sent forth a wave of gamma radiation that bathed the planet Earth for forty days. This was the time of the hunter gatherer on Earth, and man was poised to progress from fire to religion. The *Preculians* knew that Siren was spared the gamma wave and would remain a peaceful world rather than take the path of humans into great conflicts. Greed and compulsion would plague Earth, as it did the

Preculians, because religion would pave the way to money, and money would pave the way to evil.

The *Preculians* gave Earth a thorn in her side in the way of twelve sirens who proliferated into four-hundred and eighty-six conflict-perpetuating souls to stunt the evolution of mankind. Mankind had to remain blind to more advanced beings such as the sirens. That was the purpose of the sirens on Earth and the *Preculians* were duty-bound from *their* mistake to help them accomplish it.

The first step was to help the sirens construct the *Great Shield*. It consisted of eight satellites orbiting Siren, which made up a cube of photo-reflective panes rendering the planet effectively invisible. They were fueled by the decay of nuclear materials similar to plutonium, but had a much shorter half-life. In honor of a lost people, who no longer occupied this plane of existence, they named the isotope *Xerium*. But the unstable nature of *Xerium* led to the necessity of procuring plutonium from Earth to power the Great Shield. The nuclear materials produced on Earth had a much longer half-life and would supply the Shield with enough power to last until a greater technological advancement could be developed to protect Siren. That advancement was the *space/time exchange chamber*. Since no two objects can occupy the same space, even apparently empty space like dark matter, the idea of teleportation was impossible. It was discovered, however, that a finite fixed-position area of space could be exchanged with an exactly identical space over great distances. A sub-light photo-retardant pulse of ultra-violet light served as the medium for the exchange. Chambers were established, over time, in the meeting halls of the sirens of Earth, which were called alpha-omega retreats. Twelve meeting halls were constructed on Earth by the *Preculians* to facilitate the gathering and dissemination of unconscious or subconscious directives. One such directive was instrumental in supplying plutonium to the *Great Shield* of Siren. An exploratory spacecraft was built on Earth to travel to Saturn and study two of the planet's eighteen moons. It was powered by twenty-two pounds of plutonium, but the *Preculians* knew it could function properly with only half that much.

Cassini launched in October 1997 from the Kennedy Space Center with the European Space Agency's Huygens probe. The probe was equipped with six instruments to study Titan, Saturn's largest moon. It landed on Titan's surface on Jan. 14, 2005, and returned spectacular results. Cassini completed its initial four-year mission to explore the Saturn System in June 2008. The mission was then extended to the Cassini Equinox Mission, and after its completion in September 2010, the seemingly healthy spacecraft is now being programmed to make a second extended mission called the Cassini Solstice Mission.

The mission's extension, which is intended to go through September 2017, is named for the Saturnian summer solstice occurring in May 2017. The northern summer solstice marks the beginning of summer in the northern hemisphere and winter in the southern hemisphere. Cassini catapulted Earth's knowledge of haze-enshrouded Titan into a whole new realm. During the primary and extended missions, Cassini investigated the complex organic chemistry of Titan's thick, smog-filled atmosphere. On the frigid, alien surface, the spacecraft and its probe revealed vast methane lakes and widespread stretches of wind-sculpted hydrocarbon sand dunes. These lakes and dunes are used by the *Preculians* to power their outposts on Titan. Cassini researchers also detected the presence of an internal, liquid water-ammonia ocean. Since the *Preculian* outposts are beneath this ocean, there is no need to employ a shield application to hide them. It remains highly unlikely that Earth will ever have the technology to explore the Ammonian Ocean on Titan. The *Preculians* know that Cassini is about to run out of nuclear fuel and feel confident that Earth will surmise that the hard working probe died a natural death.

There was much controversy and trepidation by the people of Earth regarding the safety of such a launch. No one knew of the consequences of an explosion of a craft carrying nuclear fuel in the event of a launch malfunction. One of the sirens worked for a Houston, Texas, member of the U. S. House of Representatives who was on the President's Committee for Space Exploration. He was influenced by the beautiful siren who worked for him to ramrod the Cassini Probe Project. He gave a speech at the United Nations assuring the world that there was no danger of a radiation leak from the probe. He didn't actually possess this information for a fact, but he was helpless to resist the will of the siren. The siren's name was Christine Chalmers, and she was an extraordinary beauty. The helpless congressman looked into her eyes and saw a very rare sight. She possessed a substance called electrum in her eyes. The corneas emitted a gold and silver light when she wanted to mesmerize a human and shape his will. The source of the electrum was a metal cap on the great pyramid in the Giza Plateau of Egypt. The *Preculians* processed the metal into genetic material and introduced it into the DNA of a select group of people on Siren. Sixty of them were transformed into will-shaping Gods and Goddesses of perfection.

Twelve of them were sent to Earth to carry out the *Preculians* mission of disruption, and the forty-eight others stayed behind and tried to assimilate themselves within the societies of Siren. This became impossible. For the first time, there was discontentment on Siren. Those beautiful *Gods of Siren* were cast out and became known as *The Lost Tribe of the Valegatos*. What the *Preculians* didn't count on was the fact that *they themselves* are helpless to resist the incredible beauty in the eyes of the Earth sirens and the *Valegatos* tribe.

The natives of Siren do not have electrum in their genetic makeup and are helpless to resist the will of the Earth sirens as well. This became a source of great controversy on Siren and there was even some talk of the newcomers practicing sorcery. Some sirens spoke out against them and launched a campaign to appeal to the *Preculians* to return them to Earth. Demonstrations were held on Siren for the first time in history. They were organized outside the Great Council Chamber in the city of Creston. The name *"Crest Town"* evolved into *Creston* shortly after the *Preculians* first landed on

Siren nearly five-thousand years ago. The seat of the Great Chamber was usually a very peaceful place, but then the streets became filled with Sirens carrying signs that read "Go Back To Earth," and "Just Leave Us In Peace." *So much for paradise,* thought most of the sirens from Earth. They were devastated although they had quickly tired of any notion of their celebrity. The native sirens either loved them or hated them, but no one was without an opinion. No one would leave *them* in peace.

The group of Earth sirens were of the same mind about leaving Siren. They wanted to go back to Earth and appealed to the *Preculians* for another journey in a *space/time exchange chamber.* But the chambers in the alpha-omega meeting halls would no longer function as they once did. Their purpose was for a one-time exodus from Earth to Siren and were never intended for a return trip. There was one solution to the problem. A way station could be established in a geosynchronous orbit around Earth and could be rendered invisible by a photo-reflective shield. No ring of gas canisters would be needed to mask its magnetic signature since its relative-mass is miniscule compared to that of Earth.

The *Preculians* established the way station and were in the process of securing a pilot before ever giving the Earth sirens an answer about a return trip back home. The way station above the Earth was orbiting at one-hundred-ninety miles above sea level. It was large enough to accommodate any and all Earth sirens who wanted to return. The shuttle ship, however, was only capable of holding twenty people and would have to make as many as twenty trips to deliver all the sirens back to Earth. The *Preculians'* first order of business after establishing the way station was to build a city to house the sirens near the landing site. It was determined that a sparse community in Florida called St. Cloud was an adequate landing area that would not alarm any humans because it was principally occupied by cows. The only humans in the area were the prospective "pilot" and his newly rejuvenated wife, Carla. His name was Cap' Walker and the *Preculians* were just now securing an answer to their proposition. Cap' Walker was devastated by the loss of his wife nearly two years ago. The *Preculians* were able to regenerate her body by the use of some stem cells from the University of Florida's genetics lab (procured in the dead of night), and the DNA taken from Carla's grave site. Then, Cap' Walker's synaptic collection of every waking-moment was retrieved during his sleep one night and planted in the newly regenerated Carla Walker. She had no recollection of her life before Cap' Walker, but she remembered thirteen years of blissful experience with a man she dearly loved.

Of course, there were limitations. She only had a memory of her life through Cap's eyes and mind, although he approached life with the same sense of humor and wonder that Carla did. That was why they had found each other in the first place. Cap' was fully convinced at that point that he had his Carla back again. He knew it was impossible, and he had to work hard not to question the circumstance, but in a heart beat, his life took on more meaning than merely passing time petting his beloved Golden retriever, Isabelle. The dog didn't question

Carla's existence. She thought that her mistress smelled glorious and nudged her into a walk to the reservoir each morning to chase the ducks. Plus, Isabelle no longer had a pain in her hip. Life was good.

~

Chapter Eleven

Shelly Simon and Charles Donovan were pregnant. Shelly actually carried the fetus, but somehow Charles also had the morning sickness. There was a very special aspect to their soon-to-be-born baby: he was male and since they both were Earth sirens, he would become a *seer*. No amniocentesis was necessary to determine this fact. That had been declared by *Master Phodan* of *Preculis*. There was another male child on Siren who had been born to two Earth sirens. He was the son of Matthew Winter and Alankha Hannas. Little Zaphi was one year old, and in seven years he would begin to see the future when the Earth lines up with Siren. For twenty minutes a day, he will have the remarkable ability to focus on any individual and *see* what the future, twenty-four hours ahead in time, has in store for them. One individual was very disturbed by this ability and made no bones about voicing it. It was *Master Phodan* himself. *Phodan* felt that the future was the providence of the Creator alone, and many errors of judgment and behavior were ripe to occur through the use of this magical *sight*. He had asked Matthew and Alankha if they wanted the *Preculians* to remove this malady from their son. It was a simple matter for the advanced race of people to alter the DNA and genetic composition of homo-erectus. They could blend the genetic code of a person to be short or tall, weak or strong. Intelligence was also an element of their potential recipe for enhancement. It was not out of the realm of possibilities for the *Preculians* to produce a mind that had the total command of all thirteen-hundred cubic centimeters of his brain capacity, but they had learned that intelligence is often a double-edged sword. An enhanced being is rarely happy, *whatever the essence of happiness is*. They were not sure of the *nature of happiness* despite their obvious advanced evolution.

The *Preculians* learned the hard way that there is no shortcut to peace of mind. Sometimes a simple man, who some might consider barely sentient, had the capacity for happiness beyond that of the mass of humanity *or* sirenity. *Preculity* was not spared the shortcoming as well. Many *Preculians* had not advanced beyond the depressive state of their post-atrocity brought about by the destruction of the *Xerians*. Happiness was relative, and Mathew and Alankha requested that *Phodan* and all the other *Preculians* leave their son Zaphi to the will of the Creator.

Shelly Simon and Charles Donovan were determined to have their special progeny left alone as well. He would be named *Lorham* and their desires were for him to become a great *Priest of the Church*. Matthew and Alankha were also grooming their child, Zaphi, for a career in the clergy. Their fervent hope was that their child would never use his talent of sight to take advantage of the masses who may be blind to his knowledge. It could be a terrible temptation to approach God-like status among the masses as they well knew from their short-lived experiences of being self-aware sirens on Earth. Matthew knew that were he to have remained on Earth, he would have been able to make any man or woman see and smell and know anything that his mind could contrive, and there was nothing on God's green pastures to stand in his way. He was poised to become a God. That was instrumental in his decision to make the exodus to Siren. A God among men had to brandish the conscience of one of them. There would be no solace in being the grand puppeteer. That, he knew, would be a passing bit of fancy soon to be replaced with shame. Master *Phodan* said it best: *be very careful what you wish for.*

Shelly and Charles were lighting candles on the altar of the Church, "I wonder when Durbah and Christos Somah will be back from their adventure," said Shelly.

"It's hardly an adventure, Shell," said Charles. "They're in the grips of death as *Phodan* tells it. I'm not sure who he fears most: the creatures in the valley or the *Valegatos* themselves."

"I've heard that they are a fascinating race. It seems they can even mesmerize the animals when pushed to it."

"It must be something to see," said Matthew. "Still, *Phodan* says it's no picnic. Some never return from the valley."

"Well, it wouldn't be the first time he was wrong."

"What's gotten into you?"

"Nothing."

"What do you care about Durbah getting back?"

"There has to be a decision soon. I just want to know what I'm going to be dealing with."

"You want the position, don't you?"

"It's bigger than *what I want.* It would be the best thing for both of us, Matthew. I am the mother of a *seer.*"

"And I am the father. Maybe there should be a High Priest instead of a High Priestess."

"We've been all through that. The bloodline is carried forth by the female, not the male. The congregation has voiced their wishes. One of us will lead the direction of the prayers."

"You still covet the powers, don't you?" said Matthew.

"That's a really low thing to accuse me of. You make it sound like I just want the adoration and remuneration of a suffering people."

"Well, if the slipper fits."

"I think we're done with this conversation."

"Are we done sleeping together as well?" he asked her pointedly.

"What? Are you nuts? I'm crawling out of my skin with all this anticipation of the vote. I need you to love me."

"As you wish, High Priestess."

"Oh, so now you are a *seer* as well, is that it?"

"All I see is that you always get what you want, Shelly."

"What I want is for Durbah and Christos Somah to get back here so we can take care of business. When did *Phodan* say they would be back?"

"He said he didn't know. It was the will of the Creator. But John Poole said Christos Somah was soon to be in a *batcha*.

"God, that's horrible. Maybe we should pray."

"Seriously?"

"We should pray to *Phodan*. At least I'm sure *he* hears us."

"What about our Creator, Shelly."

"*Phodan* gets better results for the most part."

"Yeah, I guess you're right. You want to start or should I?"

"You know that he was the healer of the girl with cancer, don't you?"

"I know that we took the credit. What does that make us?"

It makes us a channel, plain and simple. The people of Siren don't have *Phodan's* ear for the most part. What's the harm in us asking for a favor now and then?"

"No real harm, Shell. But if we lie to them, we're no better than the humans we left back on Earth."

"I want the position, Matthew. Will you fight me on this?"

"I said I wouldn't, High Priestess. Just as long as I can continue to be your cabana boy."

"Keep talking like that, and you'll be going out with the tide," she said laughing.

"Come here. What was that you wanted from me?"

"What, did a horse kick you in the head when you were young?" she chided.

"I'm on it. I'm on it," he said laughing.

~

Chapter Twelve

Christos walked in bare feet across the packed-down needles of the great redwoods. His feet were calloused enough that he could kick away the huge cones without much discomfort. His sandals were hung from the silver belt on his waist. Now that Durbah knew about the belt shield, he kept it on the outside of his robe for quick access if they came upon a viper or another cat. The night was pitch-black because the canopy of the trees all but obscured the stars. Durbah followed behind him reaching out and touching his back to make sure she hadn't lost him. His footfalls were that silent. She, herself, was much clumsier trekking through the forest. Her breathing was labored, and she often tripped over a twig or branch and sometimes even a rather distasteful batch of spoor. Cat spoor and viper spoor was equal in size and could make a pretty good mess of the rubber shoes she wore for their journey into the valley. Just as she got used to feeling her way behind Christos Somah through the night, he suddenly stopped dead in his tracks, and Durbah continued on bumping into his backside. "Shhh," he told her.

"What is it," she whispered back in his ear.

"It is the girl. I'm sure of it. Listen."

Durbah listened and heard the heavy breathing of the girl called Mantah Samah. She was not crying, but her forced breathing spoke of a dehydration and a miserable state of resignation. It was a sad sound to Christos Somah's ear, and his heart went out to the girl. He told Durbah, "She is straight up."

Durbah looked up, but could see nothing but blackness. The huge tree offered footholds in the rough bark large enough to support their feet in a carefully planned climb. As long as they didn't put all their weight in one spot, the bark was sure to hold them. It was not much more difficult to scale the huge tree than to climb a flight of stairs, but this particular *flight* was over four-hundred feet high. The ascent took them nearly two hours before they reached the horizontal branch that held the nest. The branch was easily ten feet in diameter and could be walked on without having to balance or worry about falling off the edge. Durbah was amazed at the sheer size of the great tree. She figured that it must be at least a thousand years-old if it's a day.

When Durbah saw the girl, she was astonished. She no longer resembled a human form at all. A paste had been deposited across her torso, arms and legs, binding her to the nest. It was green in color, and the smell was putrid. She wondered if the girl's skin was burned by the acidity because it burned her nostrils just to breathe the same air that permeated the nest. The girl made no sound. Her eyes were wide open, yet she seemed to be asleep. Something was very wrong with her state-of-mind, and all that Durbah could think of was that the girl was in shock.

Christos Somah quickly got to work. He produced the fangs of the valegato and gave one to Durbah. "Be very careful not to prick the girl with the tooth, Durbah, but it will help us free her from her bonds. Rather than use the needle-sharp point of the tooth, Durbah used the back-end jagged root where it had broken off from the jawbone of the cat. She was able to saw back and forth and not worry about the green viscous fluid that she knew was a deadly poison. She first worked on the girl's legs. Christos Somah worked on her torso and almost had her free when he noticed one of the eggs in the nest start to crack open. "Quickly Durbah," he told her, "we don't have much time." Although the newly hatched condor would be disoriented for a short while, they knew that at nearly one-hundred pounds, the bird would soon become a formidable adversary. It would have a very sharp adolescent beak that could tear flesh in an instant. Soon a second egg began to crack. They heard the first low-pitched chirp of the condor chick and knew that it was soon to be loose from the membrane that held it to the inside of the egg. As the membrane broke, an even worse smell permeated the air around them. Durbah didn't believe that she could even imagine such a smell if she weren't being assaulted by it at that very moment. It would stay with her forever and be a vivid reminder of the gates of hell. Soon the girl's legs were free. She found her voice, "You were foolish to come for me. The condoro will soon be our end," she said miserably.

"Have faith, my child," said Christos Somah, "you will walk out of the forest this night."

"You are mistaken, my sad savior. Our bones will have a dance together in the belly of these birds this night."

"We shall see," said Christos Somah. He had gotten her torso unbound from the mass of green paste, and only one of her arms was still tied fast to the gnarly branches. Her arms and legs were bruised, and Christos Somah saw dark marks above her breasts where the huge bird had grasped her with its talons. The skin was not broken, but rendered into what must have been painful water-blisters in her soft skin. Still the girl did not cry out. She steeled her glare and resolved to do her very best to fight off the hatchlings with her bare hands if need be and try to reclaim her life if it was the will of the Creator. Durbah finally freed the girl's arm, and she knelt down in the nest and finally was overcome by fears and tears. She was so close to freedom that she allowed herself to become hopeful, and that's when the fear took hold of her. She whimpered on her knees and said, "There is not time. The condoro is soon to return, and we will never make it to the ground."

"Faith," said Christos Somah. "Tonight you will learn the meaning of the word. I know that it is your custom to pray to the Creator. But you can ask him for a favor, also. You can ask him to shine brightly on your life and promise Him that you will be grateful."

"I will be grateful. I will become a better person if I can survive this night. I will be a comfort to my people in any way that I am able."

"That is the design that He has for you, child. That you become more than you are now."

A foul smelling wind came upon them from above and they all knew its origin. The condor had returned to the nest. She beat her wings and fluttered above the nest deciding which of the three she would impale with her hellish beak and shake loose their entrails. Christos Somah told the girl to hold on to him so he could wrap the *Preculian's* shield around them both. But the shield was not long enough to hold Durbah in the circle as well. He tossed her his valegato fang, and she deftly caught it making sure not to carelessly prick herself with the poison. She held it out above her head ready to strike up with both of them into the undercarriage of the huge bird. Soon, she got her chance. She jumped up to reach the bird before it actually landed in the nest. One fang punctured the right foot of the condor above the left talon, and the other one was driven home in the great bird's belly. The squawking scream creased the night and was painful in the ears of all three of them. The bird was on the verge of madness. Hate and fury would be all she could think of at that point – determined to do the most amount of damage in the least amount of time. Then a very strange thing happened. The bird coughed as though trying to get her breath. Durbah knew that the poison from the valley cat's fangs was doing its job. The bird was dying. She collapsed onto the three of them with her five-hundred pounds of dead weight and gave one last gasp and was still. They could tell that the bird was not breathing and had killed her last victim. Her chicks would live on to continue the hell that was the canopy above the forest, but her days of horror were behind her. Christos Somah then said to the girl, "Faith, young one. It will always serve you well."

~

Chapter Thirteen

When they had made the long climb back to ground-level from the nest in the great tree, Durbah said to Christos Somah, "We were in the nest of the condor, yet that was not the prophecy."

"What prophecy?" asked Christos Somah.

"John Poole said that Bantah Somah would be in the nest of a condor. He called it the *batcha do condoros.*"

"Not much fun, is it?" said Christos Somah.

"No, it's not. I may never get that smell completely out of my nose. But the prophecy has not yet come to be. Bantah Somah still has an encounter with one of these devils. Will you lend him your belt from *Preculis?*"

"I have a responsibility to never let it out of my possession, but I will do better than that. I will be with him. The belt can fit around both of us, but not all three of us."

"What are you saying?" asked Durbah.

"I'm saying that you are going to return to the encampment and stay there until I come back with your friend."

"Like hell I am," she said. "I won't let you go off and do my dirty work."

"You will consider what I ask if you are to be my woman, Durbah."

"Please don't ask that of me, Christos Somah."

"You have fought enough monsters to last you for a while. Now you will do as I ask and wait for me in safety. I can concentrate much better on the task if I don't have to worry about you."

"You know I can change your mind, Christos Somah, if I really want to," said Durbah referring to the electrum she could wield with her gaze.

"Yes, I suspect as much. And I also suspect that you won't. You will respect my wishes and stay behind because Bantah Somah and I will be safer for it."

"Alright. I will respect your wishes this time."

"You have a responsibility now to your people, Durbah, that you never had before. You can't be selfish."

"What are you talking about, Christos Somah?"

"I was told that you are being considered for High Priestess of the Church. There is one who will oppose you, but she does not have the power to succeed."

"That position is not something that I covet, Christos Somah."

"And I do not covet being the son of a Grand Regent of the Council of Siren, but I bear my burden as you shall also bear yours."

"Yes, I suppose you're right. As the Creator wills, so shall be what comes to pass."

"You are very wise, mi corida."

"That's the first time you called me that. It sounds very nice. What does it mean?"

"When we reach the encampment, I will show you."

"Oh, I like the sound of that even better," she told him.

~

Carla Walker once again woke up singing. She surprised herself because, although she knew many songs that she shared with Cap', she never thought that her voice was particularly bursting with talent. Cap' would beg to differ with that opinion of her musical abilities. He looked forward to her morning songs and often would join in when he knew the words. At first, this morning's song was not-at-all familiar to him. It seemed like a primitive chant in a strange language, yet he found it particularly endearing. It seemed to taunt him into an action that was forbidden somehow. That's the only way he could describe it to himself. It was like some forbidden fruit like laughing in church or at a funeral. Her impish melody danced before his ears with a dare and a promise to entice him further if he were to let it. *"Ah do e na,"* she sang to him and then paused as if he were expected to answer her somehow.

"What's that you're singing, Carla?" he asked her.

"I don't really know, Nige. It was in a dream that I had I think."

"You heard a song in a dream?"

"Yes, I'm sure I did. There was more to it, too. I was one of many women singing to young men across a fire. I sang to one of them, 'Ah do e na,' and then he responded to me."

Cap' thought that he could almost hear the response in his head, but that was unlikely. How could he possibly know what was happening in Carla's dream?

"You have to time it right. It goes like this, "Ah do e na," she sang and then held out her hands to Cap' and swayed back and forth like a hula dancer.

"What is the response, Carla?" he asked her.

"I can't really remember."

"Sing it again."

She sang with the precise meter and melody of the *Valegatos* native tribe of Siren, "Ah do e na," and then Cap' suddenly answered her, "Des oo eh jo ma."

"That's it, Nigel! That's the response. How did you know it?" she asked.

"I haven't the slightest idea," said Cap'. "What do you suppose it means?"

"I don't know, but I know how I feel when I sing the words. It's beautiful. It makes me feel beautiful."

"You are beautiful, Carla. You start," said Cap'.

She began to dance back and forth swaying her hips in a seductive manner that was not lost on Cap' Walker. He liked what he was seeing. Then she began to sing, "Ah do e na," and he answered her, "Des oo eh jo mah."

"Ah do e na," she repeated.

"Des oo eh jo mah," he answered again. They established a rhythm for the call-and-answer song as well as a sensual dance that both felt were the ideal complement to each other. They could not have been more moved by the moment even if they had been touching. They continued on for some time with the taunting call-and-answer chant accompanied by the sensual dance with the swaying hips. Finally, Cap' Walker asked her, "You have any idea what it means now, Carla?"

"Nope," she said. "But I feel like I have something more to do to complete the dance move."

"And what would that be?" he asked her.

"Her reply was not verbal, but physical. She crossed the room and stood behind him, and he then said, "What now?"

She leaned over and kissed him on the right side of his neck. "I'm not sure why I am supposed to do that, but it was very clear in the dream."

"Cool dream, Carla. I like it. Next time, see if you can find out what it means."

"I think it will come to me, Nigel. I think I just have to let go and be a part of it. I sense that it is a ritual of some kind that is very old. Maybe even older than mankind itself."

"Well, I know someone who may be able to shed some light on the subject," said Cap'.

"When is the last time you saw him?"

"It was the day that you arrived. But I think he'll be dropping in on us soon. He said he'd give me three days to think over his proposition."

"And?"

"I'll do it. What do I have to lose? Plus, I'm pretty grateful that he brought you back to me."

"I'm grateful, too, Nigel. I don't remember where I was, whether it was in Heaven or in limbo or *that other place,* but I'm sure glad to be back here now."

"Don't ever talk about *that other place,* Carla. They'd never let you in."

Chapter Fourteen

When Durbah, Christos Somah and the young girl got back to the encampment, the entire tribe of *Valegatos* were gone. The ashes in the fire pit were cold, and all the tents had been packed up and carried away. Durbah and Christos Somah wondered why they didn't just leave the tents behind to return to when they once again sought out this climate. Apparently, the task of setting up was a simple one, and the *Valegatos* merely carried their houses along with them. Christos Somah asked the girl, "Which way, Mantah Samah?"

She sat down on the soft ground and looked up into the night sky. The constellations were her only clue of direction since there was no moon on Siren. She looked up at Orion just rising above the eastern horizon and turned around to search for Scorpio setting in the west. Finding it to her left, she pointed straight ahead and told them, "north, I think."

"You think?" asked Christos Somah. "You mean you don't know?"

"I know they went north because, as you can see, the water is raised from within my body and coats my skin. Christos Somah could see a fine sheen on her copper colored form.

"Although I know that my people have gone north, I am not entirely sure which way *is* north. I have to rely on an old story of how the hunter waits for the scorpion to leave the sky before he rises. Now do you see why I am unsure?" He figured her age to be about fifteen or sixteen years old, and she was beautiful in the dark night. Her eyes almost glowed slightly with the gold and silver electrum that he had noticed in Durbah's eyes as well. The only other time he had seen light in the eyes of a creature in darkness was the canos majoros, or dog-like creature that the Sirens used to watch over their young children. The *Valegatos* kept no domestic animals, but it is said that they can direct some of the ones in the wild if they so choose.

She continued, "It is the way of my people when the water comes to the surface of the skin." The girl was telling him that in order to manipulate their climactic surroundings, the tribe had moved further north where it would be cooler until the trade winds shifted again. "Lead us, little samah," said Durbah. She wanted to rejoin the *Valegatos* while Christos Somah and Bantah Somah went off in search of Alex Janzen. She had come to respect the ancient group of native Sirens and seemed to prefer their company over all the supposedly *sophisticated* native Sirens that occupied the cities like Creston at the top of the Sirenian range and Alantis located in the middle of the sea to the east. The *Valegatos* were a very sensual people ruled by the id and not the super-ego. They would be quite willing to express their desires to lay with the Earth sirens if the notion came to them, whereas the sirens of the cities were much more likely to edit their behavior to the point of ineffectuality. Their world was a mass of vanilla-flavored peacefulness; however, excitement was much more preferable to the newcomers from Earth. They wanted adventure but were presented with tedium at best and out-and-out boredom at worst. It was no wonder that Brad Early and Alex Janzen chose a lifestyle of recklessness in order to bring about some spice in their lives.

The three stragglers followed the river north for two hours before they came upon the embers of a ceremonial fire. It was apparent that they had shed their clothes because the pelts of the *valegatos* were piled around the outer edges of the fire. The girl was without clothes as well. Durbah and Christos Somah considered shedding their own clothes, but they felt that the closeness they had recently shared would be best served with some boundaries. Christos Somah wasn't sure he could interact with a naked Durbah without becoming aroused by her stunning beauty. That was something that he wasn't prepared to share with outsiders and especially the young girl. The young *Valegato* was oblivious to any kind of sexual taboos as demonstrated by her persistent practice of grabbing hold of both Christos Somah and Durbah in some very private places. Some habits die a long and painful death, and while Christos Somah and Durbah were not particularly bashful, they believed that love making was best ventured into with a certain amount of privacy.

The perspiration on the skin of the young *Valegato* maiden was dissipating, so they knew they were getting close to the next encampment. There was no reason for them to travel further north than necessary to find a comfortable climate because the bounty of the river was metastatic. There were the same fish, north or south, early or late in the day as well. They were river trout with shining green and gold scales, and they often measured as much as three feet in length. Apparently, they had no natural predators aside from the *Valegatos* tribe because they were always plentiful in number. Durbah and Christos Somah wondered why the *valley cats* didn't find them particularly appetizing. A cat and a fish is a natural match, whether on Siren or Earth or *Preculis* for that matter. But the large cats steered as clear of the fish as they did the eggs of the condors. *Perhaps it is their bloodlust,* thought Christos Somah. Once you have tasted the flesh of homo-erectus, nothing else satiates the craving quite as well. When he thought of the large fangs of the cat, and the thought of facing them without his belt-shield from *Phodan,* he shivered in the night. He was feeling very tired, but was also not quite ready to close his eyes to the night and hope for the best wishes of the Creator. He thought that perhaps they should camp for the night and that one of them should remain awake at all times and keep watch for the predators of the valley. Durbah had a better idea. "I say we keep on going until we meet up with the *Valegatos.* If you're worrying about being tired, I have a solution for that given to me by their leader Bantah."

"You've got leaves," said the girl. "I'm ready. I have no sleep in me tonight. Give me four, please."

"Four?" asked Durbah. "I was told that I would need only one or two to fight off sleep."

"You can fight off anything you want, mistress, but I want to feel good and forget about that awful creature that pasted me into her nest. Give me four, please."

Durbah handed the girl what she wanted. She gave two to Christos Somah and told him to chew them.

"I've had them before, Durbah. They will fight off sleep for us. And they give you a feeling of well being as well."

"They sure do," said the young, *Valegato* girl. "And Bantah's crop is always the best," she said knowingly.

Durbah chuckled and noted how similar youth was on both Earth and Siren. Here she was one-hundred-eighty million miles away from her home, and she felt like she was watching a high-school student catch a buzz at a party. She noticed the electrum fade in the eyes of the young girl and there was an increase of the rise and fall of her chest. She looked at the stars with a newly found interest when the drug from the leaves began to course through her veins. She looked at Durbah and Christos Somah and said, "It's beautiful. Life is beautiful. The valley cats are beautiful, and you are beautiful."

Christos Somah laughed at her demonstration of beautiful observations and said, "Let's go, samah. We can all be beautiful when we meet up with the next camp."

With that, the three night-travelers continued on in search of the *Valegatos*. They knew that Bantah Somah was eager to trek off into the valley with Christos Somah in order to rescue a flier captured by a bird. Every excursion would add to his glory as a fearless warrior of the *Valegatos*. He didn't really expect to be drawn into the senseless conflict that was continually perpetuated with the *Vipos* tribe or the *Condoros* people either, but his reputation would rise to larger than life, and he could expect a very sizable dowry from an elder when presented with a prospective mate. All three of the tribes of the valley were descended from the original forty-eight sirens who were accused of being sorcerers and banished from the cities. Each tribe identified with one of the three major animal groups of the valley: the vipers, the condors and the cats.

Bantah Somah hired a flying wing to traverse the valley in search of the lost flier. It had to fly at three thousand feet to be above the dangers of the condoros. For that reason, he wore a headset that would focus onto the treetops that were roughly four-hundred feet above the valley floor. The naked eye could never pick out a captured flier in a nest from that height. The paste that the condoro used was the same color as the nest and would mask an infrared signature as well. The headset would magnify the treetops to 20 times their normal size. It was only a matter of time before he could identify the actual tree that was holding Alex Janzen. They found it after only two hours into the grid search. He seemed to be in one piece, but Bantah Somah couldn't tell if he was breathing or not. Infrared told him that the nest was warm, but that could be a residual of the condor sitting on the huge eggs.

The hatchlings would emerge from the eggs weighing one hundred pounds and be all appetite. They were known to eat their own weight in the first three days. Alex Janzen weighed in at a little over one-hundred forty pounds since his continued addiction and self-inflicted starvation and atrophy. The chick would dispatch him in the first few minutes and then take her time. It was probably the most horrific way to die on Siren, but the bite of the coil viper ran a close second.

A small sense of solace came from the fact that there was an even worse way to die in the universe, but it was not on Siren.

It was not on Earth either. The great white shark of the Barrier Reef of Australia paled in comparison to the most insidious and deadly creature of all time. It was the deep serpent on the planet *Preculis*. But *Preculis* was light-years away from Siren and all of the perils that Bantah Somah had to deal with on this day. He would think only about his task at hand. He concentrated on the tree that he knew held the nest of the condor who took the Earth prisoner and his promise to deliver him to safety. It would be a glorious addition to the legend of the young warrior. If the truth were known, he only waged war against the creatures of the valley and had never actually engaged a rival tribal warrior in his entire life.

Bantah Somah returned to the *Valegatos* at the same time Durbah and Christos Somah had arrived with the young girl. He looked at the eyes of Durbah and noticed that there was no electrum there. She was clear of the gold and silver light source, so Bantah Somah knew she had been chewing on the leaves given to her by his father. He asked Christos Somah, "Have you begun to chew as well?"

"Yes, I have," said Christos Somah.

"Then let's go. There's no point in waiting any longer. I have the location of our quest. I hired a glider from Creston earlier in the day."

"You saw the tree?" asked Christos Somah.

"I did. We can head out now and be there before morning."

"Lead the way," said Christos Somah.

"Not so fast," said Durbah.

"You're not going to argue with me again, are you Durbah?"

"No, Christos Somah. I'm going to kiss you."

The kiss lasted a full minute and Bantah Somah was jealous of a Creston-dweller for the first time in his life.

~

Chapter Fifteen

I sabelle was barking at the screen door, wanting out. She was unable to nudge open the door as she usually did because the latch was engaged. Carla came into the kitchen saying, "What's all this racket about Belle? Oh, I see, the latch is down." *I wonder why Nigel did that at this time of day?* she asked herself. *He knows that Belle has to go out and do her business. After all, she is a businesswoman,* she chuckled to herself. Isabelle agreed with Carla's thoughts, "Rooof!" *Big business!*

"Okay, hold on, honey." Carla undid the latch at the top of the door and noticed *Phodan* rounding their mailbox at the end of the driveway and starting toward the house. Carla understood why Isabelle was barking. She opened the door and said to the *business end* of the disappearing dog, "Oh, now I get it. You don't have to go pee, you just want to see your boyfriend."

Isabelle stopped halfway down the driveway and turned around to confirm Carla's thought, "Rooof!"

"Well, go on. Tell him to come on in, Belle."

"Rooof!" said the dog and headed off to greet *Phodan*. When she reached him, she sat down at his feet and waited for him to extend his hand for her to lick. *Sooo delicious!* thought the dog. *Humans have no idea how good they taste. Preculians either, I guess.* She had asked *Phodan* if she could go to his world sometime and his answer was noncommittal. *Maybe it's a male thing,* she thought. Cap' never took her to his ships either. *But I can't help but to love them.*

Phodan extended his hand and Isabelle gave it a quick lick. The *Preculian* reached out and scratched her behind the ears knowing exactly where she liked it. He could hear her thoughts, *ahhh that feels so good, Phodan.*

"Where is your housemate?" he asked her.

"Which one, the phony captain or the waheen?"

"So that's why they call you bitches," he said playfully.

"Good one, *Phodan.* But you know I love them like only the canos majoros can."

"Yes, Belle. Indeed, I do."

"Who do you want to talk to?"

"I need an answer from Cap'."

"He's up for it. I think he's been kind of bored lately if you want to know the truth."

"Always, Belle."

"The question was rhetorical. Sheesh, you *Preculians* don't know much about figures of speech, do you?"

"I guess not, biatch."

"Touché, Masseur Rennie. Or should I call you Mr. Carpenter."

"I'm sorry, Belle. I don't follow," said *Phodan.*

"Michael Rennie."

"I'm drawing a blank."

"The Day The Earth Stood Still. Great movie! It was a 1951 American science fiction film. Directed by Robert Wise and written by Edmund H. North. It was based on the short story

"Farewell to the Master," written in 1940 by Harry Bates. The film stars Rennie, Patricia Neal and Sam Jaffe. Jaffe was good, but Neal was hot."

"I'll see if Netflix will deliver to *Preculis*."

A dog's laugh is a wonderful thing to experience. *Phodan* wasn't disappointed with Isabelle's. Snot was coming out of Isabelle's nose, "Stop, *Phodan*, you're killing me." She laughed again.

"So where is the old guy. Spill darling."

"He's out at Alligator Lake. I think he's looking for the ship."

"He won't find it," said *Phodan*.

"Just what I thought. Photo-reflective side panels?"

"Are you sure you're a dog?"

"I've got the fleas to prove it. Oh, and one more thing," she said.

"What's that?"

"Gort, Platu barada nicto!" Isabelle couldn't resist delivering the line from the classic old movie. She snickered as only a dog can.

Phodan chuckled at Isabelle's comment and told her, "I thought I could speak dog, but now I'm not so sure. Lead the way."

Carla came down the front steps from the front porch and joined them just as they were rounding the corner to the side yard. She didn't say anything to *Phodan* and greeted him only with a slight nod of her head and blink of her eyes. She knew that *Phodan* probably knew more about her than she knew about herself at this point. What was there to say? But she felt a warm heart within the sky-blue robe that clothed the mysterious man from the heavens. She was grateful to him for giving her life. He almost appeared to be a father figure for her, and in some ways she supposed he was.

When they reached the lake, *Phodan* said, "Belle tells me I have a pilot."

Cap' didn't say anything at first and just looked down at the dog. He shook his head, but still didn't say anything. In his heart, he really couldn't blame the dog for wanting to communicate. After all, Carla and he couldn't understand his dog speaking, so what was the harm in having a friend in *Phodan* to communicate with. Still, he wasn't entirely satisfied letting Isabelle completely off the hook. He looked down at her and mouthed the words that only her dog ears could hear, "You have some splaining to do."

Isabelle's ears flattened out to the sides of her head and she slinked a little closer to the ground. Carla sensed what the dog was feeling and reached down to pet her. Belle recovered in an instant and rubbed against her mistress's leg.

Cap' looked at *Phodan* and smiled at the thought of his life that had been recently put back together. He relished the thought of a life with a healthy Carla and an equally healthy Isabelle. He finally asked him, "Where is the ship. A pilot needs a ship if I'm not mistaken."

"You are entirely right, Captain. And you are not only a pilot this time, you are the sole captain of *The Pegasus Mane*."

"The who?" asked Cap'.

"Your ship. Her name is *The Pegasus Mane*. She is one of my fleet of ships that are the pride of *Preculis*. She has photo-reflective side panels, as Isabelle would tell you if she could, and a full complement of weaponry that you will never need. She also has a plus-light ion-pulse propulsion system that you will never even see. You're a smart man, Cap', and there are certain things I have brought to Earth that you have no business knowing about. I act under a strict directive to be most careful regarding what you see."

"Things like that belt around your waist," said Cap'.

"As I said, you are a smart man. What tipped you off?"

Cap' reached into his pocket and retrieved the dozen shot pellets that were given to him by Ben Mason. He held them out to *Phodan*, who just looked at them with a blank expression. *Phodan* finally said, "As you can see I've fixed my robe. You can't even see where the holes were, can you?"

"Wow, *Phodan!* We'll finally be able to unlock the secrets of the cosmic seamstresses," he said sarcastically. "Don't tell me you don't know what these are," said Cap' referring to the shotgun pellets.

"Alright, I won't."

"How does it work?"

Again, *Phodan* just looked at Cap' with a blank expression and didn't offer any information about the subject. Cap' had a sixth sense that the rule against exposing other species to the wonders of *Preculis* was the bedrock of their existence. When everyone is on a level playing field, you have to retreat back to square one. The ruling body of *Preculis* would make sure that a leak of superior technology would never come to pass.

"Would you like to see her?" asked *Phodan.*

"The ship? Yes, naturally," said Cap'.

"She is right in front of you, but to see her you will need this." *Phodan* held out a small oval stone that appeared to be made of smooth, flat black granite. In its surface were etched a number of icons which were actually active control buttons. *Phodan* said to him, "Soon you will learn the complete function of the control stone, but for now, press the large button on the front of the stone."

As Cap' did so, the ship materialized hovering over Alligator Lake just a few feet from shore. Its size was breathtaking. She certainly had room for a control cabin and about thirty passengers as well. It was all so surreal to Cap'. Where a moment before was only the stillness of Alligator Lake, now stood a sturdy mass of steel and any number of unknown alloys used to manufacture a ship capable of traveling to the stars. It was heady and unnerving at the same time, causing Cap' to become unsteady on his feet. "I think I need a beer," he muttered.

"Not a problem, Cap'," said *Phodan.* "We're not at all like the FAA. Knock yourself out."

"Isabelle nudged *Phodan's* hand and said, "Rooof!"

Phodan reached down to pet her and said, "That's up to Cap', dear. But it doesn't matter to me."

"What?" asked Carla. "What did she say, *Master Phodan?*"

"She asked if she could come along when Cap' first takes the ship up to orbit."

Carla laughed and said, "She took the words right out of my mouth."

~

Chapter Sixteen

C apt. was standing at the edge of Alligator Lake marveling at the grand scale of the ship before him. He wasn't sure because he had no way to reference it, but he thought that she displaced easily two thousand tons. For an airship, that was remarkable. He knew he was dealing with technology eons away from what would be developed on Earth. He asked, *Phodan*, "What is her propulsion system?"

"Well, there are three. A simple electro-crystal drive will give you magnetic-opposition-flow. That will take you to and from the way station. Since you will not be required to leave Earth orbit, the other drives are not important."

"Humor me," said Cap'.

"There is also a nuclear decay propulsion field utilizing *Xerium,* but there is very little left. Perhaps enough to make the journey back to *Preculis* and nothing more."

"Can't you replenish it here on Earth?" asked Cap'.

"I'd rather not. Your fuel here is too dirty for our needs. The half-life is entirely too long. We would run the risk of disease if we were exposed for any length of time."

"Cancer?"

"Yes, cancer."

"But you have the ability to cure disease, correct?"

"Yes, but in the case of long-life radiation, the disruption of cells persists beyond our abilities to interact.

"What do you say, Cap'? Are passengers allowed on board when you do your training?"

"Oh, why the hell not?" Cap' ran his fingers lightly over the stone and reached out with his senses to try to intuit the function of the carved inscriptions. Something *told* him how he could access the ramp to the control cabin. He depressed the button and a seam opened up on the ship and a ramp lowered down to the ground complete with stairs on a riser.

"Very good," said *Phodan*. Permission to come aboard, Captain?"

"Permission granted," said Cap', not missing a beat.

The four of them walked up the stairs and into the control cabin of the ship. There were only two chairs, so he told Carla to take the right seat, and he took the left one. He left *Phodan* standing behind them with Isabelle. After all, she had four feet to take her weight and was probably in the best shape of all of them.

Cap' was amazed that the controls were identical to those of the cruise ships he had been piloting for the last thirty years. There were dual thrusters, which corresponded to the mammoth drive chains of the cruise ships, along with side thrusters to make the more finely-tuned adjustments to movements in tight spaces.

"Does this look familiar to you, Capt?" asked *Phodan* knowingly.

"Yes, it does."

"Take us up," said *Phodan*.

Cap' was familiar with forward and backward, and the side thrusters would facilitate side to side, but up was a new concept that he had to wrap his mind around for a short while. Finally, he reached forward with both hands and grabbed the two thrusters and pulled slightly up. The ship began to rise. As a seasoned pilot, he knew that it was prudent to make slow movements at first, especially since he didn't completely understand the full workings of the control station. But as he reached five-hundred feet, he chanced a more forceful command of the controls and pulled up harder. Cap' and Carla were forced down into their seats with the gravitational forces, and Isabelle lowered herself to the floor of the cockpit. *Phodan* seemed unaffected and remained standing.

When they reached ninety miles above sea level, the Earth seemed to shrink into a very clear blue ball. There were no clouds to speak of and the site was beautiful. The "G" forces became neutral as they reached zero gravity and *Phodan* reached up and held himself in place by touching the ceiling. Isabelle was not so fortunate. She couldn't reach the ceiling of the cockpit and so began to float helplessly up with her paws gyrating and doing little than making her body turn into a slow spin. She belched. Cap' addressed the issue with, "Isabelle, find your sky legs or this will be your last flight."

Isabelle did, and there were no gastric accidents on that flight or any of the other twelve flights that she would make to the way station in the next month.

Cap' was getting to know the helm of the ship as though he were born to it. He thought that he could make some pretty spectacular maneuvers were he left to his flight of fancy, but he knew that was not what he was there for. He remained focused on the gratitude for rejoining Carla with him and habilitating Isabelle and applied himself dutifully and selflessly to the task at hand. *Phodan* was impressed. He said as much, "I've picked the right man."

"Thank you, *Phodan*. Where to now?"

"The way station is programmed into the con. There is an icon in front of you that says Home 1. The trick is slowing your approach and completing the docking procedure. It's not unlike nestling up to a mooring; the difference being you don't have any bumpers and line tenders.

Cap' pressed the button below the Home 1 icon. The ship closed the distance to the way station in about seventeen minutes. As they approached, the ship came to a dead stop one-hundred meters from the docking port. *Phodan* put his hand on Cap's shoulder and said, "Here is where you earn your money."

"Piece of cake," said Cap'. "Err, what money?"

"That's a figure of speech, Cap'. I don't have any money."

"Figures."

"But, one of the Earth sirens said I could get some with these," he said. He produced half a dozen large gold ingots from his pocket and said, "I'm told I can exchange these for money at a coin ship on International Drive."

"Well, you can leave a few of them at my house, too, if you want," said Cap'.

"As you wish," said *Phodan*.

"I'm gonna' get a new collar," said Isabelle, but only *Phodan* could hear her. To Cap' and Carla, it sounded a lot like, "Rooof!"

Chapter Seventeen

Christos noticed that Bantah Somah was not only wearing a small patch of fur, but also had donned a finely tailored overcoat made of pelts of the valley cats. Christos Somah had to hold himself in check because it was a forbidden amusement. To laugh at the expense of another was unthinkable to the young siren. The more he thought about Bantah Somah dressed in finer clothing than the young night-lifer's, of Creston, just tickled him to no end. The *Valegatos* were looked down upon by the youth of Siren largely because they have been taught by their elders to disregard them as savages. While it was true that they wore little clothing and their boundaries for sexual encounter were somewhat undefined, they had no instance of homicide, patricide, matricide, infanticide, doggocide or whatever-have-youicide. There were a few instances of catricide, but it went with the territory.

"Where to? Which way, Bantah Somah?" asked Christos Somah.

"Please, Christos. I give you the courtesy to step out from beneath your father's shadow when we are away from Creston. Please call me Bantah and I will not have to call you Christos Somah.

"Forgive me, Bantah Somah, but until our fathers are passed, we owe them the respect of giving them sole ownership of their names. You will own the name Bantah soon enough. If you want to talk of courtesy, please call me Christos Somah. Again, forgive me if I seem to be short with you. Our journey was very intense. We encountered a valegato. You can imagine how I felt being in charge of protecting a woman. *Delicacy du gatos.*"

"It makes me shiver, my brother. I have lived among them for my whole life, and yet I feel that I have never known them. Their heart is hidden from us, unlike the canos."

"Are there canos in the valley?" asked Christos Somah.

"Yes, but not many. They are at risk here. It is mostly the vipers who call them home to their Creator. They don't hear as well when they get older, and the viper is nearly always silent anyway."

"And what if they encounter a valley cat?" he asked.

"It doesn't happen, that's all. The only time you will see a canos in the same place as a valegato is when he is protecting a child. Otherwise, they are long-gone when they sense them. The canos is only two or three feet long. It would be impossible for the valegato, an animal four-times his size, to creep up on him undetected. He would feel the footfalls of the pads of the valegatos within a thousand paces. Then he would move accordingly just out-of-reach and eventually circle back around to his original camp. It is a dance of the ages. Many songs are written about the continuous cycle of the animals of the valley. They are all ugly, and yet they are all beautiful. The condoros takes away the disease of the fallen. The coil-vipers hold the valegatos in check so they don't grow in such numbers where they are unable to feed themselves. And the valegatos have, perhaps, the greatest role to play in the eternal production within the valley. They are the *mystery*. They are the predator that can leap one-hundred-twenty feet in the air and snag a careless flier or catcher who doesn't respect his space. There is a kill-zone from riverbed to nearly treetop level where the cats are king. The condors are formidable, and the vipers are deadly, but the *gatos* are preternatural if not ethereal. In the Darwinian sense of who gets finished - or who goes over the finish line, *the gatos are transcendental.*"

"So which way do we go?" asked Christos Somah.

"North," said Bantah. "A lot farther north than you would like."

"What do you mean?"

"You're going to need more than the clothes you have on. About twice as much, but only for a short while."

"How far north?"

"I think it's close to twenty miles."

"Then why do you think I need the extra clothing?"

"First time in the valley." He said it as a statement with never the suggestion of a question.

"How much colder could it be only twenty miles from here?"

"We're not only going north, we're going up. The elevation is about eight thousand feet."

"How cold."

"About forty degrees colder than here."

"These are my only clothes," said Christos Somah.

"I will find you a *coata do gatos*. You will be warm enough."

"What of the Earth flier?" asked Christos Somah. "Is he freezing to death up in the condor's nest?"

"I don't know. He wasn't moving, but I think he still had his jumpsuit. It was covered with the *pesta do condoros,* a glue used to bind him that should insulate him from the cold as well. I'm hoping that he is strong enough to rappel down the tree by himself. I'm bringing a separate device for him."

"Durbah said he had become weak *before* he was taken down. It is the flier's sickness."

"Yes, it is very sad. We of the valley are spared that. We may climb the trees when we are young, but we have no desire to fly."

"Why is that?"

"Have you noticed the pelts that we wear on our ankles?"

"Yes."

"Do you think they are just decoration?"

"I've never thought about it. Why?"

"They are filled with inert stones so we don't fly."

"Seriously?"

"Yes. Living in the valley makes the sand part of our skin. Notice the copper color of my skin. It is from the grains."

"Interesting," said Christos Somah.

"We do not feel that it is interesting. We feel it is a nuisance to have to weigh ourselves down."

"When do we leave?"

"Right after the ceremony."

"What ceremony?" asked Christos Somah.

"Embraces do samahs."

"A hug good-bye?"

"By all of them."

"You mean *all* the young girls will want to embrace us before we leave on our journey?"

"It may be their last chance, ever," said Bantah.

"Not the young one, too," Christos Somah groaned. "Please tell me that Mantah Samah will not be among them."

"Did you see a fire in her eyes? Was there a glitter of gold and silver when she looked at you?"

"What do you mean?" asked Christos Somah.

"Good. Then she is not yet sixteen. That one will be a handful."

"What are you talking about, Bantah? What fire?"

"It is not important, but keep this one thing in mind please. During the ceremony, when you are embraced by the young women, it is customary to close your eyes. In fact, you would do well to close your eyes during the whole affair. That would be most respectful and in accordance with our ways."

"Yes, I noticed that during the *dance do gatos* that all the men had their eyes closed."

"If you are ever again in the dance, you would do well to do the same."

~

Chapter Eighteen

Kissimmee, Florida

Chip Luger was the poster boy for the sad resignation to the fact that some necks are redder than others. His legal name, not that he was known for accomplishing anything *legal*, was Samuel "Buck" Luger III. He was given the nickname *Chip* at an early age by Buck Luger Sr.'s "associates" within a white supremacist group. The reason was, so the often told story goes, Buck III was a chip off the old blocks. He was just as hateful and ignorant as his father and his grandfather before him. Their ignorance was only surpassed by their violent nature. It was a carry-over from the original Luger who was the first to immigrate to the United States after W.W. II. Unfortunately, he never lost his taste for killing blacks and Jews as a member of Hitler's German Army.

When he had his first son in America, he protested about forced integration of schools and vowed to seek revenge along with his newly formed group of maniacs called *The Sons of Destiny*. They even had their own flag designed by Buck Luger himself. It was a red rectangle with a silhouette of a large tree with a man hanging beneath at the end of a rope. He was grateful to the American government for fighting so hard to defend his right to be the voice of atrocities. When he marched with his white sheet over his cowardly head, he was often heard to start his self-composed chant: *we will overcome right back!*

The world became a better place with the death of Buck Sr., a year-and-a-half ago, when he was within the blast radius of a nuclear explosion over Cape Kennedy, Florida. Buck had a contract to cut the seventy acres of lawn around the NASA properties, and his crew was also in charge of maintaining the sprinkler system. Chip was safely in Kissimmee shooting pool in the clubhouse of *The Sons of Destiny*. He didn't get the news of his father's death until a full day later because the electric grid was knocked out by the neutron pulse of the blast. All electricity ceased to function for a full twenty-four hours. When the news was finally on the T.V., it was all bad. Everyone had surmised that it was only a matter of time before a nuclear explosion would happen on American soil, but no one had the slightest idea that it would be a bomb of our own manufacture.

NASA sent a probe called the XB-37 up into near-Earth orbit and had programmed it to travel to a nearby asteroid and detonate at three-thousand feet above the surface. The program was altered by a short burst of gamma wave radiation, and it was sent off on a random path through our solar system. When it approached the planet Siren on the opposite side of Earth's sun, it was caught in the gravitational field, and it established a geosynchronous orbit. Since it posed no direct threat to Siren, it was merely monitored by Siren's benefactors on the planet *Preculis*. They had been looking after the welfare of Siren for over five-thousand years.

When the *Preculians* collapsed the star of a nearby enemy planet, a long burst of gamma waves was sent out into the cosmos. Earth happened to be in the path just by virtue of the fact that it was on the wrong side of the sun. Siren was spared the radiation and its effects on the fauna and flora of their planet. The unfortunate effect for Earth was a change in the basic nature of mankind. This was the time before the old kingdom of Egypt and the subsequent civilizations of the pharaohs. This was the time of the birth of emotion – both positive and negative. This was the precursor of mankind's first murder of Abel by his brother Cain. Chip Luger was anxious to follow in Cain's footsteps. He was so outraged by his father's death that he wanted to strike out at anyone or anything with every destructive force at his command. Fortunately, most people didn't follow his example, even most of *The Sons of Destiny*, and he was largely written-off as *that little whack-job Chip*. But Chip Luger didn't need a following to exact his revenge. He didn't even need a legitimate target. He was *fixin'* to strike out at his favorite target after he drank a six-pack and smoked a vial of crack. The lucky winners were, the *Mexicans*.

According to Chip Luger, just about everything that was wrong with Kissimmee, Florida, and the country as a whole, could be traced directly back to the Mexicans. They were the ones he felt were responsible for him being out of work at the masonry company where he worked. *Them Mexicans would work for less money, so he was the one let go when the work got thin.* The truth of the matter was, aside from the Mexican workers actually doing a superior job, the management of the company was just plain tired of Chip walking off the job site as soon as he had made enough money for his next vial of crack. The company was owned by one of *The Sons of Destiny* and as a favor to Buck Luger Sr., they always took him back when he slept off his drug binge. According to Chip Luger, the Mexicans were responsible for his father's death. He only had missed the mark by a matter of four light-years. The Planet *Preculis*, which revolves around the star we call *Alpha Centauri,* is approximately four light-years from Earth. It is a star that Earth astronomy chose to call *Alpha Centauri,* but the *Preculians* have always called it *Preculis*. It is located in the southern sky and is not visible to observers at a latitude greater than 25 degrees north (roughly the latitude of Florida and Egypt).

If the truth were known to Chip Luger, Earth was responsible for shooting herself in the foot. (Or the space complex as it were) When the XB-37's orbit had decayed, due to a totally random, errant meteor strike, the *Preculians* deployed a section of their newly developed *space/time exchange chamber* to return it to Earth's atmosphere. They targeted the origin of the probe, which was Kennedy Space Center, and when it reached three-thousand feet above sea level, it detonated as programmed by design.

The *space/time exchange chamber* was also instrumental in the Earth sirens' exodus back to their home world. Since teleportation is a physical impossibility, due to the fact that no two objects can occupy the same space, the *Preculians* had to explore another avenue of research. They discovered that while you cannot teleport an object into an already occupied section of *space/time,* you can *exchange* a section of space with an identical section of space over long distances on a sub-light pulse of EMR or electromagnetic radiation. Namely, slow light. An ultra-violet pulse of repeating *frozen* slow-light can connect two sections of space and exchange them.

The Americans in Washington D.C. were monitoring the situation with regard to their wayward probe and posturing to apologize for the catastrophe when all of a sudden the tables were turned on them. They essentially shot their own space complex, Kennedy Space Center, right off the globe.

Chip was cruising the strip along International Drive in Orlando, Florida, in the late afternoon looking for potential green-card-carrying targets on which to vent his hatred. He had just taken the last hit of crack in his vial and finished off the last of his six beers. Along the side of the road, he noticed what appeared to be a homeless man walking along the shoulder. The man had long hair and a beard and wore a robin's-egg-blue robe that reached all the way down to his sandals. Master *Phodan* had just emerged from a coin shop where he exchanged a three-ounce gold ingot for the ridiculously low price of five-hundred dollars. The shop owner closed up shortly thereafter and headed out for a drink to reward himself for his shrewd business acumen.

Vagrant, thought Chip Luger. *Probably a Mexican, too,* although since the man had his back to him, he couldn't really be sure enough to racially profile the man. He pressed in the clutch of his Ford F-150 truck and raced the engine. This caught the attention of the man in the blue robe, and he turned around just in time to see Chip pop the clutch and bear straight down on him at sixty miles-per-hour. Chip had done this very same thing in the past and had taken his truck in to a body-shop owned by one of *The Sons of Destiny* to remove the evidence of the hit. He though that popping homeless bodies might become his favorite sport. When the truck neared the *target* on the side of the road, *Phodan* reached under his blue robe with his left hand and extended his right outstretched in front of him. He considered the gesture a courtesy to the man in the truck, warning him that his space could not be violated due to the personal shield he had activated. *Phodan* could see the grin on Chip Luger's face as the front end of the truck imploded. Luger's drugged-up body was half-way through the windshield when the gas tank exploded. He would have been thrown clear of the blast, but there was simply nowhere to go due to *Phodan's* shield. The world, again, became a better place with the elimination of another Luger in a ball of fire along International Drive in Orlando, Florida. Some witnesses said that it was an apparent suicide when the truck hit a bridge abutment, but no one could explain how it was thrown backwards some ninety feet to where it apparently landed and burned. Also, no one could find a single scratch on the concrete structure ahead. One witness was sure of what he saw, but he wasn't sure whether or not he was losing his mind. He followed the man in the light blue robe.

~

Billy Ray Shockley pulled over to the side of the road every quarter mile, making sure to keep the man in the blue robe in sight but also unaware of his presence. He didn't know the nature of the weapon the old man used on Chip Luger's truck, but he knew it was nothing he ever wanted to deal with. *It must have been some kind of pulse laser,* he reasoned, *burning a hole right through the engine block and into the gas tank.* The explosion was instantaneous. Billy Ray saw the man leave the road and enter a building up on the right side of the road. He quickly pulled back onto the road and sped up to keep pace with the traffic. When he reached the building where he last saw the man, he pulled over into the parking lot. It was a topless bar. *Now what?* he asked himself. *Do I go in there? Has he seen me? Jesus, I wish I had never followed Chip Luger today. I was only trying to find out what he's been up to lately because I knew he wasn't working. Wasn't at the clubhouse where he was supposed to meet me to shoot pool. Wasn't working because of the damned Mexicans. It's all their fault. Chip would be alive today if it weren't for them wetbacks.*

Phodan stood just inside the door of the *Pet Palace* looking out the window at the truck parked outside. He could see one man sitting behind the steering wheel. He needed to get back to Cap' Walker's farm, but he wanted to avoid the young man who obviously witnessed him using the belt-shield to protect himself. The elders on *Preculis* would hold him in confinement if it were known how careless he was becoming. There is a reason for rules and his own bloodline was responsible for making them. The *Phodans* before him were Grand Masters as well. So was his ancestry for thousands of years that took the names, *Jhodan, Mhodan and Rhodan.* He had to be very careful with his next moves. He dearly wanted to help the Earth sirens stranded on Siren with their quest to return to Earth, but after a fruitful life of six-hundred years, he didn't relish the thought of spending his last two-hundred in confinement. A short blond woman approached him standing by the door and asked, "Would you like a drink?"

Phodan looked at the woman and was unsettled by the fact that she wore no clothes whatsoever. He gathered himself and said, "I would like a cold beer."

"What kind?" asked the woman.

"I said, cold," said *Phodan* not realizing his myriad of choices. He was still amused by the concept of beer. His world of *Preculis* had many different forms of spirits and what would be called narcotics on Earth, but no beer. He enjoyed his beer very much on Earth and was known to express the fact with a loud belch from time to time.

"Yeah, whatever," said the woman, "coming right up." She brought him a draft beer. *Phodan* hadn't yet discovered the fact that he preferred beer in bottles, not from a can or a keg. He gave the girl a twenty-dollar-bill. When she brought back his seventeen-dollars change, she asked him, "Would you like a dance?"

"I am afraid I don't know how," he told her.

"A lap dance," she said tilting her head and squinting her eyes.

"Yes, of course," said *Phodan* finally getting the picture. "How much would that be?"

"Ten dollars."

"*Phodan* looked at the money in his hand and said, "Here," handing the woman the cash.

"That's seventeen," said the woman.

"It's all for you," said *Phodan*.

"I only asked for ten," said the woman.

"Then give me the best dance you can."

"We might have to go to another room for that," she told him.

"I must stay here."

"Okay. Are you going to sit down?"

"No."

"Usually, you sit."

"Not this time."

"Whatever, honey. It's your money." The woman began to press herself against *Phodan's* body as he continued to monitor the actions of the man outside in the truck. Occasionally, she tapped him on the shoulder and said, "Hey Romeo, I'm over here." She shimmied her shoulders back and forth.

"My name is *Phodan*."

"Yeah, why do *I* get 'em?" she asked shaking her head.

~

Chapter Nineteen

The First Church of Siren

The woman waited for a full hour in the ante-chamber. Shelly Simon finally finished doing her nails and asked the young siren boy that she had chosen to serve her that day to show the woman in.

"Thank you so much for seeing me, High Priestess," began the woman.

"What is your name?" asked Shelly.

"I am Jhinduasa."

"I am pleased to meet you, Jhinduasa, but I am simply a Church member, madam. I have not been given the honor of that title as yet."

"Yes, but there is talk that it is only a matter of time."

"You are very kind. Tell me, how can I serve you?"

"It is my daughter, she is of the fever."

"I am not familiar with this fever of which you speak."

"I am ashamed to say that perhaps she has lain with one of the valley."

"The valley of the cats?"

"Yes, Jomah," said the woman raising Shelly's status to that of *mother*. The title *Jomah* is used by the *Valegatos* for wife, but among sirens, it is only used for mother. Until she gives birth for the first time, the women of Siren take the name of their men and add *"asa."*

"Was she forbidden to do this?"

"All are forbidden to lay with the men of the valley."

"Why?" asked Shelly.

"You may as well ask why up is up and down is down. It has always been so. They were once among us. Did you know that?"

"Yes, I've heard the story, but it is shrouded in mystery. Your written history leaves a lot to be desired."

"But there is the word of the Regents. It is always passed down correctly."

"So you say, but we don't have their voice in our ear, do we?"

"There is the liros-audjus."

"Yes, the audio books, I know, but there is so little time to listen when we have other duties such as prayer," said Shelly. She was driving home the point that she well-knew the purpose of this woman's visit and was pointedly telling her to *"get on with it."*

"Forgive me, Jomah. I am taking too much of your time."

"Not at all," said Shelly lying through her teeth.

"I wish there was some way to take the fever away from my Samah."

"And what is her name."

"Julianah," said the woman.

"It will be done," said Shelly.

"Oh, thank you so much, Jomah Shelly. You have made me so happy that I will serve my people more than ever before.

May I myself land in the valley of the cats if I am not pleasant and joyful when I meet with the others of my city."

"You will land in no such place Jhinduasa. Give my regards to Jhindu and may you go in peace."

The woman left the antechamber, and Charles Donovan witnessed her wiping tears from her eyes. He entered the room and said," Making promises you can't keep?"

"Who says I can't keep them?"

"Where is *Phodan*?"

"I think he's off-world, why?"

"Because it's going to come back to haunt you, Shel. One of these times, you won't deliver, and then you will have made a lot of enemies. All it takes is one broken promise, and no one will want to buy into your blessed Church anymore."

"It's not *my* Church, Charles. It's all of us. What has gotten into you?"

"Call it a reality check. Besides, if *Phodan* delivers, we're all out of here anyway."

"I may choose to stay if I am High Priestess. How could I desert my people?"

"And if I left?"

"Then you left." She was a rock with blood coursing through her veins. Charles looked at her in a completely different light than he had seen for the last year-and-a-half.

~

Orlando, Florida

The naked woman dancing before *Phodan* was a little confused. She had never had a lap-dance quite like the one she was just completing. She looked up a *Phodan,* who was a full sixteen-inches taller than her and said, "Hey I hope I didn't bore you."

"No, you were fine," he said.

"Wow, such enthusiasm! I might just get the vapors."

"Would you like to copulate?" he asked her.

"Are you asking me for a trick? You can't be a cop because that's entrapment."

"I'm pretty sure I'm not a cop."

"So, you really want me?"

"I want to leave here, perhaps through another entrance besides this one," he said motioning to the front door.

My shift ends in fifteen minutes, and we could go to my place."

"That would be fine."

~

Carla and Cap' Walker were just rising from an afternoon nap after a successful first encounter with the ship. *Phodan* was impressed with Cap's skills as a pilot and knew that he would complete the transport of the sirens from the way station without any difficulty. The only issue was the employment of the photo-reflective shield. The ship's supply of *Xerium* was dangerously low. What was left was needed to achieve plus-light speed to take *Phodan* back to *Preculis* eventually; otherwise, he might find himself stranded among humans on Earth. The prospect left a lot to be desired in his mind. Humans were harmless, provided he had his shield or could stay one step ahead of their ridiculous behavior, but he didn't embrace the scenario where he would become one of their unfortunate number, even though he was warming up to the woman from the bar.

~

Her name was Melanie, and *Phodan* was grateful to her for taking him through the back door of her workplace and to her car, so they could leave the *Pet Palace* unnoticed. The first thing she said to him when they were away from the bar was, "What's with the robe?"

"It serves me."

"Yeah, I'll bet, but it makes you kind of stand out."

"And that is a bad thing?"

"You look like a freakin' Easter egg."

"And that is a bad thing."

"Not if it's Easter Sunday and you've got some floppy ears on your head, but, yeah, for the most part, that is a bad thing. Let me shop with you. Let me shop *for* you."

"You, who does not even wear clothes, are going to show me what clothes I should be wearing," he said mechanically.

"You could do worse. I used to be into fashion until people stopped spending money on clothes."

"And now they get them for free?"

"No, you idiot, they get them at Walmart or Target now, and I'm shit-out-of-luck."

"What makes you say that?" he asked.

"Because I used to sell them to them. I used to sell six or seven square inches of fabric for two hundred dollars."

"It must have been very beautiful."

"No, it was crap. It was a freakin' bathing suit that you couldn't even get wet."

"No wonder no one wants to buy them," said *Phodan*.

"Oh, forget it, Photo-Mart."

"Why did you call me that?"

"Could I just call you Dan?"

"If you wish."

Melanie turned into the parking lot of the Northside Mall on International Drive. She took *Phodan* by the hand and led him to a store called Dillard's. When they reached the men's department, a slender, young man approached them and said, "Hi, I'm Anthony. Can I assist you with some clothing choices today?" Anthony looked at *Phodan's* robe and then looked at Melanie who rolled her eyes and nodded her head stopping just short of saying, *well, duh!*

"Something for leisure, then," said Anthony.

Melanie thought to herself, *If you bring out a leisure suit Mister, I'm gonna' kick you in the balls.*

"I suggest something relaxed like a muslin ensemble, perhaps some slacks with a black leather belt and a matching vest."

Thank you, *thought Melanie raising her eyes to the heavens. Anthony to the rescue.*

"What do you think, Madam," asked *Phodan.*

"It's Melanie, Dan. You can call me Melanie."

"As you wish."

Anthony looked at her and smiled knowingly.

"Wipe the smirk off, Tony. You don't know anything." She popped her gum, and the sound was a source of confusion for *Phodan* briefly. He let it go.

Phodan paid cash for three pairs of slacks and four Oxford button-down shirts as well as the vest and black leather belt. He stopped short of buying shoes because he was told that his sandals would be appropriate to complete the casual look he was shooting for. Looks were the last thing that *Phodan* was concerned about and just told them, "They're quite comfortable."

~

Carla was sitting at her dressing table brushing her hair. Isabelle sat dutifully by her side awaiting her turn to be brushed. She said to Cap', "Nigel, have you noticed that Belle won't leave my side?"

"No."

"For the past couple of days she's been my shadow."

"She's got good taste."

"No, it's more than that. I think she *knows* something."

"What could she possibly know?" asked Cap'. "She's a dog."

Isabelle knew they were talking about her and offered, "Rooof!"

"Yeah, roof," said Cap'. "What about the roof?"

Isabelle just panted and hung her tongue out of her mouth. She was smiling as only a dog can smile with both her eyes, and the skin of her snout pulled back to reveal a benign rack of impressive teeth. She ignored Cap's comment and continued to nuzzle up to Carla.

"I think she knows something that we don't, yet, Nige."

"Like what?" he asked her.

"Like maybe I'm cooking up a little pinball wizard."

Cap' Walker looked at Carla in a whole different light just then. Her humanity, her legitimacy was driven home by the point that she could be the mother of his child. The thought was very comforting for him. He reached down and kissed the top of Carla's head and said, "That would be very nice."

"If it's a boy, I'd like to name him *Phodan*.

"And if it's a girl?"

"Phodana."

Chapter Twenty

Shelly and Charles had just risen from their passion-tousled bed. The sheets were knotted up and had fallen to the floor. "God, you're wonderful Charles."

"Watch your mouth, Shel. There's no God here. In fact, there is a definite taboo in connection with uttering the '*word for which there is no word*.'"

"You worry too much."

"They burned sirens in Salem."

"This isn't Salem, Charles, and nobody is going to do any burning."

"Just be careful is all I'm saying. Especially with your position. The mention of God will put you in a precarious place. You don't want to deal with having to explain yourself."

"I suppose you're right. I'll be careful. But you are good," she said grinning.

"I'm inspired. What can I say?"

Let's go outside, Charles. *Preculis* is coming over the horizon."

"What? You think you can just call him up on your cell phone?"

"The nearest cell phone tower is one-hundred and eighty-two million miles away."

"You better have a good battery."

"Seriously, Charles. I am linked to *Phodan*."

"What do you mean *linked*?"

"The last time he was here. He meditated with me for a short while and told me to call out if I need him."

"You're kidding."

"Why would I kid about that?"

"He seriously told you to just call if you need him? Like with your mind?"

"He said there might be trouble."

"What kind of trouble?"

"Well, you know about the demonstrations in Creston at the Great Hall."

"Yes."

"I think that's what he was talking about. It may not end there."

"Do you think we are in danger here?"

"I don't know what to think. I saw that woman earlier today because I want to give them hope. I want to make them think that they need us. That they need the prayers of the Church."

"And what if we let them down?"

"Let's go outside."

When Shelly and Charles went out to view the night sky, *Preculis* was just coming over the horizon. It was right outside the tip of Orion's arrow. Scorpio's sting had just crawled below the western sky. Shelly locked her gaze onto *Preculis* and then closed her eyes. She remained very still for a full five minutes while Charles just stood there and watched her. When she finally opened her eyes, he said, "What? D'you get a busy signal?"

"No answer."

~

Melanie took *Phodan* to her small apartment in a modest complex situated on a lake. There were ducks and geese gathered by the shore, and *Phodan* noticed a few rowboats in the middle of the lake with young boys fishing.

"I know a girl who would love to come here," said *Phodan*. Her name is Isabelle."

"Should I be jealous," asked Melanie jokingly.

"Oh, yes."

"Remember what you asked me back at the Pet Palace?"

"Probably. I can access it if I want to."

"You're a strange one, Dan."

"In a strange land, Melanie."

"Heinlein, right? Science fiction?"

"You remind me of Isabelle."

"Whatever. *Now*, I would like to copulate."

~

"All I wanna' do when I wake up in the morning is see your eyes Phodana, Phodana," sang Carla rising from her vanity and crossing the room to Cap'. She kissed him lightly on the lips. He surprised her by chiming in, *"Meet you all the way, Phodana yeah."*

"We're not in Kansas anymore, Toto."

"No, we're not. We're in St. Cloud, and there's nowhere else I rather be right now, Carla. Just you and me and that big ball of fur over there."

"Rooof!" said Isabelle.

"You said it, Belle," said Carla.

~

Chapter Twenty-one

Billy Ray waited until the night crowd started to filter in to the Pet Palace. He saw a number of young men dressed in three-piece suits meeting their buddies just getting out of work for the night. There were also a few single girls entering the bar, and Billy Ray supposed that they were probably attached to some of the dancers.

He was just about out of cigarettes and decided that he would risk going inside to use the machine in the front lobby. He might be able to get a look at the man in the blue robe and still stay out of reach. He walked through the door and saw that there was no lobby. The door opened right up to the bar on the left and a raised dance-floor on the right. A woman was caressing a pole and showing the patrons seated around the stage her best side.

Billy Ray looked around the bar and saw no man in a blue robe. He forgot all about the cigarettes and looked around more thoroughly. Still no man in a blue robe. He went into the bathroom and looked around. There were two men in one of the stalls. *Freakin' faggots,* he thought to himself, *probably Mexicans.* Still no man in a blue robe. He then left the men's room and walked up to the bar. A new bartender was just starting her shift. She asked Billy Ray, "What can I get you?"

"Bud in a can."

"You got it," she said. She was topless and noticed Billy Ray appreciating her looks when he gave her the five dollar bill. She put down the two dollars change on the bar and said, "Nice tips, huh?"

"What?" asked Billy Ray.

"I said I deserve nice tips," she said coyly.

"Yes, darling, you certainly do. Listen, could you tell me where the guy in the blue robe went earlier tonight?"

"Sorry, buddy. That's not ringing any bells."

"You didn't see a guy in a blue robe in here. You couldn't have missed him."

"I just came on. You might want to ask Sybil. She works the shift from noon until happy hour. Then she picks up her kids at daycare."

"Where is she now?" asked Billy Ray.

"Well, duh," she said realizing she wasn't dealing with any kind of rocket scientist here, "she's at daycare picking up her kids."

"Okay, I get it. You don't have to be a wise ass about it."

The bartender looked over at a man standing by the front entrance with very large arms. Billy Ray followed her glance and then said, "No offense."

"I'll forget it if you will."

"Deal," said Billy Ray taking one sip of his beer and standing up to leave. He left her the two dollar tip and was careful not to make eye contact with the big man at the door as he left. He would be back tomorrow and thought it would be a smart idea to leave a good impression. Billy Ray was nothing if not a fast learner. He would talk to Sybil and see if she knew where the man in the blue robe went eventually. In the mean time, he thought he'd go back to the clubhouse of *The Sons of Destiny* and try his luck at some cards.

As usual, there was a game going at the clubhouse, and Billy Ray got himself a can of beer out of the refrigerator and put a dollar in the jar on top. He walked over to the card table and asked, "What's the buy in?"

"It's just ten tonight," said Roy Becker, the president of the club.

"I'm in," said Billy Ray. He took a stack of chips from the caddy and counted himself out ten dollars worth. Then he put his money in the slot and took the cards to deal the next hand. It was customary for the dealer to ante for the rest of the table and when you first joined a table, it was your turn to deal. Shuffling the cards he said, "D'you hear about Chipper?"

"Heard he bought it," said one of the players.

"They think he off'd himself," said another.

"That's bullshit," said Billy Ray.

"He was pretty upset about his old man get'n cooked over there on the East Coast."

"I said it was bullshit," said Billy Ray hotly, "I was there."

"What? You saw it happen?" asked Roy.

"Sure did."

"He hit a bridge?"

"Not that I saw. His truck just up and stopped and burst into flames."

"That's strange," said Roy. "You spose it were some kind of a gas leak?"

"Nope."

"Then what?"

"I'm fixin' ta' find out and believe me, you'll be the first to know.

"We take care of our own, Billy Ray. It'll go a long way with the members if you find out who is responsible for Chipper cashin' in his chips."

"How long is that?" asked Billy Ray.

"How about two years of free clubhouse dues?"

"That would suit me just fine, Roy."

~

Phodan got up from Melanie's bed and looked around for his underwear. She was smoking a cigarette and taking sips on a beer in a wine glass. She said to him, "That was very nice, Dan."

"Yes, it was, Melanie. Excuse me for a minute, I have to take this," he said.

"Take what?" she asked with a confused look on her face. "You don't even have a phone with you."

Phodan stepped out onto Melanie's balcony and closed his eyes. After meditating for about a minute he said out loud, *"Shelly, I hear your thoughts. I am on Earth and won't be back for another day or so. There's nothing I can do for the young one from here. But I will rid her of the death that she carries within her when time permits."*

Melanie stepped out onto the balcony and asked, "Who are you talking to?"

"A friend," said *Phodan*. "You wouldn't know her."

"No, I guess not. And it's good to hear that you are on Earth. Where the hell else would you be, Dan?"

"Actually, any number of places."

"Come back to bed."

When *Phodan* rejoined Melanie in her bed, he placed his hands on her torso just below her breasts. Melanie then asked him, "What are you doing?"

"How long have you used tobacco, Melanie?"

"I don't know, about ten years or so, why?"

"It's killing you."

"Don't start."

"I can help, just lie still." *Phodan* lowered his head to her abdomen between his hands and closed his eyes. He stayed there for about three minutes while Melanie finished her cigarette and glass of beer. When he was finished with his procedure, he sat up and said, "Your sickness has left you now. Your lungs are pink and healthy."

Melanie just looked at him with a wrinkled brow and said, "Yeah, that's good to know." *Boy, this is a strange one*, she thought.

The next morning, *Phodan* asked Melanie to drive him to the Walker farm. When she dropped him off, he reached into his pocket and retrieved a gold ingot that weighed about four ounces. When Melanie saw it, she asked, "Is that what I think it is?"

"Gold," said *Phodan*. He handed it to her.

"For me?"

"Yes."

"You certainly are full of surprises, Dan."

"I will see you again. I just now realize I left my robe at your house."

"You're going to come back for it? I thought I might just pitch it in the trash."

"That would be a terrible waste, Melanie. I have used much of a precious element to enhance its properties. The robe will offer protection now for whoever wears it."

"You mean like Harry Potter's."

"No, Melanie. Potter's robe made him invisible. The robe could do that, too, if I had more *Xerium*. As it is, I need to conserve what little I have left."

"Sure thing, Dan," she said. She didn't exactly know what to think about Dan other than the fact that he was a pretty good lover. She guessed that might well be enough.

~

Chapter Twenty-two

Christos stood with Bantah, their backs to a newly lit fire as dusk was quickly coming on, and the fire masters wanted some seasoned embers to offer the cooks. The young women knew they would be leaving soon and would not even eat with them this night. They began a procession lined up, one behind the other, and when they reached the two men, they wrapped their arms around them and whispered well wishes in their ears. Some of the wishes carried content more intimate than others, but most were just of good will and prayers for safe travel. This concept was new to Christos Somah because he had no experience with prayer. He was well aware of the wish of one siren to another for good will, but the concept that there was another entity, an *impassioned deity,* was totally foreign to him. It was long believed among the sirens that, though possibly the Creator was certainly witness to the life experience of his *children,* he was disinclined to get involved.

When Mantah Samah finally reached Christos Somah, purposely waiting to be the last in line, she said to him, "Ah do e na," and Christos Somah thought he noticed a hint of gold and silver at the very edges of the corneas in her eyes. He felt her small breasts press against his chest.

"Oh, no you don't," he said. He had let down his guard for a moment and thought he finally knew the reason Bantah had instructed him to keep his eyes closed. He thought to himself, *yes, she will become a handful indeed.*

They started north when the young women of the tribe had concluded their parting ceremony. Soon they found themselves on the path that led along the river. The air was crisp and cool, and the posi-grains were relatively thin because the path was upwind of the riverbed. Christos Somah could soon tell by the lactic acid gathering in his leg muscles that they indeed were going uphill. He found that the air had thinned out considerably in only one-thousand feet of elevation. There was a five-hundred foot waterfall in front of them. It was one of many that cascaded down the mountain to finally settle in the valley riverbed. Christos Somah considered getting the overcoat that Bantah had supplied him with out of his pack, but decided that the cold would keep him awake and alert. He had no idea what they might encounter in their trek up the mountainside to the giant redwood that held Alex Janzen in a condor's nest. When they reached the top of the waterfall, Christos Somah saw that the river continued on at this higher level and was surprised to see fish leaving the surface of the water and sailing for a hundred feet before settling back down again into the river.

"Would you look at that," said Christos Somah. "I've never seen anything like that before."

"Flying fish," said Bantah. Their bodies are full of the posi-grains. They could stay up longer if they didn't run out of river. They're feeding."

"On what?"

"Bugs. They keep the mosquitoes down, which is a blessing. Those suckers can get about an inch long when they're full grown. Their stingers inject a mild sedative and a swarm can drain a sleeping man of half his blood before he ever knows what hit him."

"Nice," said Christos Somah facetiously. "I don't understand why you people want to live in this valley in the first place."

"It is our home. We can't understand why you would want to live in Creston or Baseton. Those places are so filled with sirens that there isn't room to breathe. Out here we have the stars and all the land we would ever want. The food is here all around us for the taking and here we may live our lives without being chastised by your people. They reject what they don't understand. Just because we don't find the need for clothes, and we follow the great commandment, we are thought to be heathens."

"What great commandment are you speaking of, Bantah."

"I am not at liberty to discuss our religion with someone from the outside."

"Perhaps there is a good reason why the *Preculians* spared us your religion," said Christos Somah.

"Perhaps there is," agreed Bantah.

Just as Christos Somah was getting adjusted to walking on the path and adjusting his breathing to fill his lungs fully, the ground rose up before him and a diamond-shaped pattern emerged from it and hung there in the night. Bantah told him, "Be still, Christos Somah. We have come across a viper."

Christos Somah could see the outline of the snake against the blackness of the night. What little light there was from the stars illuminated the large serpent, and Christos Somah could see a reflection of light coming off the two large fangs that hung down from his mouth. Bantah told him, "I don't think he has seen us yet, but soon he will sense the heat of our bodies. He has two sensors on the top of his head that can detect a warm blooded animal as small as a tree rat. We're ringing the dinner bell for him loud and clear."

"Have you ever dealt with them before?" asked Christos Somah.

"Yes, many times. They are not hard to kill if you have a weapon."

"And do you have a weapon?"

"What kind of a stupid question is that, Christos Somah. I don't mean to be rude, but you surprise me sometimes with your naivety. Of course, I have a weapon. I have a sword *and* a knife."

"But that snake has to be fifty feet long. It's as thick as my waist for Creator's-sake."

"A well placed strike with a knife will bring down any animal, even a valegato or a condoro."

"What if you miss?"

"You have to put them to sleep first, then you will not miss."

"What are you going to do, sing him a lullaby?"

"Yes, precisely that."

"Even I'm not naïve enough to fall for that," said Christos Somah.

"The lullaby is not sung with the voice, but with the eyes."

"What do you mean?"

"It is electrum. That is how we sing to the beasts."

"What is electrum?" asked Christos Somah.

"I will show you," said Bantah. He took the knife from a sheath tied to his thigh and held it in his right hand. Then he started off walking toward the viper. When the snake noticed him approaching, it rose up in the air and began to sway back and forth. Its mouth opened and his forked tongue began to dart forward and back tasting the air in front of him. The pits on the top of his head began to inflate and Christos Somah knew that he was sensing the heat given off by Bantah's body. Christos Somah thought that the monstrous snake would hone-in on his target using heat rather than eyesight. Now he understood what Bantah said about the animals of the valley being ugly and beautiful. The snake was beautiful. It was coiled in a circle about five feet across that wrapped four or five times around on itself. Then the upper third of its body was lifted off the ground into a vertical dance of hypnotic beauty. Its diamond shaped pattern could be seen in the starlight and the beast's eyes were glowing yellow with fire. Bantah walked slowly forward speaking very softly to the reptile. "Close your eyes little one. It's time for sleep now."

Little one? thought Christos Somah. *Don't tell me they get bigger than this.* Then he saw what Bantah was telling him about singing a lullaby with his eyes. Bantah's eyes became fire themselves. The snake's eyes glowed with a yellow fire, but Bantah's eyes projected gold and silver flecks that had a light source behind them. It was mesmerizing to look at. Christos Somah found his own eyes beginning to close almost as though he had no control of them. He slapped himself in the face to make the visual effects go away. *It's remarkable how beautiful his eyes are,* thought Christos Somah. *Can all the Valegatos do that?* He wondered.

They say that the Earth sirens can change the look in their eyes. Is that what they mean? No wonder these people were banished to the valley. They're potentially very dangerous.

Bantah watched the snake lose the staring match and close his eyes. He walked up to the snake and patted him on the head. Then he turned to look back at Christos Somah and smiled. He wished he could take a picture of Christos Somah to show him the look on his face. Bantah had no need to kill the snake, so he just let him sleep. The two riverbed travelers then continued on their way.

After they had scaled another thousand feet of the mountain, Christos Somah began to react to the cold weather. It had dropped twenty-five degrees since they started out at dusk. He got out the overcoat and put it on. The fur was very soft and Christos Somah wondered whether it had been treated somehow or if the cat's fur is really that luxurious. It felt wonderful against his skin when he put it to his face. There was a pleasant odor to it as well. *Do the cat's smell like this?* he wondered. He turned to Bantah and said, "Can I ask you one question?"

"Certainly," said Bantah.

"You don't have to answer it if you don't want to, but I have to ask."

"Then ask," said Bantah.

"What is the commandment?"

"Do you want just the commandment, or the whole story behind it?"

"Just the commandment for now."

"To love each other."

"That's it?"

"That's enough when you think about it."

~

Chapter Twenty-three

Phodan was greeted by Isabelle after Melanie drove away. She asked him, "Rooof!" *A friend of yours?*

"Well, she is not an enemy."

"Rooof!" *Where did you meet her?* asked Isabelle.

"International Drive. I had to trade in some gold for currency."

"Rooof!" *Did you buy me anything?*

"Where is Cap'?" asked *Phodan.*

"Rooof!" *They're out at the lake looking at the ship. Cap's been singing. I wish I didn't have dog ears. I can hear him at the mailbox out by the road.*

"It can't be that bad."

"Rooof!" *Just you wait.*

Phodan found Cap' and Carla sitting on a bench down by the lake. They had moved it close enough to dangle their feet in the water. He walked up behind them, "Watch out for gators."

"Hi, *Phodan,*" said Carla. "We're not afraid of any gators. They're really very timid creatures. I think they are afraid of us."

"I guess they're not as bad as the moccasins," said *Phodan* teasing her. He noticed her draw her feet out of the water and curl them underneath her on the bench.

"I'm only kidding, Carla. There aren't any moccasins in this lake."

"Did you have a good time in town?"

"Rooof!" said Isabelle. *He met a girl.*

"Hush, Belle," said *Phodan.*

"Rooof!" *I think she's a hooker.*

"That's enough!"

~

Billy Ray had a hangover. The previous night haunted him with the fact that he lost the man in the blue robe and his money at the poker table as well. Rather than do the smart thing and drink a large glass of water, he instead drank a beer. It helped a little, but his head was still throbbing when he pulled up to the Pet Palace at 10:00 A.M. He couldn't believe that people woke up and started the day saying, *I think I'll take in a tittie bar,* but they did. He was not alone sitting at the bar talking to Sybil who looked like she could use another cup of coffee. Some of the patrons ordered Bloody Marys as well and mixed them with their beer. Salt was another staple at the bar, sprinkled into both drinks. Some of them didn't even notice that Sybil wasn't wearing a shirt. Billy Ray did. He liked the looks of Sybil's body so much that he almost forgot why he was there in the first place. Then he remembered. He placed a ten dollar bill on the bar next to his beer and asked her, "I'm looking for a man, darlin'."

"Funny, you don't look like the type who wants another man." She tried her best to do sexy, but 10:00 A.M. had its limitations.

"I'm lookin' to find him, not sleep with him," said Billy Ray.

"So why come in here?" asked Sybil.

"Cause he came in here. He was dressed in a blue robe. Looked like he just got out of the God-damned bathroom."

"I remember him," said Sybil.

"When I came in after him, he was gone. Must a' left by the back door or something."

"Possibly. Melanie ended her shift at noon. That's when I ended mine as well. I took off to get my kids, and she took off for wherever she goes. Maybe he went with her."

"Where's she live."

"Why do you want to find this guy?"

"That's my business, honey."

"Well take your ten dollars and hit the road."

"Thanks for nothing," said Billy Ray.

"You're welcome for nothing.'"

Phodan said to Cap', "Ready for your next flying lesson?"

"Sure."

"Rooof!" said Isabelle. *You're not going without me.*

"I'll make some sandwiches," said Carla. "Just give me a minute."

"And beer," said Cap'. "Don't forget the beer."

"Rooof!" said Isabelle. *And treats. Lots of treats.*

After Cap' was in the left seat of the cockpit, *Phodan* once again said, "Take her up, Cap'."

"Aye aye, Sir. And where would you like to go this time?"

"Titan." *Phodan* gave that a minute to sink in.

Cap' said, "You're serious, aren't you?"

"Yes, Cap', I have business there. It shouldn't take long."

"Rooof!" *What's Titan?* asked Isabelle.

"It's Saturn's largest moon. There's something going on there that I need to keep up with."

"Rooof!" asked Isabelle. *What's going on?"*

"There's an ocean of ammonia that I need to take a reading from. It's etching the finish on some of the polymers of the undersea station there."

"Rooof!" *Gotcha.*

Carla came back with the sandwiches and a thermos of iced tea. She also had a bottle of wine and some cheese and crackers along with a six-pack of beers for Cap'. When Cap' flew the craft close to Earth's moon, his passengers were suddenly awestruck.

"It's beautiful," said Carla. "No wonder it gives me such a pleasure to look up into the night sky and see it. Even from Earth it looks as good."

They could see the remnants of Earth's missions to the moon in the Sea of Tranquility when they passed by at less than a thousand feet.

"Careful of the gravitational attraction, Cap'. Can you feel it?" asked *Phodan.*

"Yes, I can. That was unexpected. Perhaps I flew too close. I won't make that mistake again, *Phodan.*"

"I know you won't. You can expect the same effect at Saturn, but much greater. Although Saturn is largely a gaseous mass, the sheer size of it will affect your gravitational attraction. You don't want to sling-shot around her. It's best to go straight in and back straight out. Titan will be at an apogee so you will feel the pull of the giant planet. Don't worry though, this ship can pull out of anything short of a close pass, say a million miles away from the sun.

"Rooof!" said Isabelle. *That is so cool!*

"Yes, it is," answered *Phodan.*

When they got to Titan, Cap' set the ship down on the edge of a volcano. There was a plume of smoke rising up into the thin atmosphere and sheered away from the trade winds. The ocean that *Phodan* was interested in was only a short distance away. The lava from the volcano was adding a half-acre of land a day to the Titan surface. Pillow lava was forming beneath the ammonia ocean and cooling instantly to form outcroppings of rock that would eventually host a biochemical exchange of gases to form the building blocks of life. One day, far in the future, the life of Titan would communicate with that of Earth, Siren and *Preculis,* but that day was almost too distant to contemplate. In the mean time, any readings that *Phodan* could return to *Preculis* would speak well for the use of their technology and the depletion of the treasured element *Xerium.*

"Rooof!" asked Isabelle. *Can we get out?*

"No, the atmosphere is poison. You have to just look through the viewports," said *Phodan.*

"Rooof!" asked Isabelle again. *What kind of poison?*

"It's like sulfur. Very caustic and would burn that big nose of yours."

"Rooof!" *Who's got a big nose?*

"You, that's who," said *Phodan*. "You have a big nose."

"Who would like a sandwich?" asked Carla. "I've never served lunch on a moon before."

"I'm hungry," said Cap' taking a sandwich.

"Thank you, Carla," said *Phodan* taking one as well.

"Rooof!" said Isabelle. *Don't forget me.*

"I knew you'd want one, Miss bottomless pit."

"Rooof!" asked Isabelle. *Do I look fat?*

"No, you're not fat," said *Phodan*.

~

Chapter Twenty-four

Melanie called in sick to the Pet Palace. She had caught a bug that had been going around and just couldn't see the point of giving lap dances to johns when she would herself be rushing off to *the* john every twenty minutes. When she asked if Sybil could cover for her, the manager told her to hold on. Sybil got on the phone and said, "Not a problem, honey. I'll take your set. You had a fan come by yesterday. At least I think he was a fan, but according to Julie, he acted kind of strangely."

"Yeah, in what way?" asked Melanie.

"Well, he was asking after a guy in a blue robe. You remember the guy. You gave him a lap dance. Then I left to get the kids and Julie took over. This guy asked Julie who the guy with the blue robe left with. D'he go with you?"

"What did she tell him?" asked Melanie.

"I think she told him to hit the road."

"Good for her. Tell her I owe her one."

"Will do. You coming in tomorrow?"

"I've still got bills to pay."

"I hear ya'."

"Thanks, honey, love you."

"Love you, too."

Well, that's interesting, thought Melanie. *I wonder what this joker wants with Dan. I'm pretty sure that Dan doesn't know that this guy's doggin' him or what he's after in the first place. Maybe he followed him from the coin shop cause he saw the gold he had in his pocket. I hope Dan doesn't underestimate the guy. I've seen that scenario go bad pretty quickly before.*

Melanie decided to drive on out to the Walker farm and give Dan the heads up. She still felt like crap, but she felt like she owed Dan the warning. She had gotten twenty-two hundred dollars for the piece of gold he had given her. She pulled her Honda Civic up to the front porch of the Walker ranch and parked on the circular driveway facing back out toward the street. She wasn't sure how she would be received and thought it would be prudent to position the car for a hasty retreat. Her trepidation was allayed by a smiling woman greeting her walking down the steps followed by a beautiful golden colored dog. "Welcome," said Carla. "How can I help you today?"

Melanie instantly felt at ease, got out of her car and walked toward the porch. "Hi, I'm Melanie. I was looking for Dan."

"Dan?" asked Carla. "Are you sure you have the right place?"

"Sure I'm sure. I dropped him off here yesterday. Big guy, handsome, used to dress in a blue robe."

"Ahh, Dan," said Carla understanding that his name was shortened. "Yes, he's here. I think he's down by the lake with my husband. Would you like to come inside for a cold drink, or are you in a hurry?"

"Rooof!" *Did you bring Phodan's robe?*

"She's beautiful," said Melanie. "She's a golden, right?"

"Yes," said Carla. "Isabelle rules the roost around here."

"Rooof!" said Isabelle. *You bet I do.*

"I'd love a drink," said Melanie, "but don't get too close to me, I think I've got a cold."

"Oh, I don't think we have to worry about that, Melanie. Is iced tea okay with you?"

"Sounds heavenly."

"Rooof!" *And some treats, please.*

The two women and Isabelle went inside and made their way to the kitchen. Melanie sat at the old breakfast table while Carla put the water on to boil. She said to Melanie, "I can put some basil and chamomile into the tea to help your cold, but if you really want the cure, talk to Dan."

"He's a pretty cool guy," offered Melanie.

"How long have you known him?"

"Rooof!" *They just met yesterday.*

"Hush, Belle. She does have a mouth on her," said Carla.

"I just met him recently," said Melanie, "but we kind of clicked."

"I like your taste."

"Actually, we're just friends so far."

"I mean in clothes. Dan looks pretty sharp and I think you had something to do with his choice of clothing."

"Yes, I helped. I'm glad you approve."

"That robe of his was a bit offsetting," said Carla.

"I know what you mean. I didn't want to hurt his feelings, but I knew that it had to go."

"Maybe you can get him to cut his hair and shave his beard. That would take about twenty years off his looks."

"I don't think that's important to Dan," said Melanie. "He's a little different than anyone I've ever met before."

"Perhaps you're right. I guess I have to stop trying to be a control freak. Dan has been a good friend to us, and I am grateful to him."

"Where is he from?" asked Melanie.

"Dan is a man from many places. We like to think that he is from the last place he has been."

"That's pretty vague, Carla."

"That's Dan."

Chapter Twenty-five

C hristos was the first to hear it. There was a low-pitched chirping sound coming from the canopy of the stand of large trees before them. They were Redwood-Giganticas, four hundred feet tall, but they grew alongside of a waterfall that was equally as high. Bantah told him, "I think we can swing into the canopy of these trees without having to climb them."

"Have you ever done that before?"

"Sure, I've been doing it since I was a kid. The hillside is right up against the treetops at about three-hundred feet. The nest might be eighty feet further up, but it saves us a lot of climbing."

"But how do we traverse over to the tree from the hillside?" asked Christos Somah. He was not an experienced climber as was Bantah. He did not possess finely hewn skills from experience as a young boy born of the necessity of survival rather than sport.

"It will be easy," said Bantah. "A rope will make it safer, but I could do the leap even without one."

"No need to impress me, Bantah. I'm already impressed."

"I will tie myself off to a rappel device before I make the leap."

"Thank you. I don't mind telling you that this whole affair has me a bit unsettled."

"I have done this my whole life," said Bantah.

"I encountered a condor earlier today."

"Yes, I know. The smell is bad, no?"

"The smell is putrid," said Christos Somah.

"I'm hoping that it won't be as bad with only the chicks. They are foul, but not as bad as the mother."

"Let's get this over with, Bantah. Since we can hear the chicks, it's only a matter of time before they learn to peck and find out there is food sitting before them."

Christos Somah and Bantah began the steep climb up the hillside to the treetops. "The blond one is your woman, isn't that so."

"I'm not sure what she is besides a friend," said Christos Somah.

"She is very beautiful."

'I suppose," he said. "I've never really thought about it."

"What? Are you a flier?"

"No."

"And you've never thought about the blond woman becoming your lover."

"I don't often take a lover, Bantah."

"That's a shame."

"Could we talk about something else?"

"As you wish," said Bantah though he thought it was strange that Christos Somah did not want to talk about women. It seemed like that's all he talked about with his friends. The only other thing he liked to talk about was the hunt.

The cats were the most formidable adversaries. They were least susceptible to the electrum in the eyes of the

Valegatos. The Tribe of the Viper and the Tribe of the Condor also had the ability to display the gold and silver in the corneas of their eyes, but it was not often used in the hunt. The cats moved too fast and wouldn't look the tribesmen in the eyes long enough to become mesmerized. The young men had to strike quickly and with deadly accuracy. The crossbow was the weapon of choice while hunting the great cats.

It was the mark of a very skilled hunter to take them down with only one shot. They would have to place an arrow precisely in the heart, and the only way to insure a heart-shot was to fire when the cat was in mid-leap. Obviously, a miss meant that the hunter was likely to be pierced by a fang or a claw. They would survive being raked with a claw, but a bite was nearly always lethal. When they had climbed another two-hundred feet up the steeply rising precipice, Christos Somah asked, "How many cats have you taken?"

"Dozens," said Bantah. "My father used to take me when I was very young."

"Weren't you afraid?"

"Yes, I was very afraid, but my father never knew it. I was careful not to show my fear."

"Are you still afraid of the cats?"

"Afraid is not the word I would use. I am very careful during the hunt, and when I am on the path of the river, I always try to stay downwind. That way I can smell the cat before he ever smells me."

"But you don't fear them?"

"I respect their power. I know that they carry the *death spirit* and can take a *Valegato* in the blink of an eye so I am wary, but not afraid. The only way I stand to lose a battle with a cat is if he catches me asleep."

"What do you do, sleep with one eye open?"

"I sleep when I am among my people. During the hunt or on a quest such as this, I chew the leaves that drive away sleep."

"The leaves make me kind of jumpy," said Christos Somah.

"Jumpy is good when you are on the path of the riverbed. Sleepy is bad. Here," he said handing Christos Somah another leaf, "it is time for you to have another."

They only had fifty more feet to climb to reach a high branch that almost touched the hillside. Bantah got out two of his thin braided ropes made of cat hide. Christos Somah could see they were no thicker than his little finger, but Bantah assured him that they were very strong. "If need be, they could carry the weight of two men," said Bantah. "And there is another good feature of the corda-gatos, or cat-ropes. They can stretch. They are *dynamic* so that if they have to catch your fall, they can do so gradually and not all at once."

"That's very smart," said Christos Somah.

"My people have used them for centuries. They learned to utilize all the elements of the valley from the very beginning. It was a matter of survival."

"What else do you get from the animals of the valley?" asked Christos Somah.

"Do you know about the fixed wing of the condor?"

"No."

"There are bones where the wings of the condor meet its body. They are like your two hands and lock together into a fixed-wing. Then the bird can hang from it for hours with no exertion. They just catch the thermals and circle around as they rise. Then they can glide as long as they want hanging beneath their wings until they need to catch another thermal. The only time the condor actually needs to land is when they eat and sleep. They spend the rest of their lives in the air."

"So how do you use the wings of the condors?" asked Christos Somah.

"We hang from them as well and can glide from the peaks of the Sirenian Range to the base of the valley. It's quite enjoyable; you should try it sometime."

"Don't your gliders stink like the condor?"

"They are not so bad after you soak them in the river," he said.

Bantah attached one of the ropes to his shoulder-harness and handed a rope and harness to Christos Somah. "Have you ever used a rappelling device?"

"No, I haven't."

"There's nothing to it. Just put the harness on like I have. Then take the rope and feed it through the oval hole in the metal place attached to the front." Christos Somah did as Bantah instructed and said, "Now what?"

Bantah tied Christos Somah's rope to a branch on the redwood that was only a few feet from the hillside and told him. As you climb up the tree, pay the rope out behind you. Then, when we reach the nest, we will attach the other ends of the ropes to it, and loop the rope under our thighs and over our shoulders. When you take hold of the rope, you'll be able to hang your full weight on the device and just let go of the rope to rappel down. Our progress will be a slow or fast decent depending on how tightly we grasp the rope. It's a lot simpler than it sounds. Don't worry about it. I'll show you how when the time comes."

"I should have practiced it closer to the ground," said Christos Somah.

"C'mon, where's your sense of adventure?" asked Bantah.

"I think I left it back at the encampment."

"I thought you didn't want to talk about her."

"If you like her so much, why don't you ask her to become *your* woman, Bantah?"

"Why don't I ask the sun to stop shining?"

"What are you talking about?"

"The woman. I've seen the way she looks at you, Christos Somah. I feel that she has only one thing in mind."

"She wants her flier back safely," said Christos Somah.

"Alright, two things. But the thing she wants most of all is you."

"I'd rather not talk about it."

"So you said."

~

Chapter Twenty-six

Billy Ray Shockley hit pay dirt when he talked to one of the other dancers at the Pet Palace. A girl named Crystal was giving him a lap dance when he said casually, "I sure am glad my uncle Eddie turned me on to this place. He told me I would like it, and he was right."

"He a regular."

"Naw, he just found this place the other day," said Billy Ray. "Maybe you danced for him. He wears a blue robe sometimes."

"No, that was Mel," said Crystal.

"Mel? Is she one of the other dancers?"

"Yeah, Melanie. She works the day shift, but she called in sick today."

"Well, I'd like to meet her. My uncle said she was pretty impressive," said Billy Ray.

"What am I, chopped liver?" asked Crystal.

"No, honey, I like you just fine. I just don't want to go steady."

"Me neither, pal. Besides, I already got an old man."

"Good for you."

"You want another dance?" she asked as the song ended.

"Maybe later," he said getting up from his chair. He went into the bathroom and wrote the name Melanie on an envelope he fished out of his back pocket. He then left the bathroom and walked over to the bartender to give her the envelope. It was sealed. He said, "Could you give this to Mel when she comes in, please?"

"Sure, no problem," said Sybil. If Julie, the other bartender, had been working that shift as well, she could have told Sybil that Billy Ray was the same guy trying to bird-dog Melanie the day before. As it was, Melanie would learn the hard way that trouble was coming her way.

~

"Could we go down to the lake?" Melanie asked Carla after they had finished about half of their iced teas. "I need to give Dan a message."

"Sure. Follow me." Carla and Isabelle led Melanie out the back door and down the steps to the back yard. There were huge oaks adorned with Spanish moss all across the back lawn. They could see the two men down by the water's edge sitting on a bench and drinking bottles of beer. When *Phodan* saw Melanie, he rose from the bench and approached her. "How is my pet today?" he asked.

"Not so well, Dan. I think I caught a cold or something."

"Oh, I'm sorry to hear that."

"He can help," said Carla knowingly.

"Be still, Carla," said Cap' in a forced whisper leaning down toward her ear. "We don't know how much she knows about our guest."

"Can I have a word with you in private, Dan?"

"Yes, I suppose so," said *Phodan.*

"Rooof!" *You know I won't say anything. My lips are sealed.* She sat up and panted.

"Oh, all right, Belle, you can come, too." He turned to Cap' and asked, "Would it be okay if I talk to Melanie inside the house for a little while?"

"Go right ahead," said Cap'.

"We won't be long," said Melanie.

"Rooof!" *Did you bring the robe?* asked Isabelle.

"Yes, did you?" asked *Phodan* on their way up to the house.

"Did I what?"

"Did you bring my robe?"

"Yes, it's in the car," said Melanie. The three of them made their way up the back porch steps and into the kitchen. They sat down at the table, and Isabelle lay down on the floor at their feet.

"She's beautiful," said Melanie referring to the dog.

"Rooof!" *Thanks,* said Isabelle. *You're not too bad yourself, Melanie.*

"Yes, she's also a good friend, said *Phodan.* "Now, what is it you came to tell me?"

"There was a guy who came into the club looking for you. Asked about a guy in a blue robe."

"And what did you tell him?"

"I wasn't there, but my friend Julie told him to get lost."

"So, what's the problem?"

"He's not going to give up that easily. I think you need to lay low for awhile."

"I always lay low."

"That's good. Man, I feel like crap warmed over. I think it's going in-and-out of air-conditioning that's the problem. I'm always catching a chill."

"I think the problem is you don't wear any clothes at work. You should at least bundle up between your performances."

"Yeah, you're probably right."

"Would you like me to make you feel better?" he asked.

"What do you mean?"

"Your cold. Would you like to be rid of it?"

"Yeah, right. What are you some kind of doctor?"

"Oh, no. Much better than a doctor. I'm a healer."

"A healer, huh? Well, go ahead, knock yourself out. Heal me."

"Stand up," said *Phodan.*

Melanie stood at the kitchen table, and *Phodan* stood as well and placed his two hands on her ribcage. He lowered his head until it was touching his hands and stayed that way for about a minute. When he rose back up, he said, "Done. Now please go and get my robe out of your car."

Melanie shook her head. She was surprised to find that her sinuses were clear, and her bronchioles and lungs were completely devoid of the phlegm that had stuffed her up just minutes before. She also felt energetic and somewhat euphoric. Before she left to retrieve the robe, she said to him, "My God, you weren't kidding. You really are a healer. I feel totally better. What is that like faith healing or something?"

"Something like that," said *Phodan.*

"You want to come back to my place and fool around?" she asked him.

"Not today, Melanie. I have some work to do with Nigel, Carla's husband."

"Okay, but don't forget about me. You know where to find me."

"Yes, Melanie, I know."

After Melanie got *Phodan's* robe and brought it into the house, she kissed him and said, "Tell Carla thanks for the tea. I hope we meet again soon."

"I'll tell them," said *Phodan.*

Chapter Twenty-seven

The Planet *Preculis*
An Emergency Meeting of the
High Council in the Great Hall

The room was buzzing with heated conversations back and forth across the large table. The sounds echoed off the marble walls and floor creating a situation where there seemed to be twice as many council members as there actually were. In the absence of their elected Grand Master *Phodan*, his two distant cousins, who were designated *Great Masters,* presided over the meeting. Their titles were Great Masters *Rhodan* and *Jhodan.*

Rhodan tried to bring about some order in the room, "Please, Councilmen and Councilshama *Oshiana,* I beg you to compose yourselves and respect the venue of this meeting. This Great Hall has been the source of reason and order for thousands of years. To hear heated emotions within your voices brings me great pain in light of the charge we have been given to govern our great people. No wise decision was ever made in the heat of judgment."

"How can we not come to judgment, *Rhodan?*" asked *Lojahn,* The Minister of Precious Artifacts on *Preculis.* Your cousin, *Phodan* has threatened our very existence."

"Minister *Lojahn*, I believe you are overstating the importance of the issue at hand. We have never encountered a race that posed a threat to *Preculis*, thanks to our technology. We remain eons ahead of any or our neighboring solar systems."

"But an imitative culture could discover the specific workings *behind* that technology if it is ever allowed off-world. Your careless cousin has absconded with not one, but three *Preculian* artifacts and taken them off-world. This action is simply unprecedented. I move for his dismissal as Grand Master."

"Absconded?" questioned *Jhodan*, "How can one steal what one already owns? The artifacts in question are *the property* of *Phodan*." Both *Rhodan* and *Jhodan* were shooting daggers with their eyes at *Lojahn* after his comment about their cousin *Phodan*. *Jhodan* reminded him, "You will need a majority vote to dismiss the Grand Master as you well know." A chill ran through the room and down the spines of the council members. The power in the room was immense. The accumulation of wealth and power by the six seated councilmen and councilshama was unprecedented in the history of *Preculis*. Any negative emotion was sure to bring about animosity and future consequences to anyone who was foolish enough to voice it. The mere fact that three of the seven council members were of the same bloodline was certainly daunting. A personal attack on any one of them was thought to be political suicide by the five men and one woman seated at the table. There seemed to be a collective cringe among them when *Lojahn* spoke of *Phodan's* carelessness.

"Well, if we are to entertain a motion for dismissal of our Grand Master," began *Rhodan,* "perhaps we can give him the courtesy of actually reviewing the charges. You may proceed, *Lojahn.*"

"Thank you, Great Master *Rhodan.* The issue I bring before you will be examined in three parts."

The two cousins, *Jhodan* and *Rhodan,* looked at each other and rolled their eyes. *Here we go, cousin,* each of them seemed to be saying, *and the witch-hunt begins.*

"First," continued *Lojahn.* "Grand Master *Phodan* has taken one of his ships to a neighboring solar system, namely Sol, for the purpose of Shuttling the Earth Sirens back to Earth from a way station he established without the sanction of this body. It has further been determined that the way station does not have *Xerium* in sufficient supply to shield its appearance for more than one Earth month. He risks detection and unwarranted observation by the humans if he is not successful with his transfer within that time."

Jhodan tried to downplay the importance of the charge, "Earth is four light years away, *Lojahn.* The humans haven't even come close to establishing light-speed let alone eclipsing it. We have determined that it would take them nearly thirty years to travel to *Preculis.* Furthermore, once they have, our *space/time exchange chamber* would send them back in roughly fifteen of their minutes."

"That's precisely the point, *Rhodan*. The humans don't have light-speed capability. If for some reason *Phodan's* ship was to fall into their hands, who is to say that they wouldn't figure out the plus-light drive?"

"The Chamber recognizes and concedes the point of *Lojahn's* Complaint Part One," said *Rhodan*. *Jhodan* looked at his cousin curiously and thought to himself, *be careful, Rhodan*.

"Thank you, *Rhodan*," said *Lojahn* with a self-satisfied smile. He continued, "Secondly, Grand Master *Phodan* has traveled to both Siren and Earth with a *Xerium*-powered Shield Robe. We can only assume that he intended to use it for self-protection thereby demonstrating a precious *Preculian* artifact off-world. That action is in direct violation of our charter. We have all taken an oath, to the point of our own peril, to prevent any deliberate exposure of the superior technology of *Preculis*."

"The robe has a time-line safeguard," argued *Jhodan*. "That's right," agreed *Rhodan,* "if the robe remains out of the bearer's possession for two rotations of a celestial body, the shield generator becomes inert. All that the humans or the sirens would have is an ordinary robe with no protective powers at all."

Lojahn cleared his throat, "If I may continue, please."

"By all means," said *Rhodan*.

"Thank you. Thirdly," continued *Lojahn*, "Grand Master *Phodan* has also taken off-world a *Xerium*-powered belt-shield that isn't tied to the cell structure of his body and can be used by anyone on Siren or Earth. I'm sure you can all understand the seriousness of that circumstance. Our own technology is unable to compromise the artifact. It would remain impervious to all of our weaponry. If *Phodan* were to lose possession of the belt-shield, the one who wears it would be as invulnerable as any one of us. A single entity could essentially wage war on us with our own technology and might very well win."

"All this talk of weaponry and war," shouted *Rhodan*. "Have we grown so little in our wisdom? Our ancestors made a grave error in the *Xeries* conflict, but who is to say that other worlds haven't grown beyond that mindset. Just because a race can do something, doesn't mean that they will. Where is it written in stone that we are the only ones who will evolve? I am sure that *Phodan* would never allow the belt or the robe to fall into the hands of a malevolent entity. It simply would not happen."

Lojahn was ready for this argument, "The law is not subject to your opinion, Great Master *Rhodan*. The law was put in place by councilmen and councilshama much older and perhaps wiser than we are. The laws were put in place so there would never be a place for opinion. Their very design is to take the decisions out of our hands."

"Very well then, call for your vote, *Lojahn*," said *Jhodan*.

He began, "If there is no further discussion, I call for a vote to . . ."

"I have further discussion," said Councilshama *Oshiana*. "It has not been determined whether or not your worst fears have come to pass, *Lojahn*," she said. The others in the room were convinced that she left the title *Councilman* off of his name for a reason. With one statement, the powerful Shama reduced him to a mere person with a petty complaint instead of a revered councilmember. She continued, "We will wait until *Phodan* returns to us either with his artifacts safely in tow, or it has been determined that he has compromised our position of superiority throughout the cosmos. Furthermore, I wish to spare you a failed motion on your record because I will vote with *Rhodan* and *Jhodan*. The most you could have achieved would have been a tie. With that, Council Members, I shall take my leave." Councilshama *Oshiana* rose from the table and walked quietly out the door of the Council Chamber in the Great Hall of *Preculis*.

There was a smile on *Rhodan's* face as he addressed the other councilmen, "Well, I suppose *that*, as they say, *is that*."

~

Chapter Twenty-eight

Capt. Walker and *Phodan* were scheduled for another training session in the ship parked beneath Alligator Lake. In the interest of conserving *Xerium, Phodan* decided that the ship must remain visible to the eye and not employ the photo-reflective shield. For that reason, the ship had been hidden beneath the water of the lake since the last excursion to Titan.

Carla decided not to make the trip because she had some grocery shopping to do, and Cap' didn't want the bother of Isabelle occupying the cabin that didn't have an adequate seat for her. Before leaving for the training session to learn how to dock with the way station, Cap' put Isabelle inside the house and engaged the latch on the back-screen door. Isabelle had her nose out of joint having been left behind, but Cap' put her in her place, "Isabelle, you stay inside the house and no funny business. I don't want to hear any complaining because I've taken you to Titan for God's-sake. How many dogs do you suppose will ever be able to say they've visited one of Saturn's moons?"

"Rooof!" *It's not fair.*

"Get over it," said Cap'. "End of discussion."

~

Christos Somah and Bantah were climbing the last fifty feet of the great redwood. The sun was just coming over the horizon down the slope at the base of the valley. They could see condors taking flight in the light of the new day. Soon they could expect the mother condor to return to the nest above them and regurgitate posi-grain charged dust into the throats of the chicks. Then she would pick up the pieces of the eggshells and throw them over the side of the nest to the forest floor below. The chicks would then find their legs and be able to walk around the nest and explore their new world. That was the time when Alex would know the hell of being captive in the *batcha do condoros*. He would become living food for the young.

The two men crept up the tree finding hand-holds in the huge sections of bark. Occasionally the bark would come alive with a two or three square-inch section and move onto their skin. Ticks! They had to be quick about brushing them off or they would risk the *tick disease* that was prevalent in the *valley do gatos*.

Finally, they could look over the edge of the huge nest and see the captive flier, Alex Janzen, pasted into an immovable glob of protein for the chicks. When Alex saw them, he didn't react at first. He blinked his eyes, and then they closed partially as if he was drifting off to sleep. His body was covered in the same crusted-over paste that Christos Somah encountered earlier when the other condoro fused the young girl to her nest. Christos Somah reached in and grabbed him by the shoulder, "Alex," he shouted. "I have been sent to find you by your friend Durbah Purness."

Alex was groggy as though coming out of a hypnotic trance. "Durbah?" he asked weakly.

"Yes, Durbah, your mate. Now quickly, you have to wake up and we have to get you out of here."

"My God Christos, it's you!" said Alex when he realized he wasn't dreaming. It seemed like the paste had a sedative effect when it came in contact with his skin.

"Yes, Alex, it's me. On Earth I was called Christos, but here I am called Christos Somah out of respect for my father." The two men began tearing away the paste from Alex's jumpsuit. The smell was horrible, but they put it out of their minds and breathed through their mouths.

"How are you doing? Do you think you can climb down the tree?"

"I have no use of my legs, but that may just be because of the paste."

"Bantah has brought a rappelling device for you in case you cannot climb."

"Bless you, friend. But first things first. Destroy these eggs before the chicks hatch and start pecking at us," he pleaded.

Bantah looked around the nest at the four condoros eggs and said, "They are not our enemy, flier. They perform a vital function in the valley."

"What function?" asked Alex.

"They take our bodies back to the land for the Creator to use again and make more living things. They are beautiful in their own way."

"Yeah, well, beautiful or not, I don't want to be their breakfast."

"Calm down, Alex," said Christos Somah. "We've almost got you free."

The two men worked feverishly to tear away the foul-smelling regurgitation of the condor paste and eventually were able to extract Alex Janzen to the point where he could move freely. There was still some paste adhering to his arms and legs, but he had full movement for the time being.

"I can't believe you came for me," said Alex. He started to cry.

"It may be all for nothing, flier," said Bantah. "We are at least eighty feet from the crest of the hillside. A fall from this height could kill us as surely as a fall from the canopy to the ground four-hundred feet below. This is the time for action. We don't know when the bird will be back."

All three of the men felt the jolt beneath their feet at the same time. A valegato had abruptly landed from forty feet above them to the branch that held the nest. Despite its huge girth, the branch shuddered under the weight of the cat. It must have weighed at least seven hundred pounds and was close to twelve feet long. Bantah quickly retrieved some wire from his pack and fashioned a cross of timber to make a crude crossbow. He knew it would be close. A *Valegato* warrior could construct and fire a crossbow in under a minute, but he had been taken by surprise. The number one rule of Bantah's *Valegatos* creed of the valley had been broken. He was upwind of the great cat. The cat approached them on the large branch where they stood just outside the nest of the condor.

The huge valegato licked his large lips, and his whiskers quivered in anticipation of a lethal bite following a burst of muscle into a fast leap for his prey. The cat envisioned the neck of his quarry collapsing beneath his fangs and a satisfying sink into yielding flesh as a reward for his stealthy approach. Bantah was just pulling back the wire to set the arrow of his crossbow when the cat jumped. He realized too late that there was nothing to stop the onset of death from this great creature. He was remarkably calm, and instead of pulling forth his sword or knife to strike at the cat, he simply issued a prayer to the Creator.

Christos Somah was not ready to concede to the cat just yet. He had an ace in the hole in the way of *Phodan's* belt-shield. He jumped in front of Bantah at the last moment and simply held up his forearms before him. Alex and Bantah thought that either he had lost his mind, or he wished death to come to him quicker than all the rest. They were mistaken. The cat seized Christos Somah around the head, and for a moment, Christos Somah seemed to have no head. Christos Somah shook his head back and forth, and the cat let loose and fell aside rolling to the side of the branch. Christos Somah moved closer to the cat and nudged him over the edge. The cat let out a scream and disappeared briefly only to reach back up in the last second and grasp the branch with two of his great claws. He hung precariously there until Bantah woke from his temporary stupor and charged to action. He drew his sword from the scabbard on his hip and struck down, severing the two claws of the great cat.

The scream of the gato tore through the night and stirred every bird within a half-mile radius to take to the sky.

Bantah walked over to the edge of the branch and pried the two huge claws from the tree. He brought them over to Christos Somah and held them out in his hand. "These will make a fine necklace for your woman, Christos Somah."

"Thank you, Bantah, but perhaps they should be presented from the flier."

"Again, you disappoint me, Christos Somah."

~

Chapter Twenty-nine

Billy Ray pulled his truck up the gravel drive of the Walker farm. He parked in front of the front porch and retrieved his rifle from the rack behind the bench seat on the rear window. Melanie's broken body was duct-taped at the wrists and ankles and had rolled around in the bed during the rough ride, painting it with her blood. She had held out for nearly three hours while they beat her, but finally, her frail body was no match for the jackboots of the zealous skinheads. Her jaw was broken and one of her eye sockets was fractured and swollen shut. She was beyond tears or any resistance to Billy Ray and his cohort, Joey Berger, who was the son of the president of *The Sons of Destiny*. When Billy Ray determined that there was no one at the house, he hatched a plan to send a message to the man in the blue robe from *The Sons*.

~

Billy Ray had followed her back to her apartment where he and Joey had rushed her before she could close the door behind her. Billy Ray asked her casually, "You got any beer, bitch?"

"Get bent, Gomer"

"Oh, I'll bend more than that, Mel. I'll bend whatever I want including your skanky ass."

"The money is in a jar in the freezer. I've got about two thousand bucks. That's it."

"I don't want your money, you scabfest. And I don't want your body. I wouldn't touch that thing with a ten-foot-pole."

"Lucky me," said Melanie miserably.

"I want Blue Robe, Mel."

"I have no idea what you're talking about, scumbag."

"You'll pay for that comment, Mel. And eventually, you'll tell us where to find old Blue Robe. Otherwise, you won't tell anyone anything again in your whole scanky life."

"Get bent," said Melanie.

She said the same expression for another ninety minutes until she was teetering in and out of consciousness. She muttered, "I don't care anymore."

Actually, she did care. She cared for *Phodan* and for the Walkers and their beautiful golden colored dog. But she reasoned that perhaps *Phodan* would know how to deal with these primitive jerks in a way that she could not.

She figured that they would eventually kill her anyway, so she had nothing to lose. She also figured that *Phodan* would want to know if her situation became critical because of him. There was a part of her that *knew Phodan* would be very glad to give the son-of-a-bitches their due, even though he seemed to be a very peaceful man. She sensed that there was something just below the surface that was not to be fooled with. She felt that *Phodan* was a person of great power, although she didn't exactly know why.

When Melanie finally told them where they could find the man in the blue robe, Billy Ray Shockley called Roy at the clubhouse and said, "We've got him. He's living out by Alligator Lake. Joey and I are on the way there now."

"Do you want help?" asked Roy.

"Nope. Free dues for two years, remember?"

"You get em' and you got it."

After opening the tailgate of the truck, they dragged Melanie's body by the arms to the backyard of the Walker farm. When they dropped her, she lay at the foot of one of the great oaks by the lake, and she was not moving. Isabelle saw her through the back screen-door and was livid. She began to bark furiously over and over telling the men in the back yard that she would find a way to kill them if she could. Isabelle saw the black eye on Melanie and how her listless body had lost all direction from her brain. Isabelle was on the brink of becoming crazy. She had never been there before, but she was a fast learner. She jumped up on the latched screen door and found that it only rattled against the hinges. This outraged her. She jumped up once again and almost reached the latch that had been installed out of her reach. Still the door rattled in its frame and she was held inside. One further try almost reached the latch at the top of the door, but she fell back and heard the door rattling once again against the hinges.

Hell with the latch, thought Isabelle. She backed up into the kitchen and ran full force into the screen door with her paws and nose. Unfortunately, her nose caught more of the door than her paws and she was pierced by a nail that was supposed to be driven home to hold the screen. She ignored the wound and the blood trickling down her nose. She backed up and lunged again. This time, the door gave a little bit more as the top hinge came apart from the doorframe. Isabelle looked out the door and saw Billy Ray and Joey throwing a rope over one of the high branches of the great oak. They meant to leave a message for *Phodan.* They meant to hang Melanie by the neck until dead. But Billy Ray somehow didn't think Melanie had suffered enough. He ripped her shirt off and Isabelle could see the dark bruises along her thin ribcage. She was cut under the left breast and the blood had dried into a tear-drop shape as though her torso was weeping for the sad state that mankind had achieved.

This scenario was simply impossible in the life of Isabelle. She was very calm all of a sudden. She weighed her options and took a few long and slow deep breaths. Isabelle was the master of her universe. She never before in her life felt so in control of a situation. It gave her heat. It gave her thanks to her Creator. She thanked him for the great muscles in her flanks that would render the screen door to splinters. She thanked him for her great teeth that would sink into the skin of the assailants who tormented Melanie. But most of all, she thanked the Creator for the ability to transform herself in an instant into a precise killing machine. She would kill for God. She would kill for Cap'. She would kill for Carla, and she would kill for Melanie and *Phodan.*

Isabelle backed all the way into the dining room, a full twenty feet away from the back screen-door of Cap' Walker's house. She ran at full speed and hit the door in the middle stringer, and it exploded from the hinges of the doorframe. She trampled over it and in a bounding leap, jumped over the back railing of the porch and onto the lawn. She didn't growl and conserved all her energy as she traversed the distance from the porch to the tree stealthily and expertly. She was upon the surprised skinheads in an instant.

"What the hell!" exclaimed Joey. "Where the hell did that dog come from?"

"I'll take care of the dog," said Billy Ray. He held his belt that he had just used to make another cruel stripe on the tattered chest of Melanie. The large buckle was at the business end. He swung the belt around in the air hoping to frighten the dog off. It whistled through the air with a pain-spoken warning of damage to come, but Isabelle was having none of it. She charged him. Billy Ray's belt caught Isabelle on the snout just below the left eye, the buckle cutting the skin and issuing forth a raised welt soon weeping blood. Isabelle yelped uncontrollably, but it didn't stop her resolve in the slightest. She charged forward again and despite taking another buckle on her flank, sunk her teeth into the ankle of Billy Ray.

"Son-of-a-bitch!" he screamed. Billy Ray had no idea how painful a dog bite could be, but he learned a very fast lesson. He swung the belt again at Isabelle. She jumped in the air and briefly caught the belt in her teeth. When she couldn't hold on, she backed away and sized up the situation to make another run at Billy Ray from a new angle. Joey was getting spooked. "That bitch is not gonna' back down, Billy Ray. We've got to get out of here."

"It's just a dog," said Billy Ray.

"Well, then you kill the dog, and then I'll help you hang the bitch," said Joey Berger.

"Okay, I will," said Billy Ray. He charged forward towards Isabelle and made a feint with his belt to the left, and kicked out with his jackboot to the right. His foot caught Isabelle on the left front paw, breaking it, and continued into her ribcage breaking four ribs then as well. He then made the mistake of approaching Isabelle to finish the job. She jumped up despite all the pain in her body and clasped Billy Ray on the forearm and shook her head for all she was worth. His skin began to shred away and a mist of frothy blood issued forth that seemed to want to continue until there was no evil blood left in the evil man. Isabelle knew that she could kill him then, and she prayed to the Creator to give her the chance.

Joey came up behind Isabelle and kicked her in the ribs on the left side. She let go of Billy Ray's arm and rolled over to catch her breath. The two men grabbed Melanie by the arms and dragged her back to the gravel drive and threw her back into the truck. Isabelle gathered her breath and made it around the house to the front porch in time to hear, "Freakin' dog. We'll take the bitch back to her house and do her there."

Chapter Thirty

*P*hodan and Cap' Walker missed Billy Ray and Joey Berger's retreat by a mere twenty minutes. It is not a perfect world. If it were, *Phodan* would have come down upon Alligator Lake witnessing a woman he was intimate with being strung up to hang by the head until dead. The fireworks that would have ensued would have eclipsed any Disney display by about a hundred-fold. *Phodan* would have gathered Melanie into a pod of protection and then vaporized the immediate area to the point that Cap' Walker and Carla would no longer have a place to live. As it is, their neighborhood was spared that conflagration because Billy Ray had taken flight to another location. Namely, Melanie's apartment.

~

Cap' Walker and *Phodan* came ashore and sent the ship out to the middle of the lake to bed-down beneath the water. When Cap' saw the broken screen door, he was livid. "Damn! That dog is high maintenance sometimes. The little shithead broke out of the house. She used to break through the screen with her nails from time to time, but now she's broken the whole damned door down!"

Phodan noticed the rope hung over one of the branches on the large oak tree. *That wasn't there when we left.* He also noticed the drag marks from Melanie's feet across the lawn that led around the side of the house. The hackles on the back of his neck began to stand up and a chill ran down his spine even though the temperature was a comfortable eighty degrees. He walked the line of the drag marks and saw Isabelle laying on her side by the front porch. Cap' followed behind him, and when he saw the dog, he said, "What is wrong with you, Isabelle? What the hell did you do to my door?" Cap' reached down and grabbed Isabelle lightly on the snout. Isabelle made no sound. She stumbled to her feet and placed her head against Cap's thigh waiting for him to pet her. Cap' looked up and said, "*Phodan*, you want a dog?"

"Yes, Cap', I certainly do."

"I'm so mad at her I could almost let you have her," he said.

"Yes, I do. Cap' I want a dog. How many ways can I tell you that I want your dog. How many words in the English language mean yes? I would like to tell them all to you. Yes, indeed, I want your dog."

When Cap' saw Isabelle holding her paw up off the ground, he became concerned. "What did you do to yourself, Belle? Are you alright?"

"roooof," said Isabelle weakly. *they've got Melanie.*

"Where did they take her?"

"rooooooof," *back to her house . . . they mean to kill her there . . . hurry there's no time . . .*

"You are injured, my friend. Let me help you," said *Phodan.*

"roooooooof," *there's no time . . . go . . .*

Phodan said to Cap', "I need your truck. I have to go help a friend."

"Take it," said Cap'. He threw *Phodan* the keys. "Do you want me to come along?" asked Cap'.

"No." *Phodan* started for the truck and Isabelle gathered up all the strength she had left and said, "ROOOF!" *The Robe, Phodan! Take the robe!*

"Yes, of course, thank you, Belle," he said.

Cap' was confused and just looked down at Isabelle. He was still mad at her for breaking down the screen door. He looked down at his hand and saw there was blood on it. Shaking his head, he said, "What'd you do, cut yourself on the door?"

~

Phodan pulled Cap's pick-up truck into the parking lot of Melanie's apartment complex. He walked around the building and silently climbed up to the second floor balcony that faced the lake. He made no sound at all and could see through the sliding glass doors that Melanie was tied up in a chair and bleeding from the face. One of her eyes was closed, and there was a large bruise beginning to spread across her face and forehead. One arm hung as an angle that was not natural for the human form and his heart began to manifest a fury unlike he had ever felt in his six-hundred years of existence. He had only one thing in his mind at that point. He was saddened by the fact that he could only kill the bastard once. *Indeed,* he thought to himself, *it is not a perfect world.* When he reached the sliders, he tried them and found that they were unlocked. He had determined that there were two young men in the living-room with Melanie. When he slipped inside, Melanie opened her one good eye and saw him. She wanted to cry out and warn him that the two men were after him and only using her as a means to get to him. Of course, *Phodan* knew the situation very well because he was told a great deal by Isabelle. He brought his index finger up and held it vertically to his lips telling her to be quiet and don't let the men know he was there just yet. Then he motioned to her that she had to tip the chair over and lay down on the floor to get as low as possible. He made a gesture with both of his palms close to the floor. Melanie nodded her head that she understood what he was telling her.

Phodan had donned the blue robe and wrapped it fully around him. Just as he stepped into the room, he whistled. "Hey, idiot boy. What stagnant gene-pool did you crawl out of?"

"What the hell?" said Joey Berger.

"Well if it isn't old blue robe his-self," said Billy Ray. "We been waitin' for you. Sorry that we started the party without you, cause you da' man of the hour."

"No problem, piss ant. I can catch up pretty quickly." *Phodan* motioned to Melanie to hit the floor and stay low. He quickly walked to the center of the room and stood between the two men. Taking his hand out of his pocket, he held it up to Billy Ray and made a shooting motion with his fingers. Billy Ray made a motion of his own. He had a 357 Smith & Wesson revolver in his hand. He fired off two shots at *Phodan* who pulled back as though he was dodging the bullets. Joey Berger was struck in the chest by one of Billy Ray's shots. Billy Ray shouted to him, "Shoot him, Joey! What the hell are you standing there for? Kill the son-of-a-bitch!"

Joey pulled his big Colt 45 from his belt and aimed at *Phodan*. He pulled the trigger twice. The room exploded with cordite and smoke. *Phodan* was briefly blinded by the muzzle flash, and the first thing he saw when he regained his sight was Billy Ray backed against the wall with a large hole in his forehead. He slowly leaned forward and then fell face first to the floor striking his now ruined head on the coffee table. Joey clutched his chest and sank into the sofa dropping his gun and moaning from the pain of a gut-shot. "Son-of-a-bitch," he mumbled softly and then his head lolled to one side and he was still.

Melanie raised her head off the floor and looked at *Phodan*. She managed to ask, "Are they dead, Dan?"

"Very dead, Melanie."

"Good."

"Yes, it's very good. This world just became a better place."

"You're what makes it a good place, Dan. Did I tell you that I love you?"

"Not in so many words, but I got the idea."

~

Phodan drove Melanie back to the Walker farm after he spent a considerable amount of time healing her wounds. She had a fractured eye socket, a broken jaw, four broken ribs, a compound fracture of her arm and a number of lacerations on her face and breasts. When he was through, she looked at herself in a full length mirror and was unable to speak. She cried. When it seemed like her tears could come no more, she asked weakly, "How?"

"Shhhh," said *Phodan*. "How is not important now. We have to go help a friend back on the Walker farm."

"She saved my life, Dan," said Melanie through her tears.

"Yes, I know."

~

When Melanie and *Phodan* reached the Walker farm, Carla had returned from her grocery shopping. She scratched her head and asked, "What happened to the door?"

"The dog," said Cap' with little more of an explanation.

Carla then asked, "Why?"

"Who knows," said Cap'. "That dog is high maintenance sometimes, Carla."

"Well, she had to have a good reason, Nigel."

"What would you have me do, ask *her* why she broke down the door?"

"If we only could," said Carla.

"Maybe someday, but not today. Now all she says is Rooof!" said Cap'.

Phodan took Isabelle into a bedroom of the Walker house. He healed her wounds on her head and set the broken leg and knitted the bones together. He also healed her broken ribs and the cut on her nose. When he was finished, she jumped down off the bed and shook herself vigorously from head to toe. She panted loudly and her face was pulled back into a big grin. She told *Phodan,* "Rooof!" *Thank you for healing me, Phodan. I love you.*

"I love you, too, Belle."

"Rooof!" *How is Melanie?*

"She's fine."

"Rooof!" *She didn't look too fine the last time I saw her.*

"Honestly, she's fine," said *Phodan.* "She's out in the living room talking to Carla. Come and see for yourself."

"Rooof!" *I'm sorry I called her a hooker.*

"I knew you didn't mean it."

Later that day, *Phodan* took Cap' Walker down by the lake with a couple bottles of beer. He told Cap' why Isabelle had broken down the screen door. He also told him that he brought Melanie and Isabelle back from the threshold of death's door. It was close going there for both of them for a while. He told Cap' that he explained to Isabelle he could give her a very long life compared to the five or six that remained for her here on Earth. *Phodan* had another two hundred years of life left, and Isabelle could easily see half of them. She could be the oldest dog in the universe and see wonders beyond her imagination. *Phodan* told him, "I explained it all to Isabelle and how you jokingly said you were tempted to let her go with me after she broke the door down, and do you know what she said to me?"

"What?" asked Cap'.

"She said, "Rooof!" *I'm Cap's dog.*

Then I said to her, think about it. Just think about what you'd be giving up. And you know what she said then?"

"What?"

"She said, ROOOOF!" *I said I'm Cap's dog DAMMIT!*

Cap' Walker was a man of few tears. He had been wounded in battle serving his country; he had been tortured by pirates off the coast of Indonesia while with the Merchant Marines; he had watched his beloved Carla wither away with a cancer eating her up little-by-little, day-by-day, and he never once cried.

Sitting out on that bench under the oak tree with *Phodan* – looking down at his hand and seeing Isabelle's dried blood, he cried that day.

~

Chapter Thirty-one

I t took longer to get Alex Janzen into a harness and rappelling device than it took to descend to the ground. When they reached the foot of the tree, they saw the big cat lying there misshapen and quickly growing cold. Bantah had rights of the trophy and so he pulled his knife and began the laborious task of taking the pelt. Christos Somah was surprised to learn that the skin of the cat had a sweet smell like honeysuckle and gardenia mixed with musk. It was also very soft to the touch, and he understood why the *Valegatos* might covet the pelt even though they did not often wear clothes. He knew that the pelts were for sleeping on even before he asked the question. Bantah told him, "Since I was a small child, my earliest memories are of sleeping on the gatos fur. It warmed me when the night turned suddenly with the trade-winds, and it was a soft place to land when I was learning how to climb the trees. We pray to the Creator with thanks for the gatos. Although he carries the *death angel*, he is our friend and we love him."

The next things that Bantah took from the cat were his long teeth. He left the smaller teeth knowing that they would be there for a tribesman to retrieve after the ants cleaned all the flesh from them. Bantah told Alex and Christos Somah that the trophies of the pelt and the fangs belonged to the ones who took the cat's life, in this case he and Christos Somah, but the small teeth belonged to the valley. They were to be left for a tribesman to find and fashion a necklace for his mate called the *bonesgatos*.

The last things that Bantah took from the great cat were the bones of the tribesmen. When he opened the long underbelly and dragged out the stomach of the gato, Christos Somah and Alex were both surprised and nauseated. They couldn't imagine the reason why Bantah would take his knife and release all the foul-smelling gasses of the huge cat's entrails. Bantah's eyes began to water, and he threw up all the contents of his stomach right then and there. *Nothing could be worth going through that agony,* they thought. Christos Somah and Alex resisted the urge to gag and vomit as well even though they were standing well away from the gruesome procedure. Christos Somah spoke up, "Bantah, what are you doing? Get away from that foul thing!"

"I will get away when I have retrieved all the bones that are lodged in this beast." With a ceremony that spoke of a great reverence, Bantah retrieved a shiny, white cloth from his pack and said a prayer kneeling over it. He touched all four corners and then his forehead and his heart. He pulled the bones from the stomach lining of the cat with his bare hands and placed them on the cloth. Then he folded all the corners to the center and tied it with a small braided rope that was made of the hide do gato. He spoke to the two men standing twenty feet away who watched confused by his actions. "This is something that we must do when we take one of the gatos. This is the only time when it is possible because the condoros will take what we leave and bring it to her nest for the young ones. I have taken the bones of the tribesmen for the *bone ceremony*. It is, perhaps, all that keeps the peace within the three tribes."

"What is the bone ceremony, Bantah?" asked Christos Somah.

"It is a time when all three tribes come together in peace. It is the only time of peace, so it is of great importance that the ceremony is passed down from the elders to the young warriors. Otherwise there would never be any hope of one day living with peace in the whole valley."

"What are the bones for?" asked Alex.

"Obviously, we don't know who the bones belong to. They could be from the *Valegatos*, the *Viperos* or the *Condoros* tribe. There is no way to tell. So during the bone ceremony, all tribesmen and tribeswomen pray over the bones. It is very significant that we pray over the bones of each other. Then they are placed in a large pile and set afire. All three tribes perform their ceremonial dances around the fire at the same time. Christos Somah, you took part in the *call of the gatos* of my tribe the other night."

"Yes, I remember. What is this prayer you speak of? You said that you pray over the bones."

"Yes, it is true. We speak to the Creator with our voices and our hearts. We feel we are in communication with Him."

"That's very strange," said Christos Somah. "I have heard of that practice, but it has disappeared from my culture. We know nothing of this prayer."

"It is done to wish for something. In the case of the *ceremony of the bones,* we wish that the tribesman are free to have another body."

"That seems quite unlikely, Bantah. Once you live no more, that is the end."

"Or, perhaps it is the beginning."

"Very strange, my friend."

"Perhaps it is strange to my people that you have no prayer."

"Perhaps. But the different ways of our people make us unique, even though they serve to keep us apart."

"We have prayer on Earth," said Alex. "Some of us have brought it here to Siren. It's something that I have not done enough of lately."

"You had your feet firmly planted in the air," said Christos Somah.

"Yes, I'm afraid I did."

"The woman who sent us to find you said she has lost you to the valley, even if you return."

"I can understand why she would feel that way. But with any luck, I can change. The experience with the condor has shown me what I have been missing."

"It may be too late for that," said Bantah.

"What do you mean?" said Alex

"Your love may be lost."

"This love you speak of is as thin as the air," said Christos Somah.

"You wouldn't understand," said Bantah. "My people have taken love into the valley because your people had rejected it so many years ago."

"What you speak of is primitive, Bantah, at least according to my people," said Christos Somah.

"If love is primitive, then primitive is good. If the Creator is good, then the Creator is primitive," said Bantah.

"You speak in riddles, Bantah."

"Let us go now. We should return to the encampment. I will add these bones to the cache that we have collected since the last ceremony."

"One more thing, Bantah. What makes you say that I may have lost my love?" asked Alex.

"Perhaps she loves another," said Bantah pointedly looking at Christos Somah.

"Him?" asked Alex. "How can someone love he who knows nothing of it?"

"Perhaps he is willing to learn."

~

Chapter Thirty-two

*P*hodan told Cap' and Carla that he would leave for Siren shortly. When he heard the call of Shelly Simon on Melanie's balcony, he told her that he would soon return and attend to the needs of the Church. Again, he felt a sense of responsibility for the Earth sirens and the native sirens as well. Religion was taboo on Siren and the people from Earth had brought it with them. They hadn't been on Siren for more than a month before they felt the urgent need for prayer. It was as though they were going through withdrawal from a powerful drug that had a hold on them. At first they didn't know what it was. They just woke up each day and couldn't find any peace within their hearts.

The people of Siren were always in a peaceful state. They had known nothing else for centuries. There was no conflict of any kind. They had knowledge of the primitive tribes of the valley, but always steered well clear of them. When the Earth sirens witnessed the perpetual state of peace and well-being that the native sirens demonstrated, it only served to irritate them. They couldn't find any semblance of peace until Durbah suggested that they pray for it. The transformation was immediate. It was as though a veil had been lifted, and a great truth issued forth. They felt like they had a purpose in life for the very first time. Durbah began to speak to the other Earth sirens on the lawn outside the Great Hall in the city of Creston.

Christos Somah's father, Christos, was the local member of the Council of Regents on Siren. As such, he was the governing leader of the entire city of Creston and the surrounding areas of the Sirenian Mountain range. It was to him that complaints came about the newcomers and their pagan ways.

Prayer was rejected on Siren nearly five-thousand years ago when the sirens first left for Egypt by way of the *Preculians*. It was also at that time that the tribes of the valley were established. Those that didn't go to Earth also had the mark of electrum. Their eyes would become lit with a fire of gold and silver on the edges of their corneas. The result was a mesmerizing trance brought to the people of Siren. It was rumored that the tribesmen of the valley still possessed this ability so they were feared and avoided at all costs.

The son of Councilman Christos was taking a huge risk to help Durbah Purness journey into the valley, but she had released her powers on him, and he was helpless to resist her. There was a residual effect that he still felt even though she reined in her pheromones and the projection of electrum in her eyes. Christos Somah longed for Durbah although he didn't understand the origin of his feelings. Siren had peace and consideration for all members of society, but there was no love. There was also no God. To speak the word God was thought to be blasphemy. It was the word for which there is no word. The sirens believed in a creator who was a dispassionate observer of their lives, but that's as far as it went. To suggest that a being took an interest in their well-being was absurd. When the sirens witnessed the prayers of the newcomers and the actual mention of the word for which there is no word, they were furious. They insisted that the Council of Regents decree that public display of worship be strictly forbidden, punishable by banishment to the monopole valley. That is where the tribes originated in the first place. They were banished to the valley by the fears of the sirens over five-thousand years ago. What was even a greater threat than prayer was a powerful force that all of siren feared. It was the concept of love. There was no defense against love. It would creep into the soul and grow until there was no controlling one's own feelings. To lose control of your mindset was unthinkable and feared worse than death.

Now the newcomer sirens from Earth were worshiping unabashedly in public and it was even considered possible that they had gone the extra mile toward destruction and embraced love. Love threatened the very peace that Siren had enjoyed for thousands of years. It was dangerous. It had to be guarded against and watched with a careful eye so as not to be exposed by possible contamination. The sirens feared that their young people might become infected by the strange practices and concepts of the newcomers. They were threatened by a doxology. A doxology could undermine the very foundation of their world, and they would make sure that their young people were not exposed to it.

The Church of Siren was established in this way. The Church, built by the *Preculians,* was permitted to function just outside the Creston City limit. It was situated on a hill overlooking the monopole valley, which was due east of Creston and stretched out nearly five-hundred miles to the Alantis Sea.

The sun would rise over the valley and shine on a huge crystal situated at the top of the steeple. This was a symbol of both power and warning for the people of Siren. It was very similar to the metal, pyramid-shaped cap that was on Khufu, the Great Pyramid of Egypt on Earth. That metal was called electrum, and it was made of gold and silver. The *Preculians* mixed the electrum atoms of Khufu's capstone-cover with carbon based molecules to make epigenetic alterations to the DNA of the sirens who would travel to Earth. That was the source of the strange power that was displayed by their eyes. Once again, the *Preculians* were careless with their technology. They created a monster. Their intention was to make the sirens more beautiful for their own protection and to enhance their influence over humanity, but the effect became much more. The combination of electrum along with increased pheromones became an irresistible attraction. Even *they* could not resist the powers that the sirens had to shape the will of others.

Thirteen of the enhanced sirens were taken to Earth, and the remainder tried to blend into Sirenian society, but that idea was doomed from the start. The remaining enhanced sirens, nearly fifty of them, with the electrum in their eyes were sent to the monopole valley. There they divided into three groups that eventually became the tribes that thrive there today. They were free to practice their traditions of prayer and strong attraction for one another. Thus, love was able to thrive in the valley. But along with love came other emotions that were detrimental to the peaceful coexistence of the tribal members. They began to spread apart, and each tribe laid claim to a certain section of the valley.

The *Valegatos* tribe went west, almost dangerously close to the outskirts of Creston itself. The animals of the valley were dangerous, but the sirens of Creston even more so. What the sirens lacked in love, they made up for in fear. There was an unnatural phobic avoidance to the tribes of the valley by the sirens. Christos Somah begged Durbah and Alex not to divulge the fact that he had interacted with the *Valegatos*. If it were learned that he actually took part in one of their primitive ceremonies, he would be banished to the valley as well.

~

Chapter Thirty-three

Christos, Bantah and Alex had been walking the path along the river for about an hour in total silence. Finally, Alex couldn't contain himself any longer. He reached out in front of him and grabbed Bantah's shoulder.

"Did he sleep with her?" he asked motioning to Christos Somah with his eyes.

"What?" asked Bantah. He grabbed Alex's hand and pulled it off his shoulder. "You are hurting me. That is a strange way to reward me for your freedom from the condoros."

"Did he sleep with her? Come on, tell me. I'll find out anyway."

"You mean, the light-haired woman, correct?"

"You know exactly who I mean. Her name is Durbah."

"Yes, she is very nice."

"Are you in love with her?"

"I am *in love*, as you say, with everyone," said Bantah.

"That's not an answer," said Alex.

"Yes, it is, Alex," said Christos Somah. "Take it from me, the people of the valley, at least the *Valegatos*, are in love with everybody. I should know because even *I've* felt it, and I am in love with no one."

"Then you're not in love with Durbah?" asked Alex.

"No," said Christos Somah.

"But Bantah is. Is that right?"

"It is the same with all the tribes," said Bantah.   "They love all the people on this world and all the animals. The only ones they will not show it to are the other tribes. We *Valegatos* are fearful of the *Viperos* and the *Condoros* tribes. We love them, but we will not show that love because of our fears. It has been that way for thousands of years."

"But you love all sirens," said Alex matter-of-factly.

"Yes."

"And you love me."

"Yes, but you are not a siren."

"And what about you, Christos Somah? You say you don't love Durbah?"

"No, I don't."

"You say you love no one. Do you mean that literally?"

"Yes."

"Why not? Why don't you love anyone?"

"It is not something that we . . . do."

"None of you?"

"None of us."

"Nobody cares about anybody else on all of Siren. Is that what you're saying?"

"No, not at all. We care a great deal for each other. We extend ourselves so much that we are beyond the concept of individual ownership. Whatever I have, I give to all of Siren. They may have it because I care so much for them. But that is not love. Love is a painful thing that we once had in our history, but it no longer lives in our hearts today."

"God is love," said Alex.

"Maybe that is why," said Christos Somah, "we don't use that word, and we don't have that concept as well."

"You have no love and you have no God."

"That is correct," said Christos Somah.

"What about sex?"

"We have that, yes."

"Did you have that with Durbah?"

"Why do you ask?"

"Because I just want to know, dammit! Yes or no?"

"No."

"I don't believe you."

"You seem upset," said Christos Somah.

"You're damned right I'm upset."

"And this makes you feel good?"

"Of course, it doesn't make me feel good. It makes me feel terrible."

"And this is what love does for you," said Christos Somah. "You may be better off without it."

"Oh, you wouldn't understand," said Alex hotly.

"I could say the same to you," said Christos Somah.

"I understand," said Bantah. "I love the woman, Durbah."

"You stay out of it, Bantah. You can't have Durbah because you live in different worlds."

"She came to my world once. Perhaps she will do so again."

"Don't bet on it."

The three men walked the path of the river in silence once again.

~

Alligator Lake - Kissimmee, Florida

Melanie was sitting with *Phodan* on the bench by the edge of the lake. I can't believe what just happened today. It seems like just a bad dream. Those men almost killed me. I would be dead right now if it weren't for you."

"And Isabelle," *Phodan* reminded her.

"Yes, I know. She's wonderful."

"I wish I could take her back home with me, but she turned me down."

"She talks to you?"

"She told me where to find you, remember?"

"Yes, I guess she did. I wondered how you knew where I was."

"It was Belle. She was injured also battling the evil ones. When I healed her, I was able to gather some stem cells."

"So?"

"I asked her if I could grow them into a companion."

"You intend to clone a dog?"

"It's more than that. I intend to give her the memories and personality of Isabelle herself."

"Did you tell her that as well?"

"Of course."

"I wish you could make one for me," said Melanie.

"In a sense, I will."

"What do you mean, in a sense?"

"I want you to return with me to my home."

"You want me to live with you?"

"Yes. Would that please you?" asked *Phodan.*

"Yes, I think it would. I know I can't go back to my apartment. There are a couple of dead guys there, and it must be swarming with cops who have a lot of questions."

"So come away with me. I can show you some things you would never see otherwise."

"Alright, I will. I just wish I could get the memory of this awful day out of my head."

"I have a friend named Shelly who can do that for you. Soon you will meet her, and this day will leave your mind forever."

"Where are we going? Where do you live?"

"I'm glad you're sitting down."

"Why do you say that?" she asked.

Phodan reached into the pocket of his vest and retrieved the control stone. He held it toward the lake and pressed the etched icon for the ship to rise out of the lake. He then said to Melanie, "You're going to love this."

The woman's jaw dropped when she saw the top of the ship break the surface of the water. It was a curved canopy that glistened in the afternoon sun. The body of the ship began to appear, and it rose slowly up to nearly fifteen feet high. The length was easily four times as long as it was high, tapering down to a sharply pointed nose cone. It hovered just a few inches above the surface of the lake and looked to Melanie like a cross between a very large motor home with short wings and a sleek sports car without wheels. *Phodan* pressed another icon and a ramp broke away from the side of the ship and lowered to the ground just beyond their feet.

"Oh, my God," said Melanie. "You're kidding me," was all she could manage to say.

Just then, Carla had walked up behind them and put her hand on Melanie's shoulder and said, "Ain't she a beauty?"

"Am I dreaming, Carla?"

"Yes, honey. I am, too. Careful now, you don't want to wake us up."

~

Chapter Thirty-four

*P*hodan landed the ship on the lawn outside the Great Hall in the city of Creston on Siren. The sirens flocked to it just as they had five-thousand years before when the *Preculians* first came and told Siren of Earth's existence. They told of the accident that produced the gamma rays, and how Earth would come to be a war-like planet and be plagued with greed, the need for conquest, and of religion. This time the news would be better.

Now, they would be transferring the Earth sirens back to Earth if they chose to go. Most of them would, the exceptions being the very old and the very addicted to either the lavish lifestyle they enjoyed on Siren or to flying over the monopole valley. Although he dearly loved Sarah Poole, who would choose to go, Brad Early would choose to stay behind. His addiction to flying was at the critical stage, and now he could think of little else.

Phodan and Melanie were met by Councilman Christos when they walked down the ramp of the ship to the lawn. He embraced *Phodan* and then held both of Melanie's hands in his, "Welcome to Siren, Grand Master," he said to *Phodan*. "And welcome also to your friend."

"Her name is Melanie, Christos. She has agreed to come home with me to *Preculis.*"

"How nice," he said, but Phodan didn't think that he really meant it.   He knew that the concept of desiring someone's company was entirely foreign to Christos and all other sirens.

"I have come to meet with the newcomers at the Church. We are to make arrangements for their departure."

"Just how will that take place, Master *Phodan?* I know that they cannot all fit on your ship."

"We will not use the ship until we reach Earth orbit. The transfer will take place with the use of a *space/time exchange chamber.* The Church was constructed with the precise dimensions of the way station in Earth orbit.   We anticipated this eventuality when we first brought them here. We had high hopes that they could blend in with your society here on Siren, but some compulsions are merely too strong to suppress.   It seems that prayer is one of them.   We felt confident that their extreme emotions, although somewhat distasteful to you, would pose no actual threat.   But religion is another matter entirely.   We realize your young people are impressionable, and we feel responsible, once again, to act in your best interests."

"And once again, we thank you Master *Phodan.*   It seems as though your people have been our benefactors throughout time itself.   We will all breathe a sigh of relief when our newcomers are transferred back to their home planet."

"They had hoped that Siren could be their home, but I suppose that was our fault.   We on *Preculis* have made many mistakes throughout the centuries, and it seems that history always repeats itself."

"No one on Siren holds any ill-will against you, Grand Master."

"Please, Christos. Dispense with my title. We have known each other a long time. I remember when you were born. I used to confer with your father and your grandfather before him. Please don't call me Grand Master and I won't call you Councilman."

"As you wish, *Phodan.* What will become of the Church? Will you dismantle it?"

"That will be transferred as well. I have found a place for it by a lake where I am sure they will be happy. The climate is a little warmer than here, but they should get used to it eventually."

"Perhaps one day I can see it for myself. I've never been off-world, but as you know, my son, Christos Somah, has been to the city of Cairo on Earth."

"Where is your son now? I hoped to say hello to him while I am here," said *Phodan.* He was very interested in saying hello to young Christos Somah and also interested in retrieving the belt shield he had loaned him for his journey into the valley of the cats, vipers and condors.

When Alex Janzen fell prey to one of the condors, Durbah reached out to *Phodan* for help finding him. *Phodan* in turn reached out to Christos Somah to take her into the valley and seek the help of a *Valegato* tribesman.

At first, Christos Somah was adamant in his refusal to be exposed to *"the savages,"* but Durbah unleashed her powers and he was helpless to refuse her. She would have to use her powers once again when Alex and Christos Somah returned to Creston to purge the memory of his experiences in the valley. She made a promise to *Phodan* to expunge his contamination and retrieve the belt shield.

"My son, Christos Somah, will be coming to Creston soon. He has been traveling in the valley with one of the newcomers. She asked to see the source of the mag-belts and Christos Somah agreed to show her the posi-grains."

"Will you send him to the Church to see me when he arrives, please?"

"Certainly, *Phodan.* I'm sure he will be very pleased to see you. It is because of you that he is the only siren to have traveled to the planet Earth. That makes him quite a celebrity."

"If he is a celebrity, it is because he is your son."

"You are most kind, *Phodan.* If you have any needs during your stay, please be sure to ask me for assistance."

"Thank you, Christos. I certainly will."

Phodan and Melanie closed up the ship and began to walk up the hill to the Church. It was less than a mile, and they arrived in about twenty minutes. Melanie used the time to ask a few questions, "What's with all this Grand Master stuff?"

"It is merely a title. They show respect when they address me as such."

"But what does it mean?" she asked.

"On my home planet, there are Masters of the different districts, much the same way there are elected officials on Earth. Think of it like calling someone Senator."

"But Grand Master means something else, doesn't it?"

'There has to be one official who oversees the rest of them. It is for the purpose of breaking a tie when voting and things like that. For now, I hold that office."

"So now I have to call you Grand Master?" she asked shaking her head.

"Only when we're in bed," he said jovially.

Shelly Simon was lighting candles at the altar. Charles Donovan was seated in the first pew reading from a copy of the Old Testament. When Shelly heard *Phodan* open the front door to the Church, she quickly blew out the match and rushed up the isle to greet him. "Grand Master *Phodan,* you heard my prayers," she said excitedly.

"Yes, Shelly. I heard you loud and clear."

"All the way from Earth! That's amazing. I heard you as well. It was as though you were standing in the same room. Introduce me to your friend," she said motioning to Melanie.

"Forgive my manners, Shelly. This is Melanie and I neither know nor care what her last name is."

"It's Cook," she said.

"Hello, Melanie," said Shelly. "I'm very glad to meet you. Welcome to *The First Church of Siren.*"

"It's very nice," said Melanie. "It reminds me of the old South."

"I know what you mean. I think that's what Master *Phodan* had in mind."

"Is that what you had in mind, Grand Master?" asked Melanie accenting his title for emphasis.

"Call me Dan."

"Is that what you had in mind, Dan?"

"Not exactly, but now that you mention it, it does look like the old South. South Carolina to be exact."

"That's it," said Shelly. "Charleston."

~

Chapter Thirty-five

Christos and Bantah had to slow down to Alex's pace because his body was emaciated from being a flier too long. Christos Somah tried to comfort him, "Don't worry about it, Alex, we're in no hurry." They were words he was not completely behind. Actually he was concerned about staying in the valley too long. There were so many perils around them that it was just a matter of time before something fatal would befall one of them. They didn't have long to wait. Because their slow pace made them easy targets, hell rained down on them from the trees.

Ticks and recluse spiders fell on all of their shoulders. The only way to survive the assault was for them to stand in a tight circle and swat the vermin away from each other. Bantah was the most at risk because of his bare shoulders. Christos Somah and Alex were sure to swat away the spiders first and then deal with the ticks. The ticks were larger, but the brown recluse spiders were much more perilous. They were only half-inch wide, but their bite carried a flesh eating bacteria that would eat large holes in Bantah's flesh in less than a day. There was no known antidote for the spider bite, and the tick bite was likely to impart the disease that atrophied the muscles of the victim over a period of weeks.

The three men were sure not to move because it would only put them in the position of providing more prey for the insects. They stood in a tight circle until all were clear of the invading forms of creeping death. The experience brought them closer together, and Alex was ashamed of his actions a short while earlier. He told the two men, "I'm sorry for my emotions. I had no control of my voice. I was jealous. I displayed a side of humanity that was far from its finest hour."

"There is nothing to apologize for, Alex," said Bantah. "I understand perfectly. That is the reason why we resist contact with the other tribes. If our women lay with them, it brings on the madness."

"Well, I don't mind telling you it was a rather distasteful discussion for me," said Christos Somah. "My people don't speak of such things. We hold no ownership of others. If it is the choice of our women to lay with a man, it is none of our concern."

"Yeah, we get it," said Bantah. It was the first harsh expression that Alex ever heard issued from the gentle tribesman. It seemed that he was close to rejecting Christos Somah's people as much as they rejected him. It was a love/hate position thought Alex. He knew the *Valegatos* loved the Sirens, but they were frustrated that they could not share in the feelings that they held most dear. Alex was starting to understand Bantah's position regarding the opposite sex. He found that he was actually a little envious because, to hear Bantah tell it, the whole of the *Valegatos* tribeswomen were *his* women. *Must be nice,* he thought.

Christos Somah came up with a plan. He turned to Bantah and said, "The pelt of the gato. We can use it for a cover for you and Alex."

"It is not big enough for all three of us if we are to drape it all the way to the ground."

"It only has to be big enough for you and Alex. I have my own way to be protected."

"What are you talking about?" asked Bantah.

"Do you remember when the gato attacked up in the tree?"

"Yes."

"Why didn't he bite me?"

"I thought he fell from the branch."

"Have you ever known a gato to fall from a branch before?"

"Never."

"And he never will. They are superb acrobats and would never fall from a tree."

"But that one did."

"No, he didn't. I pushed him off the tree with a personal shield."

"You talk nonsense, Christos Somah. There is no such thing."

"There is, and I will show you."

"What are you saying? Are you mad or something?"

"Take your sword and attack me with it."

"You are mad. I knew it."

"You cannot hurt me, Bantah. Nothing can. That is how I tripped the gato over the side of the branch. I have a powerful shield, strike me and get it over with."

Bantah drew his sword and tapped Christos Somah on the shoulder testing the strength of the shield.

"Harder," insisted Christos Somah.

Bantah struck a bit harder. The shield held fast.

"Harder," demanded Christos Somah. "Bantah, strike me as hard as you can!"

Bantah did as he asked and was amazed as his sword just bounced off Christos Somah's shoulder. He finally was convinced.

"That is sorcery," he declared.

"Perhaps. Just be glad that I am on your side."

"I am glad," said Bantah. "You could defeat anyone or anything with that shield of yours."

"That's true. But the one who gave it to me has made me promise not to abuse it. It is a promise that I will surely keep."

"Thanks be to the Creator for that," said Bantah. "Alex and I alone will use the pelt for protection from the insects. You have no need of our protection. That much is sure."

The three men continued on down the path of the river to the point where they needed to cross over to travel west toward Creston. Bantah told the other two men, "Thanks be to the Creator that we have protection as we cross the river. The pelt should work for Alex and me, but I'm afraid it may be damaged on the way."

"Damaged," asked Christos Somah, "from what?"

"Teeth. You saw the fish that fly above the water. The whole time they are in the air, their mouths are open. They will surely smash into us although they do it by accident. They can't steer themselves once they take to the air."

"They're catching insects, is that it?" asked Christos Somah.

"Yes," said Bantah. "Thank the Creator that they do. Otherwise there would be millions of them swarming over the river and they would suck us dry in an instant."

"It surprises me how you are thanking the *Creator* for all the things that happen in the world. There are things called the forces of nature. They are of an ancient design that keeps changing over time. All creatures learn to survive the best way that they can. The ones who don't learn die out. It has always been that way, and it always will. I'm sure that your Creator has nothing to do with it."

"You are wrong, Christos Somah. So wrong that it saddens me that you cannot see what is right in front of your face," said Bantah.

"What about you, Alex?" asked Christos Somah. "Do you believe in this all-powerful being who helps out us wretched creatures from time to time?"

"I used to."

"And now?

"I'm not sure. But one thing is sure: I will rejoin the members of the Church whether they decide to stay on Siren or not."

"If my father has anything to say about it, they will surely choose to go. There is great unrest among my people because of their openly wanton practices," said Christos Somah.

"Like what?" asked Bantah. "What do they do?"

"Well, for one thing, they pray out in the open. And there is also some talk of fornication among the members of the Church."

"How could the Creator hear you unless you pray out loud?" asked Bantah. "It all sounds pretty baseless to me. They are committing no crime."

"My people see it differently, and my father has to hear about it from a great deal of them."

"They would be welcome here in the valley with my people. We do the very same things every day," said Bantah.

"I don't think the valley would appeal to the members of the Church, Bantah, but thank you anyway," said Alex.

"Bantah, you talked about the last commandment when we spoke before. Now I would like to hear the whole story if you don't mind."

"But you are not a believer, Christos Somah."

"I don't have to be a believer to take an interest in your culture. I've studied your people in school, in fact, all of the tribes, my whole life."

"Aren't you afraid you will become corrupted?"

"I'll chance it."

"All right. I'll tell you. The Creator sent Her son to live among the tribes one at a time to be an example for them. He would show them the ways of peace and love and living in accordance with the Creator's wishes. Those wishes were imparted to the people of the tribes by a list of commandments. There were ten of them initially, and then he added the final commandment, which we spoke of earlier. Actually, the eleventh commandment is the most powerful of all. If followed, there seems to be little use for all the other ten."

"What is the eleventh commandment?" asked Alex.

"To love each other," said Christos Somah speaking for Bantah.

"Spoken like a true *Valegato,* Christos Somah. Too bad it is not part of *your* life," said Bantah.

"What are the other ten commandments?" asked Christos Somah.

"What difference would it make to you?" asked Bantah.

~

Chapter Thirty-six

Shelly Simon had finished showing Melanie around the Church and the surrounding grounds when she asked *Phodan,* "I have a Church prayer request for you, Master *Phodan.*"

"Yes, as you said when I was back on Earth. Some young person needs healing. Isn't that so?"

"Yes. She has a problem with her blood. It is a cancer that I think has invaded her blood. Can you help her?"

"Bring her to me as soon as you can," said *Phodan.*

"I will."

Shelly sent a message to the woman known as Jhinduasa to bring her samah Julianah to the Church to have a session with the healer *Phodan.* She arrived within the hour. Shelly brought her to the rectory where she had placed *Phodan* and Melanie in one of the many rooms for their stay on Siren. *Phodan* received the young girl and asked Melanie to give them some privacy. Melanie was quick to agree and was anxious to see whether or not *Phodan* could actually help the girl. She knew that he had healed her and Isabelle from their episodes of trauma at the hands of *The Sons of Destiny*, but a blood disease was another matter entirely. Still, after the events of the past few days, there was nothing that she felt was outside the realm of possibility where *Phodan* was concerned.

~

When the three men, Christos Somah, Bantah and Alex Janzen walked into the encampment of the *Valegatos,* there was much celebration. *Here we go again,* Christos Somah said to himself. *More excuses for hugging and pressing their young bodies against us. These people are nothing if not exuberant. You can't help but to feel warmth for their pitiful savagery,* he thought. *But I wouldn't want to spend a lot of time among them. Their exuberance could be contagious.*

The young women were wild with excitement at the prospect of having Bantah back among them. Aside from the fact that he was the son of the tribal elder, his fame was reaching never-before heights as there were rumors he had subdued both a viper and a gato on the way to rescuing a citizen of Creston. All of them had dreams of taking him to their bed, and Bantah would do his very-best not to disappoint a single one of them.

~

Durbah was somewhat subdued when she first saw Alex walk into the encampment. She calmly walked up to him and said, "I am relieved to find you well, Alex."

"That's it?" he asked her. "No, oh, Alex, thank God you're safe. I've missed you so!"

"I guess not."

"You haven't missed me?"

"I started missing you months ago."

"I know, and I'm sorry," he said.

"And that may not be enough."

"Is it this Christos fellow? Do you love him now?"

"He is called Christos Somah, Alex."

"Just answer my question, Durbah. Do you love him?"

"Of course, I do. I asked him to risk his life. No, wait, let me tell it the right way: I *willed him* to care about your life even above his own. I shaped his needs to my needs, and you know I don't have that right. I just didn't know what else to do. When he acquiesced, I couldn't have been more grateful. It didn't matter whether or not I gave him a choice in the matter. If he had wanted me then and there, I would have torn off my clothes and satisfied him knowing that I might be the last lover he ever enjoyed. So, to answer your question, do I love him? You bet your sorry-flier ass I do. I'm just sorry that he doesn't return the sentiment. He is incapable of loving me in the same way that I love him. I'm sure you are relieved to hear that."

"What I want to hear is that you still love me."

"I'd love to tell you that, Alex. Perhaps, in time. Please don't pressure me to jump right onto that horse that threw me. I was devastated that you would choose that Creator-forsaken valley over me. That's not something that you soon recover from."

"I know, Durbah. I won't pressure you or rush you to take me back. But I just want you to know that I've taken my last flight and if you give me a chance, I will make it up to you."

"Welcome back, Alex. Come on, let's join the ceremony and try to keep an open mind."

~

Chapter Thirty-seven

*P*hodan and the young samah, Julianah, walked out of the rectory and crossed the large lawn to the Church on the hill. The girl was smiling and looked over at *Phodan* with reverence. She seemed to be taking in her surroundings with a renewed appreciation as though she were awakening from a long slumber. Her eyes followed the birds up into the trees and the butterflies lighting on the flowers that were in bloom. She said to *Phodan,* "It's all so beautiful here on this hill."

"Yes it is, Julianah. And you are a beautiful child as well. You should have a long and healthy life as far as I can tell."

"Then you have healed me."

"Not yet, child, but you shall be healed."

"Why do you say not yet?"

"Your blood still has the sickness, but now the Creator has been made aware of it. It is the *Prayers of the Church* that will heal you, not me."

"But I saw you praying over my body, Master *Phodan.*"

"That was merely to start the process, my child. I have no power to heal the sick. I have the power to ask *She* who can. That is all."

"But you say I will be well again."

"I am sure of it."

"When will the Church pray for me?"

"Come, it starts today."

He led Julianah over to the Church door and opened it for her. She walked inside and saw Jhinduasa sitting by the votive candles patiently waiting with her hands in her lap. The woman didn't understand why the healer couldn't meet them in their home, and she felt uncomfortable being in the Church with all of the forbidden symbols surrounding her. There was an ancient symbol of torture made of two timbers joined together standing in the front of the room. There were also crude candles of some pagan rights, long outlawed by civilized society. She really didn't understand why these awful reminders of a distasteful past could be tolerated. She made a mental note to complain to Christos of The Great Council of Regents.

She rose from the bench when she heard the door open and held out her hands to her daughter, Julianah. "My darling, come to me and give me your hands."

The girl rushed up to her mother and said, "Oh, Jomah, there is hope for me now. Master *Phodan* has called forth a wish for healing that he says will come to pass."

"What?" asked the woman. "What do you mean that *will* come to pass?" she was confused by what she was hearing.

"The Church will pray for me, Jomah. The Creator will hear them and bring about my cure."

"What is that nonsense you speak of, child. You are risking great punishment to speak thus."

"Don't you want me to be well, Jomah?"

"You know I do. But there was no mention of prayer. Primitive ceremonies will not heal you, Julianah. They will only get you banished to the valley of the cats."

"No, Jomah. They will heal me. It has been assured to me by Grand Master *Phodan*."

The woman looked *Phodan* in the eye and said, "What is this pain-spoken nonsense that you are filling my Samah with. How can it serve you to issue empty promises?"

"They are not empty, Jomah. Your Samah will be well again in time."

"Not by any crude rituals. I was told that you were a healer. I was assured that the healing comes from you."

"The healing *starts* from me, Jomah. It *comes* eventually from the Creator."

"I will hear no more of this." She grabbed her daughter by the hand and led her toward the door of the Church. She shouted over her shoulder on the way, "Primitives! Savages! There will be no prayers for my Samah. Not now, and not ever!"

She didn't hear the next words from *Phodan* as she closed the huge oak door behind her. He had said simply, "Oh, yes, there will."

Shelly Simon and Charles Donovan looked over at *Phodan* and shook their heads. "You can cut it with a knife, Grand Master," said Shelly.

"I thought we could leave intolerance behind us when we came to this backward place."

"You can't outrun something that you bring along with you," said *Phodan*.

"What do you mean," he asked.

"What did you just say, Charles?"

"I said that this planet is backward. There has been no procession toward Godhead in thousands of years."

"And you sound intolerant of their present condition."

"Oh, I see what you mean," said Charles. "I suppose you are right."

"I'm intolerant of such idiotic superstitions about savagery," said Shelly. "I don't mind telling you that I can choose to discriminate. The Creator gave me that choice. God gave me that choice. There I said it. String me up on a cross for mentioning the word for which there is no word, for God's sake."

"Not for His sake, Shelly. And not for yours either, but for the sake of some very frightened people, that's all."

"We can't stay here," said Shelly.

"No, you can't."

"We had such hope, Grand Master."

"You can still have hope. And you can still have your Church and The Prayers of the Church. You can pray for the young Samah as well, but you may have to do it from Earth."

"Earth sounds pretty good to me right now," said Charles.

"I would imagine many of the newcomers feel the same way," said *Phodan*. "Certainly the Church members do."

"Yes, Grand Master," said Shelly.

"How many are members of the Church?"

"There are about one-hundred thirty of us."

"And there are another two-hundred some other Earth sirens as well. They will all be given the chance to make the transfer in the *space/time exchange chamber,*" said *Phodan.*

"Where is the chamber?" asked Shelly.

"We are standing in it."

"Oh," she said, "and where is the chamber on the other end?"

"In orbit around Earth. Do you remember the way station where you stopped briefly on your journey here?"

"Yes, I remember it. That was about half-way to Siren, but not in Earth's orbit."

"Correct. We have found the need to establish the way station in Earth orbit to make the transfers to the ground."

"Why not just establish a chamber location on Earth?" asked Charles.

"There are none at the present time," said *Phodan.* "They were all dismantled on the last transfer out. They were filled with concrete if you remember, all except for Khufu's Horizon, the chamber in the great pyramid at Giza. There, it was dismantled when Alexander was returned to his final resting place. "

"So how do we get from Earth orbit to the ground?" he asked.

"With the ship that now stands on the lawn in front of the Great Hall. I have found you a pilot who will fly you all home to Earth in groups of about twenty-five at a time."

"And where is our final destination?" asked Shelly.

"Well, that's up to you. You can live wherever you like, but the initial port you will arrive at is a lake in Kissimmee, Florida."

"You're kidding?" said Shelly. Isn't that where there was a nuclear explosion recently?"

"It was a little over a year ago. The lake in Central Florida is outside the fallout area. I assure you it's quite safe."

"And who is our pilot?" asked Charles.

"His name is Cap' Walker. He lives on a farm by the lake with his wife, Carla, and his dog."

"Sounds very nice," said Charles.

"Yes, it is. It is also the new location for your Church. At least until you decide to move it somewhere else."

"Somehow I think Kissimmee, Florida, will be just fine," said Shelly.

"I picked it out personally," said Grand Master *Phodan*.

~

Christos Somah took Bantah aside during the welcome home ceremony of the *Valegatos*. "You people and your ceremonies. Is there anything you don't celebrate?" he laughed.

"When we make a new friend, we don't celebrate if they leave us. We probably won't celebrate when you and Alex travel back with Durbah to Creston."

"I'd like to hear the rest of the story," said Christos Somah.

"What story?"

"Come on, Bantah. Don't play with me. Tell me the story of the commandments."

"There isn't all that much to tell that you already don't know. As I said, the Creator sent Her son to live among the tribes. He taught them how to catch fish in the river and how to purge the posi-grains from their lungs. He taught them to revere the animals of the valley and to fear them as well."

"Keep going."

"The Creator gave him ten commandments that would make life easier and more pleasant for Her children. We are all the Creator's children. We are all equal in Her eyes and none more or less important than Her son whom She sent to live among us."

"What happened to the son?"

"He was killed."

"That's terrible," said Christos Somah. "Was it the *Valegatos* or the *Condoros*?"

"No."

"The *Viperos*, then," said Christos Somah.

"No."

"Then who?" asked Christos Somah.

"It was the *Sirenos*."

"What? What are you saying?"

"It was the sirens. Your people."

"I don't believe it," said Christos Somah.

"Okay."

"How was he killed?"

"The sirens came into the valley and interrogated him. They asked him if he was the son of the Creator."

"And what did he tell them?"

"He said we are all the sons and daughters of the Creator."

"And for that they killed him?" asked Christos Somah incredulously.

"It was not only that. They said he was dangerous."

"How was he dangerous?"

"Some of the sirens would come to the valley to listen to him. He told them that they could choose how to live their lives and make their own decisions."

"And what were the commandments?"

"Basically, to be good to each other.

Do not take what is not yours.

Do not harm others physically.

Do not resent your brother for what he has.

Do not speak poorly of the Creator.

Do not suggest that the Creator is indifferent.

Do not harm Her creations for sport.

Do not say things that are untrue.

Do not disparage the tribes in the valley.

Do not do harm to other worlds.

Do not do harm to the planet Siren."

That's it?" asked Christos Somah.

"Yes, and then the final commandment. The eleventh one, love each other."

"What did the sirens do to him after he was interrogated?"

"They tied him to a tree and left him for the animals of the valley to eat. But the animals would not touch the son of the Creator, and he just stayed tied to the tree for forty days. The tribes brought him food and water, but he told them to leave him alone and that he would go home to the Creator. It was his wish to go home to the Creator. After a while, he stopped eating the food and drinking the water that the tribes brought for him."

"And what happened then?"

"One day, he was gone. Just like that. Simply gone."

"That's it?" asked Christos Somah.

"That's quite a lot. He was destroyed at the hands of your people. When he was gone, the one who gave the order to take his life also took his name. He used it as his own name and passed it down through the centuries."

"What was his name?"

"Christos."

~

Chapter Thirty-eight

arla Walker saw Cap' sitting on the bench down by the lake. The ship had been moved off some time ago when *Phodan* and Melanie made the trip to Siren. He said there were some last minute details that he had to take care of prior to the transfer of the Earth sirens to the way station. He also asked Cap' for a parcel of land on the lake where *The First Church of Siren* could be relocated. Cap' was only too happy to comply. He offered the five-acre lakefront building site for free, but *Phodan* insisted in paying him twice fair-market value in gold.

When Cap' learned where *Phodan* intended to place the Church, he arranged for underground utilities to be run up to the site of the buildings. *Phodan* told him that there would be the Church proper and two other out-buildings, a twenty-room rectory and an underground complex of temporary housing units that were accessed by elevator within the Church. The housing units could accommodate over three hundred people for as long as a year, but *Phodan* expected that most of the Earth sirens would be leaving soon to reclaim their former walks of life. There would be many questions raised about their eighteen-month disappearance, but the sirens had ways of dealing with controversy or any unwanted attention. They knew that it may be necessary to shape the minds and wills of a few troublesome humans, but that could be accomplished in a matter of minutes.

Cap' Walker seemed to be lost in thought. He was somewhat overwhelmed by the events of the past two weeks. First his beloved wife simply walked back into his life after he had lost her to illness a year before. Then meeting *Phodan* and eventually accepting the position of pilot for a spacecraft that would establish a port on his property. Then finally, agreeing to share his quiet life with a group of new settlers on his lake in Kissimmee, Florida. It was all a bit much to take in.

Phodan told Cap' that the newcomers had a way to make the changes to his life seem *natural*. Cap' tried to call it brainwashing, but *Phodan* assured him that it was nothing of the sort. He told him that he and Carla could choose what to remember and what to forget in order to obtain peace of mind in their lives. They could remember all the details of the past few weeks if they chose to, but somehow *Phodan* didn't think that they would. There was one thing, one memory that Cap' would be better off without. He would like to erase the memory of him being unkind to Isabelle.

Carla wasn't sure why, but when she saw Isabelle walk up to Cap' sitting on the bench by the lake, she thought that they needed some time alone together. Isabelle put her head in Cap' Walker's lap and just stood there in silence for more than a minute. Finally, Cap' said, "I was wrong, Belle. You're a good dog, and I don't deserve you."

Isabelle seemed to disagree with that assessment. She raised up her head and licked Cap' on the face.

~

Phodan asked Shelly to follow him outside for a minute to speak in private. Charles sat back down on one of the Church pews and continued his reading. There was a large fountain in the garden behind the Church where Melanie sat on a bench. When she saw *Phodan* and Shelly approach, she asked, ""How'd it go?"

"It went well," said *Phodan*. "The girl's mother was upset because she didn't understand that prayer would be involved in the healing process. But it doesn't really matter what the woman thinks. The important thing is that the girl will be healed."

"What is the mother's problem with prayer?" asked Melanie.

"There is religious persecution on this world. The people who openly practice religion are banished from the cities here and have to live in a rather dangerous place called the monopole valley."

"But what about the Church? They can't be too thrilled about that."

"They aren't. That's why the Church will soon be relocated."

"Let me guess," said Melanie, "to the Walker farm."

"That's right."

"You could do worse," she said to Shelly. "It's a nice setting." There wasn't anything else that Melanie wanted to say about the Walker farm because she had some unsettling memories about the place. That is the reason that *Phodan* brought Shelly out to the garden to talk. He explained the ordeal that Melanie had recently gone through and Shelly said, "The poor dear! I'll help her Phodan. I know that you can heal her broken bones, but I can heal her broken soul."

"I knew you would, Shelly. May the Creator bless you."

"God bless you, too, *Phodan*."

~

Chapter Thirty-nine

*P*hodan had returned to the city center of Creston to prepare the ship for departure. There were many curious onlookers, although no one came within fifty feet of the strange craft. Some thought it would bring bad luck to touch it and others thought that even to look upon it for very long would bring bad luck as well like looking into the sun. *Phodan* invited a few sirens to enter the ship and take a look around, but he had no takers. Not even the small children would satisfy their curiosity and enter the strange machine from another world. They probably thought that they would be spirited away never to see their loved ones ever again. They were taking no chances.

When he was satisfied that everything was in order, he closed up the ship and climbed the hill back up to the Church. He found Melanie sitting with Shelly on a bench in the garden by the fountain. Melanie smiled at him and said, "There you are, Dan. I've missed you. Is everything well with the ship?"

"Yes, it is. We should be able to leave right after we begin the transfer process from the Church chamber to the way station. We'll need to leave before the transfers start to be at the station when they arrive. Their transfer will only take about seventeen minutes, but our journey by ship will take over an hour."

"It's all very exciting. I can't wait to get back to Earth and see the Church in its new home."

"And the Walker farm? How do you feel about that place?" he asked.

"It's beautiful. I especially love the old oaks by the lake with the Spanish moss."

"And do you remember the people there, dear?"

"Yes. I remember a very nice couple. Their names were Cap' and Carla Walker, isn't that right?"

"That's right, Melanie. And is there anyone else you remember?"

"Well, of course. My good friend Isabelle!"

Phodan looked at Shelly who just smiled at him. He nodded his head and mouthed the words, *"Thank you."*

~

Durbah sat with Christos Somah by the ceremonial fire and took his hands in hers. "I have much to thank you for, Christos Somah."

"It has been a true adventure for me, Durbah. I have read about the people of the valley, but I have never had the experiences of the last few days. I don't think I'll ever be the same."

"That's what I need to talk to you about, Christos Somah. You *will* be the same. I need to ask one more favor."

"What is it?" he asked.

Durbah released her pheromones which quickly got Christos Somah's attention. She also released the electrum in her eyes, and Christos Somah saw the gold and silver flecks in the corneas. She then held his hands in hers and said, "I need you to forget the experiences of the last few days."

"No, Durbah, please don't ask that of me."

"I am asking, and it pains you greatly to refuse me. You can't refuse me anything. All you want is for me to be happy at this point. Right now the only thing that will make me happy is if you give me *Phodan's* belt shield and forget the experiences of the past few days. You have no choice in the matter. I have taken your mind out of the decision. Now give me the belt."

He handed *Phodan's* belt shield to her, and she coiled it up and put it in her pocket. Then she told Christos Somah, "That is not all I want from you. I need you to feel elated about your experience in the valley. I need you to have warm feelings and know that the people of the valley are not a threat to you, although you don't really remember much about them. You kept me from them for the most part and just showed me the origin of the posi-grains used to make the mag-belts. That is all you will take from this valley. Do you understand?"

"Yes, I do."

"Good." She reined in her pheromones and the electrum in her eyes. They were once again blue-green and reflected the firelight in the warm humid night. Finally, she asked him, "How do you feel, Christos Somah?"

"I feel good. I'm glad I got to show you the valley and the posi-grains. These *Valegatos* are a strange people though.

I'll feel better when we're back in Creston. You don't suppose we're in any danger here, do you?"

"I wouldn't worry about it," she said truthfully.

~

Carla walked up to Cap' Walker sitting on the bench by the lake. She reached down and stroked Isabelle's soft coat and said, "You should go for a swim, Belle. It will cool you off."

"Rooof!" *With alligators? No thank you.*

Cap' laughed as though he knew what was on Isabelle's mind. Of course, he didn't. He just knew that she was a very good dog, and he was blessed to have her. He lowered his head and kissed her on the head. She smiled.

Carla asked him, "Have you decided what to keep of your memories, Nigel?"

"Only one thing for sure. I'm keeping you."

Carla smiled as well.

~

Chapter Forty

Walter and Edith Purness lived on an exclusive area of homes near Vero Beach, Florida called John's Island. Their eighty-foot Ribovich fishing yacht was often seen cruising down the canal that surrounds the island on their way out to the Intra-Coastal Waterway. Walter was an avid fisherman and often would take along his good friend, Senator John Poole, Sr., who had traveled to the planet Siren along with his wife Johanna and John Poole, Jr. John Jr. was a *seer* living among the *Valegatos* tribe on Siren. He was a *seer* because both his parents were sirens who just happened to be currently making plans to return to Earth. They were part of the original exodus from Egypt to Siren eighteen months earlier. Their son, John Jr., would also make the journey back to Earth with his parents. He was currently accompanying Durbah Purness, Alex Janzen and Christos Somah out of the monopole valley back to the city of Creston.

As the mother of Durbah, Walter Purness's wife Edith was, of course, a siren. But Walter was a human and even though he had the chance to travel to Siren, he chose not to. He decided he had too much responsibility on Earth as the Chairman of the Virginia Coal Consortium. Their organization was fighting to stay above water in light of the new resurgence of natural gas as well as personal nuclear generators that were just being developed. But natural gas and the competition for his coal consortium was the last thing on his mind. What was on his mind was a telephone call that he recently received from the president of the United States. The president chose to be a man of few words for that phone call, simply saying, "Walter, I think I need to talk to Edith."

"I understand Mr. President. Actually, I've been expecting this day for some time now."

"Not over the phone, Walter. I'm sending *Marine One* for you and Edith. Please do me the honor of joining me and Sean for lunch at the White House."

"Certainly, Sir. Where do we catch *Marine One*?"

"Patrick Air Force Base. Just call the switchboard and ask for General Hightower's aide."

"I understand," said Walter and hung up the phone. He went outside to where his wife was sitting by the pool and said, "It's happened. I just got the call from the White House."

"We could always just deny, deny, deny, Walt. That's something that they well understand."

"Is that what's really in your heart, Edith?

"No, Walt. You're right, as usual. I will meet with them and put their minds straight, if not at ease."

"I knew you would," he said.

About fourteen months ago, Edith Purness met with the Director of NASA and The President of the United States to inform them that the XB-37 probe would soon be entering Earth's atmosphere. It was originally launched from Kennedy Space Center complex 41 A, on April 17th, 2009. The probe's programming guided it out of Earth's orbit and to a Near Earth

Asteroid to be detonated 3,000 feet above its surface. It was a nuclear device. The probe was sent off in an errant direction and landed in orbit around Siren. When a meteor struck the probe by random chance, the orbit decayed and it plummeted toward the surface of Siren. The *Preculians* intervened and used a *space/time exchange chamber* to send it to Earth's atmosphere as soon as it entered Siren's.

Durbah Purness had just recently immigrated to Siren along with nearly 400 other souls, but she was still in contact with her parents who chose to remain on Earth. She warned them that Cape Canaveral would be receiving a nuclear payload in the near future and suggested that the president and the director of NASA be given fair warning. Edith Purness directed them with the powers of a siren to relate the tragedy to the American people and the world in general as an accidental detonation of a space probe during a launch that had gone awry. This was false information, but it was necessary to conceal the existence of the planet Siren and their ultimate benefactors the *Preculians*. The *Preculians* had protected Siren from Earth for thousands of years and would continue to do so.

When Edith Purness met with the director and the president, she told them of the imminent delivery of the nuclear device aboard the Earth probe and instructed them to impart disinformation about the origin. If it were learned that the planets Siren and *Preculis* were responsible, a campaign of directed fury and retribution would surely follow.

Siren and *Preculis* had little to fear from Earth, but there is always the possibility that situations change. Who is to say that Earth will not develop the *space/time exchange chamber* technology in the future and then all bets are off. Revenge is a dish better served cold, and cold was something that humanity was well versed in. Walter and Edith had no other choice but to travel on *Marine One*, a special helicopter used to transport the president. It would take them right to the front lawn of the White House where there was some explaining to do.

~

When Walter and Edith disembarked from *Marine One* and were led by secret service personnel to the Oval Office, the president met them at the door. "I would say welcome, but I'm not really sure that would be appropriate."

"Mr. President," began Edith . . .

"Edith, please," said the president. "I'm sure we're on a first name basis now. Call me Hussain since you have the blue-print to my mind. Would you like me to bark like a dog or I know: since I'm black, why don't I teach the chickens how to walk."

"Please, Mr. President. What I did was for your benefit and that of Mr. O'Keefe. I couldn't change what was about to happen. The only thing I could do was alert you to the situation and give you time to compose a suitable explanation short of exposing our near neighbors in the solar system."

"Yes, I suppose that makes it fine and dandy, doesn't it? I could have you tried for treason and executed."

"I could walk out of this room, and you would be teaching the chickens how to walk."

The president took out a handkerchief and wiped his brow. "Let's start over, Edith. You are the one who did this to me and Sean, correct?"

"Correct. Walter had nothing to do with it."

"Okay. Now what exactly did you do to make me forget our meeting?"

"I merely wished you to."

"That's all?"

"Yes."

"No drugs or hypnotic suggestions?"

"No."

"What tipped you off?" asked Walter.

The president motioned to Director O'Keefe and said, "Sean and I were having recurring dreams about the explosion at Kennedy. In every case, we knew about the blast beforehand but did nothing to warn anyone about it. Then one day I was in a meeting with Sean, and he just said, 'Edith Purness'."

"Interesting," said Walter.

"Yeah, you bet. We both had met Edith, but had no conscious recollection of having been in the same room with her."

"So what did you do?" asked Walter.

"Hypnosis. For both Sean and I. We had separate sessions with the same therapist, and he came up with the same visions. That led us to the conclusion that something in our memories has been suppressed."

"I see," said Walter.

"Well, I'm glad you do, Walt. Care to tell us what the hell is going on?"

Chapter Forty-one

Sarah Poole was an Earth siren whose parents had also made the exodus out of Egypt to Siren. Her father was a United States senator until he decided to return home to Siren. His young son, John Jr., was a *seer* in the sense that he could see tomorrow when the Earth lines up. Every twenty-four hours, the Earth lines up with the exact rotation of its sister planet, Siren, and for roughly twenty minutes, John Jr. can see twenty-four hours ahead in time when he focuses on a particular individual.

He was ostracized for having this ability when the sirens learned about it. They once had *seers* in their society, but they were banished to the monopole valley thousands of years ago. John Jr. didn't wait to be banished. He chose to go to the valley and live among the *Valegatos*. They embraced his gift and called him a great shaman who would be an asset to their tribe. He would be sorely missed because he has been asked by his parents to return to Earth with them and his sister.

Unfortunately, his sister's lover, Brad Early, has become hopelessly addicted to flying over the monopole valley with the aid of the mag-belts. He neglected his body; he neglected hydration; he neglected nutrition; but worst of all, he neglected Sarah Poole. She was an extraordinary beauty that any man would be ecstatic to call his lover, but Brad was uninterested. He had a one-track mind on a one-track destination for emaciation and death. Many of Siren suffered the same fate. Sarah told him that she would never give up on him and that perhaps, when he found himself again, he could rejoin her on Earth.

John Poole, Jr. returned to Creston with Durbah Purness, Alex Janzen and Christos Somah. They made their way to the Church and settled into rooms in the rectory for some sorely needed sleep. They had chewed entirely too many leaves of the drug to chase away sleep and were teetering on the brink of hallucinations. Although Durbah Purness slept in the same bed with Alex Janzen, her mind, if not her heart, was in the next room where Christos Somah slept. There was something they shared in the valley that she couldn't quite shake out of her mind. Perhaps it was the *call of the gatos* dance ceremony, or perhaps it was the rescue of the young *Valegato* in the condor's nest. Whatever it was, it just wouldn't let go. She also felt close to him when she unleashed her preponderant pheromones and electrum. He was as helpless as a baby in her arms. He was a beautiful young piece of clay to be molded into a trophy to be carried on her arm. The only problem was he was indifferent to her charms unless she unleashed her powers. When she met with *Phodan* to return the belt shield, he said to her, "Thank you, Durbah. This is a very important artifact of my planet, and I see now that loaning it to Christos Somah was the right course of action. I knew as soon as you purged Christos Somah of his memories of the experience in the valley, you would retrieve it from him."

"It is I who should thank you, Grand Master. The shield saved our lives. And it saved the lives of Christos Somah and Alex a second time. You were very wise to give it him. I don't think he could have survived the valley without it."

"I'm glad they could find your friend and bring him back to safety."

"I am glad, too, and yet I have mixed feelings about our relationship. I need to be at two places at the same time. I know I am expected to return with the Church members to Earth, but a part of me wants to stay here and win the heart of a siren."

"That may not be possible, Durbah. The hearts of sirens have built walls of protection around them centuries ago."

"Yes, but you know I am capable of breaking down those walls. You know I can shape the will of Christos Somah. I've done it before."

"I sense that your interest in Christos Somah is more than just the physical. I sense that you see yourself at his side for another reason, Durbah."

"I know that one day he will replace his father on the Supreme Council of Regents. He will become The Regent of Creston and could use the help of a persuasive mate," said Durbah.

"You would use your powers for politics? Isn't that what you did back on Earth?"

"Back on Earth it was Siren's agenda. Here on Siren it would be mine."

"Perhaps there is a way to do what you ask," said Phodan.

"What do you mean?"

"There may be a way for you to be two places at one time."

"A replication?"

"Precisely."

"But which one would be the real me? The original Durbah or the replication?"

"Both initially."

"That's too much to hope for, *Phodan*. Could you really do that?"

"There are limitations. The new Durbah would retain *your memories,* but be responsible for *her own emotions.* There is no guarantee that she would have your values. But it could be done."

"What about my powers of persuasion?"

"They would stay with you. The new Durbah would be effectively human, not siren."

"What would I have to do to make that happen?"

"You would have to show me what is inside of your heart. I would have to see that your intentions are for the good of this planet and not only to serve yourself."

"How is this done?"

"Give me your hands and hold nothing back from your mind," he said.

She opened up her heart and presented her conflicted feelings to him. It was as though she could almost feel him probing around in her brain and her past emotions. Her life passed through her eyes with images from Earth, Siren and the monopole valley in particular. She could see the young girl who had been taken by the condor, and she relived gathering up all her courage to face up to the beast. She recalled thrusting the valegato tooth up into the underbelly of the huge bird and the prayer she issued to the Creator: *God, give me the strength for this!*

When Durbah sensed that he was done with probing her mind and emotions, she said to him, "*Phodan*, you have done so much for us in the past few years. First enabling the exodus from Earth and then having the foresight to leave the back door open as you did in case things didn't work out. We are very grateful to you. Perhaps I don't have the right to ask this of you."

"You have the right, Durbah. You are one of the few who do."

"Then you intend to make a second Durbah Purness?" she asked hopefully.

"Yes."

"Will it hurt?"

"I already have what I need, and you didn't feel a thing."

Phodan enlisted the help of Charles Donovan, Shelly Simon, Matthew Winter and Alahnka Hannas to coordinate the schedule for *space/time exchange chamber* transfers. When *Phodan* and Melanie had departed in the ship, the Earth sirens began the transfer process to the way station. The station had a housing complex that could accommodate all of the arrivals until they could board Cap's shuttle back to Earth. Some of them would stay on the station enjoying the solarium viewports and the hospitality of the station caretaker, *Zo*.

Although he has not yet a member of the *Church of Siren,* Alex Janzen was in the first group to the Alligator Lake Port Housing Area, or ALPHA. With him was the perfect Durbah Purness. She seemed perfect in every way. Her long blonde hair framed the angular features of her high cheekbones and flawless complexion. It fell gracefully down to her full shapely breasts and accentuated the curve of her hips. Her timeless beauty would be sure to hold the attention of any man in a room. Her smile was warm and genuine with slight dimples at the corners of her mouth. Her blue-green eyes had a sparkle that was very captivating and would melt the heart of Alex Janzen or any other man she would choose. But they would never again display the gold and silver flecks of electrum. That Durbah Purness was still back on Siren.

~

Chapter Forty-two

*P*hodan and Melanie made a quick stop at the Walker farm to check in with his pilot. Cap' Walker and Carla were sitting out by the lake when the ship came down. They waved and Isabelle wagged her tail as well to welcome them. The ship settled down on the surface of the lake long enough for *Phodan* and Melanie to use the gantry to shore; then it closed up and slipped beneath the surface of the lake.

"I'm making paella said Carla. Fresh Florida shrimp, scallops and Maine lobster. Any takers?"

"Rooof!" said Isabelle. *You bet!*

"If I had known what you were cooking, I would have picked up some saffron from Europa. Jupiter's moons have the best saffron."

"I never know when you're kidding, *Phodan.*"

"He's kidding, Carla. There aren't any spices grown on Europa."

"You sound like you've been there."

"You betcha. Master *Phodan's* Wild Ride."

"Think Universal Studios would be interested?"

"Without a doubt," she said laughing.

Phodan told Cap', "I'd like to set the Church's location. All I need to know is where you want them to be."

"You own the parcel, *Phodan.* It's your choice. But I would appreciate it if you don't disturb any of the trees."

"Never, Cap'. I feel the same way you do about them."

"They're beautiful," said Melanie.

"Yes, they are," said Carla. "Come help me in the kitchen, Mel. You can peel the shrimp."

"Rooof!" *Yum. Stinky shells in the trash can.*

~

When the first group of Earth sirens got to the way station, they were greeted by a kindly old man who had been brought by *Phodan* from *Preculis*. He was serving as care-taker of the station until all of the sirens were transferred to Earth. He had dark clothes and stark white hair. When the pulsing blue light of the transfer stopped, he opened the door to the chamber and said. "Welcome sirens. I am *Zophan,* but my friends call me Zo. You are welcome to do so as well."

Shelly stepped forward and said, "Hello, Zo. Very nice to meet you."

"Nice to meet you, too, Shelly. And you are Charles, correct?" said *Zophan* to Charles. "I have been anticipating your arrival and everything is in place for a comfortable experience here on the station."

"We've been here before, *Zophan.* "It's certainly a trip."

"We are facing the Eagle Nebula. I had my lunch today before the portal screens. I looked back so far in time that I ate my salad with the *big bang.*" He laughed heartily and Shelly and Charles instantly warmed up to the old man.

"That's funny, *Zo,*" said Shelly.

"I tickle myself sometimes," said the ancient *Preculian*.

"When can we go down to Earth, *Zo?*"

"I'm not exactly sure, but it will be soon. *Phodan* is with your pilot now. I think he is making plans for the compound of your community."

"Have you been down there, *Zo?* To Earth?"

"No, I don't think that Earth is ready for me just yet."

"Why do you say that?" asked Charles.

"Because I am only half here. The other half of me is still on *Preculis*."

"I don't understand," said Shelly.

"Give me your hand," he said.

Shelly held out her hand and reached for *Zophan's* hand. When she expected to make contact, there was nothing there. She saw her hand pass back and forth *through* the hand of *Zophan*.

"Wow, that's something I've never seen before. Does that hurt you?"

"Not at all. As I said, I am not really here. I am asleep on a planet four light-years away called *Preculis*. I think that your planet calls it Sirius. It's just outside the constellation of the great hunter, Orion."

"I know it well," said Shelly.

"Perhaps one day you will travel there, and I can shake your hand with the other half of me. The physical half," he said jovially.

"Yes, *Zo*. Perhaps one day I can."

"Let me show you to your suite. You can choose any that you like, but I recommend the screens facing the Eagle. But the Crab nebula is beautiful as well."

Shelly turned toward Charles and said, "Is this place cool or what?"

Zophan said to them, "I can adjust the temperature to anything that suits you."

"That's not what she meant, *Zo*," said Charles. "She meant that she likes it here."

"I like it as well," said *Zophan*.

~

Cap' told *Phodan* that the utility lines had been run underground to the property and there would be sufficient three-phase power to supply the whole community. Water would be supplied by the lake through a filtration system, and the sewer lines were connected to the Orange County Waste Treatment Plant. Everything was in place. He asked *Phodan,* "When will the Church arrive?"

"Tomorrow," said *Phodan*.

"So soon?"

"Yes, of course. Are you having second thoughts?"

"No, of course not."

"Well, I'd just like to tell you something. After the community is settled here, then you can decide how you feel about having so many new neighbors. Your decision is never set in stone in perpetuity. You can change your mind at any time, and I will re-locate the Church somewhere else."

"No, I think it will be fine. I'm sure Carla and I will embrace our new neighbors. We've been all cooped up all to ourselves for too long now."

"That's fine," said *Phodan*. But always remember, you can go back to your old lifestyle at any time."

"Thank you, *Phodan*. You are a good friend."

"And you as well, Cap'."

~

Chapter Forty-three

Just as *Phodan* had promised, when Cap' and Carla woke up the next day, there was a beautiful Church on the other side of the lake. Its reflection was mirrored in the glass-like surface of the still water at sunrise, and the birds had already accepted their new perch and were sitting high on the steeple. Carla found herself singing again, *"All I wanna' do in the middle of the evening is hold you tight, Phodana, Phodana . . ."*

"Or, Phodan," said Cap'. "I know it's too early to know which."

"Oh, no it's not," said Carla musically. "Our friendly neighborhood space traveler would beg to differ with you, Nigel."

"Really? He told you?"

Carla nodded her head.

Cap' began to sing, *"All I wanna' tell you is now you'll never ever have to compromise, Phodana, Phodana . . ."*

Isabelle had to join in as well, "Rooof!" *Meet you all the way . . . Phodana yeah . . .*

~

John and Johanna Poole were in the group behind Alex Janzen, Durbah's replication, Shelly Simon and Charles Donovan arriving at the way station. Their daughter Sarah was with them as well as their son, the *seer*, John Jr. He was not happy about having to leave the monopole valley as he had become quite accustomed to the ways of the *Valegatos*. He told his mother, "I wanted to stay on Siren, mother. Just because you and Dad couldn't handle it, why did *I* have to leave?"

"Because you are our son," she told him.

"Bantah, the tribal elder, was like a father figure to me. And I had a girlfriend for the first time."

"What do you mean you had a girlfriend? You're too young to have a girlfriend. You're only eleven years old."

"Bantah's wife, the Shamana, said I am an old soul."

"She doesn't know you as well as we do. We see you as a young soul."

"I miss my girlfriend already. I may never see her again."

"How old is she, John?"

"I asked her that question, and she said she didn't know. I don't think they have birthdays in the valley."

"How old do you think she was?"

"Well, I know she wasn't sixteen because she didn't have electrum in her eyes yet."

"Sixteen? She better not have been sixteen. That's entirely too old for a boy like you. What could you possibly have in common with a girl that age?"

"We liked to dance."

"Please tell me you wore clothes when you were with the *Valegatos*, John," said Johanna Poole.

"I wore shorts. Gosh, mom, what did you think, I ran around naked?"

"Did your girlfriend wear shorts?"

"Do we have to talk about this?"

"I've heard that the *Valegatos* tribe is quite primitive in some ways, John. Did you find that to be true?"

"Nope."

"Is that all you have to say about the subject?"

"Yup."

"Did you use your sight to tell them what tomorrow would look like?"

"Yes, I did. They thought I would become a great shaman. Now I have to go back to Earth and be in the sixth grade," he said miserably.

"I just feel that your place is with us, John. Don't you agree?"

"Yeah, I guess. But if I ever get the chance to go back to Siren after I'm eighteen, I'm going."

"After you're eighteen, you can do whatever you want, John. Until then, you just have to believe that we know what's best for you."

"Do we still have to talk about this?"

"Now that we're on our way to Earth, I guess not. But I think that we took you away from Siren just in the nick of time."

"What's that supposed to mean?" asked John.

"We're not going to talk about it, remember?"

"Yeah, I do, but still I miss her."

Johanna Poole looked at her husband and rolled her eyes. John Sr. just smiled.

Chapter Forty-four

Walter and Edith Purness were sitting in the Oval Office of the White House with President Hussain Amalah and Director O'Keefe of NASA. They had been served a light lunch and were gradually working into the conversation that would explain once and for all how they had been so completely compromised by a little old lady from Florida. The implications were not lost on either of the two men. Never before in their lives had they had their mind altered and their personal histories revised within their own personal recollection. It was scary stuff. A part of the president coveted the control of such a process for the protection of his beloved country. *What a weapon! Imagine how we could control the Russians or the North Koreans with such power, not to mention China or the Middle East! If I could pull off the acquisition of something as great at this thing that Edith does, I would go down in history as the greatest president of all . . .*

"Excuse me, Mr. President. You were day-dreaming," said Edith.

The president caught himself and hoped that his thoughts were not as transparent as they would appear to be. He came back into the moment with kid gloves. "Please, Edith, call me Hussain, at least inside the walls of this office. I am Mr. President out in public situations, but in this room, it's just Hussain."

"As you wish, Hussain."

"And please call me, Sean," said the NASA director.

"And you can all call me, Mr. Purness," said Walter.

They all just looked at him for a long moment and he said, "I'm kidding, I'm kidding. I was just trying to lighten the atmosphere in here. I don't mind telling you, Hussain, it's not every day that we are summoned to the White House via *Marine One*. Landing on the White House lawn in a helicopter is a bit much. I'm just glad we're all on the same side here."

"Are we, Walter? Boy, I sure hope so." He turned to Walter's wife and said, "I can tell you that Sean and I have had a rough time of it lately at your hands, Edith. I, for one, doubted my sanity for a while there. I'm sure Sean felt the same way."

"Absolutely," said the director.

"I'm sorry about that," said Edith. "But I assure you it was necessary, and once you hear the whole story, I'm sure you will agree with me."

That's good, Edith. Keep going, thought the president. *Give us the whole story this time and no more witchcraft.*

"Tell us, Edith. What is the whole story?"

"Well, I should start by telling you that I'm not a human being."

The statement just hung in the air for a pregnant few seconds and then the president said, "You're not," with a blank expression.

"No, I am Siren. The origin of my people is a planet called Siren on the opposite side of our shared sun."

"How come we have never detected it, Edith?" asked Director O'Keefe.

"It has been hidden for as long as this planet has had the application for space travel. Since it is located on the opposite side of the sun, it was obscured from visual observation until humans had the ability to see what's on the other side."

"You say humans like we're the enemy," said the president.

"If the shoe fits, Hussain. You are the ones who launched a nuclear device that was descending on Siren. The *Preculians* told us it would have destroyed one of their major cities called Creston."

"Who are the *Preculians*?" asked the director.

"I'm getting to that, Sean. Bare with me. When humans were able to see on the other side of the sun, it was necessary to employ a device to hide the planet. It took thousands of years for an advanced race called the *Preculians* to develop. They did so because they felt responsible to protect Siren from Earth."

"Why did they feel responsible?" asked Amalah.

"Because they accidently caused a wave of gamma-radiation that bathed Earth and changed the nature of mankind from benign to hostile."

"Okay, let's say I buy all that. How did they manage to hide a whole planet?"

"The device was named *The Great Shield*. It was composed of eight satellites in a geo-synchronous orbit around Siren. They formed a huge cube of six photo-reflective planes so that when you looked at any part of the cube, you would see what is on the opposite side. The planet Siren appeared invisible."

"Believe it or not, I'm somewhat familiar with the technology," said the president. "I've been briefed about a similar application for our military aircraft. It would seem that we may be catching up to the *Preculians*."

Edith looked at Walter and was amazed at her self-control to resist rolling her eyes. Humanity was to *Preculity* what the amoeba was to humanity. She continued. "Then they hid the magnetic signature of Siren with a very large belt of gas canisters that ringed the planet in a counter-rotation."

"Fascinating," offered Director O'Keefe.

"Yes, Sean, we think so, too."

"Is this shield still in place?" asked Amalah.

"No, Hussain. Now there is no need for it, which brings me to the point of why I had to change your will and recollection of the past."

"Shape our will."

"Yes, Hussain."

"Mind control."

"You could call it that, but I don't. Think of it this way: everyone wants something from your behavior. Both sides of Congress are battling back and forth across the aisle for your attention and to address their agendas. I simply wanted you to address the agendas of the Sirens and the *Preculians*. Everything we do, all our actions are directed to address cause and effect. I didn't employ mind control as much as I merely asked you to do me a favor. And in doing so, you did a favor for Siren, *Preculis* and Earth as well."

"I'm still not getting it, Edith," said Amalah.

"It goes back to why *The Great Shield* is no longer necessary. Now the *Preculians* have developed a process that makes them invulnerable to any possible attack from any world. They merely extended that protection to Siren as well. Now, they don't care whether or not Earth knows about Siren."

"And that's why you feel comfortable about talking to us about it. You feel that we are no threat to Siren now. Tell us, what is the nature of this new process?"

"You remember when the XB-37 was launched into space with a warhead intended for an NEA, or Near Earth Asteroid?"

"Yes, I remember," said Amalah.

"And you remember the explosion over Kennedy Space Center fourteen months ago?"

"Yes, of course."

"Well you did have prior knowledge of that occurrence, just like in your dreams. The device that exploded was the same warhead launched aboard the XB-37. When it entered the atmosphere of Siren, the *Preculians* detected that it was programmed to detonate at three-thousand feet. Are you with me so far?"

"Yes, go on."

"When the military craft reached four thousand feet, the *Preculians* sent it back into Earth's atmosphere in roughly twenty minutes. When it entered Earth's atmosphere, it was also at four-thousand feet and descending fast. When it was only one-thousand feet away from detonation, there was obviously no time to warn anyone on Earth to take cover or leave the area so we didn't." All it would have accomplished is alert Earth to the fact that Siren shares its solar system. Due to the aggressive nature of humankind, we felt it was in our best interest to keep silent. But the explosion had to be explained. The world had to have someone to blame, so we placed the blame firmly on its own shoulders. Check out the radioactive signature, Hussain. That will confirm that the nuclear material came from your stockpile of enriched plutonium."

"We already have, Edith. That's why your revisionist-history farce was so convincing. If it weren't for the recurring nightmares, we wouldn't be having this conversation at all."

"Why Kennedy?" asked Amalah. Why not send the damned thing into the Pacific Ocean?"

"They simply went for the point of origin. They returned your property."

"You're telling us that when the craft entered Siren's atmosphere, the *Preculians* made it enter ours, is that right?"

"My God, they've curved space!" said Director O'Keefe. I've heard about the theoretical calculations, but we are centuries away from that kind of technology."

"That's precisely what we have come here to tell you, Sean," said Edith. She let them believe that *Preculis* could curve space, which was not even close to the *space/time exchange chamber* technology, but they had no need to know.

"But as you said before, you could shape our wills again. What made you come forward and divulge this information, Edith?"

"We need your help, Hussain."

"My help? You mean you need the help of the United States government? Whatever for?"

"Protection, for one thing. The sirens completed an exodus from Earth to Siren about eighteen months ago. Some of them have made the adjustment and are living relatively happy lives there, but some are not. Some of the newcomers have been persecuted for their religious beliefs and intend to come back to Earth. They want to come to the United States to escape religious persecution. Sound familiar?"

"History repeats itself."

"It sure does," said Walter.

"So what kind of protection are we talking about here? What do they need from us?"

"They need to be left in peace. That's all. What they don't need is to be hunted down like the witches of Salem, or any curious onlookers dogging their every movement. They need your help in preserving their anonymity. They want to blend in with society when needed and stay peacefully isolated when not."

"And what does the United States get in return, Edith?"

"How about a ride to the International Space Station?" She winked at the president.

Chapter Forty-five

C apt. Walker was getting antsy to begin the process of transporting the Sirens to their new location. He and Carla liked the looks of the Church compound across the lake, thinking that it looked like it had been there for years. The Church proper was situated beneath a huge Florida oak with Spanish moss and majestic, fat limbs that hung low to the ground. The squirrels loved the old tree and often chased each other up and down and all around the limbs in a frenzied miasma of chirping energy. The morning doves that weren't perched on the steeple of the Church seemed to be well acquainted with the tree also. It was a complete ecosystem within itself and was a fitting representation of the future harmony that life might present the Church members on Alligator Lake. The idyllic picture would make a perfect postcard with the cows in the background and the egrets on their backs. The caption over the cross on the top of the steeple might read: *Holy Cow.* Cap' took a hold of Carla's hand and said, "I think the young kids will find a nice home here."

"Yes, Nigel, I agree. At least until they choose to relocate."

"Why would they want to do that? This is a beautiful lake."

"You seem to have gotten used to them already, and they're not even here yet."

"Well, I just think it might be good to have some young blood around here for a change. Maybe even somebody for little *Phodan* to play with."

"Or *Phodana*," said Carla.

"Or *Phodana*," agreed Cap'.

"It wouldn't bother you for our child to play with siren children?"

"From what I understand, we could do a lot worse. *Phodan* said they're very gentle people and also very beautiful."

"I'm not sure I want to share you with beautiful girls, Cap'."

"Relax, Carla. At my age, I'll be invisible. Trust me."

~

"The International Space Station? You're serious aren't you, Edith?"

"Yes, Hussain. Here's what I have to propose, and by the way, it's non-negotiable: The sirens are establishing a settlement on a small lake in Central Florida. They have already relocated the *The First Church of Siren*, their house of worship. Alongside the Church is a rectory with sleeping quarters for roughly fifty people. In addition to the rectory, there is an underground housing unit with over one-hundred-fifty two bedroom suites. They have all the amenities they will ever need. There are exercise rooms, theaters, restaurants, medical facilities and daycare. If need be, it can become a totally self-contained, self-sufficient complex in the event of emergencies, but for the normal course of business as usual, they could use some help."

"What kind of help?" asked President Amalah.

"Underground utility lines have been run to the Church and the outbuildings, but they have yet to be connected to the power grid. Water and sewer lines have been run also, but they need to be put online with the Orange County Water District and Water Treatment System. They would appreciate it if their utilities are free of charge, and they don't expect to pay any property taxes to the United States Government."

"Oh, really?"

"Really. They have gone ahead with the construction of the compound unbeknownst to the Orange County Board of Planning, and, obviously, they have pulled no permits to do so. They request complete amnesty from impact fees, taxes and a moratorium in perpetuity from utility fees. Do you get me so far?"

"Go on, I'm enjoying this," said Amalah.

"Good, Hussain, so am I. Well, next there is the matter of security. There are two main accesses to the properties on and around the lake. The first is the driveway to the farm of Nigel Walker and the second is a newly paved road around the lake to the grounds of the Church Compound. Both entrances are on the same road roughly two hundred yards apart. Walter and I feel that it would be in the best interest of the United States Government to build a ten-foot-high concrete wall completely surrounding the forty-acre parcel of land that surrounds Alligator Lake."

"Oh, is that all?" asked the president facetiously. Just a ten foot wall around forty acres, free utilities, no taxes or fees, and I suppose you want armed security patrolling the property at all times," he said sarcastically.

"Yes, Hussain. I'm sure you will want to do that. But please be tactful about it. And I think that the wall should be painted to blend in with the scenery."

"Well, of course!" said the president. "We wouldn't want some eyesore of a wall mucking up the scenery. Let me ask you one thing, Edith: why on Earth would I ever want to submit to your requests if you didn't use your powers-of-persuasion on me?"

"Oh, I don't think I'll have to persuade you at all. I'm sure if you knew the totality of the situation, then all of these ideas would be yours as well."

"I have one question, Edith. Why?"

"Because Alligator Lake is going to be Sean's new Space Port. Of course, if I were you, I wouldn't advertise the fact, but it would seem you might be able to use an ace in the hole now that you no longer have a delivery system of your own. How much are the Russians charging you to take astronauts to I.S.S. Alpha?"

"About sixty million a man give or take."

"I'd say Alligator Lake is a bargain, wouldn't you?"

"You're a remarkable woman, Edith," said the president.

"I tell her that all the time, Hussain," said Walter.

~

Chapter Forty-six

Melanie liked staying behind on the way station. Her thoughts went to dreaming about being a member of an idyllic society floating above the Earth with all of the cosmos at her fingertips. But it was no dream. It was all true. She grew to love *Phodan*, not only for saving her life, but for saving her from a dead-end life going nowhere. Now she felt like she was a part of something, and most of all, a part of *someone*. For the first time in her life, she considered having a child. She wanted to have *Phodan's* child and show him the wonders of the universe that *Phodan* was showing her. *Could that be possible?* she wondered. *Could the dream reach that far?* She found herself immersed in prayer just like the Church members when they looked to the stars and wished that the Creator would keep them all well. She prayed for the first time in her life. Melanie had never been a church attendee and neither had her parents. She simply had no influence to attend. She had nothing against religion, but it simply didn't play a part in her life. She was not a particularly sinful woman, although some would say, her choice of profession would demonstrate the opposite. But dancing made her feel special, and it seemed to be the only job she could get to make enough money to keep her own apartment.

Phodan changed all that. *Phodan* showed her that he loved her and didn't look down on her for being a dancer. All

Phodan could see was a pure heart in Melanie and a young woman who needed his protection. Those feelings grew into a desire to have her accompany him to his home world and possibly have his progeny for the first time. He had never taken a mate, and public service seemed to dominate his time and energy throughout his more than six-hundred years of life. Now it was time for a change. He was thinking of stepping down from his position as Grand Master of the Supreme Council of *Preculis*. Although it was a life-long appointment, he had the right to step down for medical or personal reasons. He supposed that having a family with Melanie was personal reason enough.

Phodan was having dinner with Melanie in an observation lounge on the way station. They had chosen to scrutinize the Crab Nebula back in time. It was beautiful. A billion years ago, there was a succession of supernovas that lit up the galaxy in a glorious burst of green and gold colors. The swirling spiral almost made them dizzy looking at it unless they tore themselves away for short periods of time to center themselves. The food was wonderful. It was a mixture of Cajun Jambalaya and fruits from Hawaii. *Phodan* asked her, "Would you like to deliver the ship to Cap' Walker with me, or stay here until I can take you to *Preculis* in an exchange chamber?"

"Oh, I definitely want to go with you to Cap's. It will give me a chance to see Carla and Isabelle again."

"You can also check out the new location of the Church."

"It's there already?"

"Yes. The whole complex is in place, and there is a siren who is arranging the final details as we speak."

"That was fast," she said.

"Time is relative, Melanie. It has already happened, but it is still happening depending on where you observe it from. From Alligator Lake, it has happened. From the Church Hill of Creston on Siren, it is still happening because the chamber is still being used. The only difference is the building no longer surrounds the *exchange chamber.*"

"I don't understand, Dan."

"You will in about a hundred years."

~

Carla and Cap' were discussing the future with Isabelle. Neither one could communicate with the dog with words, but they felt confident that Isabelle could understand what they were saying to each other. Cap' asked Carla, "Have you thought about what memories you want *Phodan* to leave with you?"

"I want it all, Nigel. I've only got a piece of my past life inside of me. It's a pretty large piece, but it's still just a piece. I don't want to surrender anything that I have now as far as memories go."

"I feel the same way, Carla. I know that shuttling the sirens and befriending *Phodan* is turning my life upside down, but I don't mind. I think that if anyone should have a six-hundred year old space man for a friend, it might as well be me. I think I can take it all in and keep a sensible perspective on my life."

"Rooof !" *I have faith in you, Cap'.*

"You see?" said Cap'. "Belle thinks I can do it."

Carla laughed. "I think you're right. It's almost as if I can read her thoughts."

"Maybe someday we will."

"Do you honestly think so?" asked Carla.

"I don't know, but stranger things have happened. After these past two weeks, nothing would surprise me. I'll talk to *Phodan* about it."

~

Chapter Forty-seven

Mantah Jomah was sitting in the waiting room at the Creston Healing Center reading a magazine to take her mind off of her samah's grave illness. The healers had told her that there was nothing they could do to take away the girl's blood sickness, but she refused to accept that and brought her in for another battery of tests. When a healer entered the waiting room, he was smiling. He said to Mantah Jomah, "It is a miracle, Jomah, or perhaps a big mistake. I've never seen this happen before, but a mistake is always possible."

"What do you mean?" she asked the healer.

"Your samah is well. There is no longer the blood sickness that she exhibited before. Perhaps our tests were giving us false results."

"No, healer. Perhaps you made her well with your tests."

"No, Jomah. You don't understand. We did not heal your samah. There is no cure for the illness your samah had. It's called Siren Immunodeficiency Virus or S.I.V. All I can think of is that the tests we ran were in error. No one has ever been cured of S.I.V. If they were, it would be a great day for Siren. The person's blood could be used to create a vaccine, which would save millions of souls. Perhaps even billions because this particular disease spreads like wildfire."

"Where did it come from?" asked Mantah Jomah.

"No one is really sure, but there is suspicion that it came to the tribes of the valley from eating the flesh of the viper. They are all *carriers* of the disease, but none of them actually contract it."

"And you say no one has ever been cured?" she asked.

"I have heard of things like this, miracle cures, but I have never actually experienced them."

"You are too modest, healer. I will thank you until the day I die for the health of my samah."

"Ask your Mantah, Jomah. He is a healer as well. He could not heal your samah. Then you brought her to us. He will tell you that we did not heal your samah. Perhaps you need to thank someone else. There is one more thing that I feel I need to mention, Jomah," said the old healer.

"Yes?" she answered.

"Perhaps your samah is not yet out of the woods so to speak."

"But you said she no longer has the virus," said the jomah.

"That is true; however, although I don't believe that she was ever really infected, some might conclude that she was and is now well. They will seek her blood at all costs. Your samah might find herself running for her life."

"I think you exaggerate, healer."

"Just the same, if it were my child, I would be very quiet about her medical history. No one must suspect that she carries the cure whether or not she actually does. Do you understand?"

"Yes, healer. Thank you for your advice and for the life of my samah."

The healer just shook his head as she left the room. He guessed that he just didn't make his point clear enough to the jomah. She still didn't understand that her Julianah was never healed. No one is *ever* healed of S.I.V.

The young girl knew the truth. When she left the Creston Healing Center, the first thing she did was go up to the Church on the Hill and seek out the old man who called forth the prayers to heal her. When she got there the Church was gone. A group of people were standing in a tight group when suddenly a pulsing blue light came down from the heavens. It bathed them in a soft blue light and seemed to beat like a heart. There was no sound, but the people in the group became obscured in a hazy mist. She ran up to them and said, "Please, where is the old-one called *Phodan*. I want to thank him for giving me back my life."

The others didn't answer her. They were incapable of speech just then. The young girl was suddenly incapable of speech as well. When the platform cleared after the final transfer from the *space/time exchange chamber,* the last of the Church members were gone . . . and the young girl was gone as well.

~

Chapter Forty-eight

*P*hodan landed on Alligator Lake just as the sun was setting and a green and orange afterglow painted the sky like a watercolor wash. He extended the ramp down to the shore and led Melanie to Cap', Carla and Isabelle waiting on the bench below. "Greetings, pilot. I bring you your ship."

"It's about time, *Phodan*." said Cap' with false anger.

"Behave yourself, Nigel. Is that any way to welcome guests?"

"He knows I'm just kidding, Carla, don't you *Phodan*?"

"Of course. How are you all doing? Well, I hope."

"Very well, indeed, *Phodan*. And we are glad to see you. And you as well, Melanie. How have your travels been?" he asked.

"Wonderful, Cap'. *Phodan* has shown me the stars."

"He didn't pull that old trick of running out of gas, did he?"

"No, Cap'. He knows I'm too smart for that." They all laughed at the ridiculous notion.

Phodan looked Cap' in the eye and said soberly, "I think we need to talk about something, Cap'."

"Oh?" he asked, his interest piqued.

"Yes, I have something to ask you. Carla can hear this if you want. It concerns her as well in a way."

"Sure, go ahead, *Phodan*," said Cap'.

"You know I promised you that I would purge any recollection of our encounter if you want, right?"

"I've been thinking about that, *Phodan*, and I don't think that I want you to."

"Are you sure?"

"Yes. Carla and I talked about it. I want to retain the memories. I want to remain friends."

"I'm glad you said that, Cap', because I have another proposition for you."

"I haven't even started the first one," said Cap'.

"That doesn't matter. I have complete confidence in you."

"What's this other proposition?"

"I'd like you to be a pilot for the space program of your country."

"Me? An astronaut?"

"You're already an astronaut, Cap'. One of the sirens who has been in contact with the president has intimated that we can deliver the astronauts to the space station. In exchange, they will give your farm and the Church compound increased security and complete anonymity. As you know, they have to depend on the Russians now out of Star City for any rides to the space station. If you were to shuttle them, they would owe us a great deal."

"Are you saying that you would leave your ship with me indefinitely?"

"We'll just take it one day at a time, okay?"

"Okay, *Phodan*. I'm your man. I'll shuttle the astronauts up. Is the docking port similar?"

"It's the same one. You won't have any trouble handling it."

"Good, then it's settled," said Cap'. "This calls for a drink. Beers all around."

"I'd like a Virgin Bloody Mary," said Carla.

"Me, too," said Melanie.

"Rooof!" said Isabelle. *Sounds good.*

"That's three of us girls want cosmopolitans," said Carla laughing. "You guys can have the beer."

~

When Matthew Winter and Alankha Hannas got to the way station on one of the last transfers from Siren, they were surprised to discover a stow-away. Mantah Samah looked around at her strange surroundings and started to smile. "Is this what I think it is?" she asked looking out a viewport to the beautiful blue planet Earth below.

"It sure is," said Matthew. "This is a space station in orbit above the planet Earth. Where did you come from?"

"From Siren, naturally," said the girl.

"You're Julianah, the girl we prayed for."

"Yes, I am Julianah, and I am cured. I no longer have the blood disease. The healers on Siren say I should live a long and healthy life."

"I think you need to live a long and healthy life on Siren, Julianah," said Alankha holding little Zaphi. The toddler's eyes were as big as saucers at the incredible sights he was seeing. He seemed to grasp the concept of being in space. The wonder could be seen all over his little face. The young girl, Julianah, looked up at Alankha and asked her, "Can I hold him?"

"Sure, why not." She handed little Zaphi to Mantah Samah.

~

Chapter Forty-nine

Roy Becker called an emergency meeting of *The Son's of Destiny*. There were eleven club members in attendance, and Roy made it an even dozen. They had recently lost three members due to violent deaths, and Roy meant to get to the bottom of it. He was especially upset because one of the most recent fatalities of a club member was his own son, Joey. Billy Ray Shockley and Joey Becker were found shot to death in a small two-bedroom apartment in a complex called Lakeside Villas.

The apartment belonged to Melanie Cook who was a performer at the Pet Palace on International Drive in Orlando, Florida. The girl has vanished from the scene, and no one has heard from her since. Police have no leads in the murders and have sealed off the crime pending further investigation. Roy Becker had no real evidence how or why his son was killed, but he had a theory. "Here's how I think it went down," he told the club members. "Billy Ray said he knew how Chip Luger was killed last week, but he didn't know why. He told us during a poker game that he was in the process of finding out. That meant that he had a lead he was working. Everybody with me so far?" he asked.

The group all nodded their heads as one. Roy continued, "Billy Ray called me here at the clubhouse and said he knew where the guy was who killed Chip. He had picked up my Joey, and they both were plannin' to drop in on the guy. He said something about Alligator Lake. Anybody know it?"

"I do," said Bob Ellis, one of the members. "St. Cloud, off 192."

"Okay, that's a start," said Roy. "Now here's how I think the girl fits in: I think it was the Mexicans again."

"Mexicans?" asked Ed Carter, another one of *The Sons*. "Well, I'll be damned."

"Sure as shit, the Mexicans. Here's what happened. I think Billy Ray was dating this girl Melanie Cook, and the Mexicans knew about it. When Chip Luger was complain'n about all the Mexicans getting the work and not him, they got pissed at him and blew up his pickup truck. I'm pretty sure it was a bomb planted under the gas tank when he wasn't lookin.' Those Mexicans are sneaky bastards."

"They sure are," said a number of *The Sons* all at once.

"So Billy Ray grabs Joey and follows this lead that takes him out to the Mexicans on Alligator Lake and confronts them about killing Chip. Somehow they must have got the drop on them and took them back to the girl's apartment. She might even have been there when they killed those two, the poor girl. Now she's missing because the Mexicans have kidnapped her and plan to sell her into white slavery."

"Man, that's awful, Roy," said one of *The Sons*. What do you think we should do?"

"Only one thing *to* do. We've got to go out to Alligator Lake and find us some Mexicans. See how they like it when we get the drop on them."

"Yeah, you betcha," said a number of *The Sons.*

"So here's what we're gonna' do: Since you know the place, Bob, why don't you take old Ed there out to Alligator Lake and take a good look around. See if you see any Mexicans. But if you do, don't confront them alone. You call back here to the club and holler for the rest of us. Them sneaky Mexicans will come out of the woodwork and before you know it, you'll be outnumbered."

"Sounds good, Roy," said Bob Ellis. "C'mon, Ed, we'll take my truck."

~

The Army Corps of Engineers had begun clearing the fence line with chainsaws and stump grinders. It would take them less than two days to prepare the perimeter for the mile and a half of fence sections. They would be ten feet long and ten feet high and there would be six-hundred twenty of them in all. They would have barbed-wire along the top, and one of the strands would carry an electric charge of 300 volts. The ALPHA complex would be completely secure in less than three days.

Bob Ellis and Ed Carter drove up to the entrance of Cap' Walker's driveway and parked the truck. "See any Mexicans?" Bob asked Ed.

"Not yet, but I'll bet they're around here someplace. Trust me, if Roy thinks they're here, then they're here. We just can't see em' yet. That old Roy's a smart guy, Ed. He showed me this book he read cover to cover."

"Get out, he read the whole thing?"

"Swears he did."

"What's the book about?" asked Ed.

"It's a book what makes you smart. It's called *Dionestics* by a guy named L. Dom Hummer er' sumpin.' Anyways, it made him smart for sure."

"I guess that's why he's the president of *The Sons*."

"I guess you're right," said Bob. "You reckon we should get out and take a look around?"

"D'you bring a gun, Bob?"

"No."

"Me neither," said Ed.

"Now, why the hell not?" asked Bob.

"Why didn't *you* bring one?"

"Cause I'm the driver. You was shotgun, dammit."

"Aw, hell," said Ed. "Take me back to the clubhouse so's I can get my gun."

"By then it'll almost be dark," said Bob.

"Then let's just sit here a while. Look for Mexicans."

"Sounds good to me," said Bob. "Got any weed?"

Ed Carter did have some weed, and it was pretty good weed at that. By the time the sun went down, they were sitting heavy-lidded in Bob's truck at the end of the driveway to the Walker farm. They had completely forgotten about any Mexicans or what they were doing there in the first place. It was lucky that Bob made it home all right because the next day, he didn't even remember driving home.

~

The ballistics report came back on the two shooting victims of the Lakeside Villas murders, and it was determined that each man was shot by the other one's gun. Melanie Cook was still missing, but the police have indicated that she is not wanted in connection with the crime other than for questioning. It is not believed that she was involved in the shooting, but until she surfaces, no one will know for sure.

"Shot with each other's gun?" asked Roy reading the story in the *Orlando Sentinel*. "How the hell do you think that happened?"

"Beat's me," said Bob Ellis.

"What'd you guys see out there at that Alligator Lake?"

"Not much. Just some old couple and a dog. No Mexicans."

"Well, just because you didn't see'm that time, doesn't mean they ain't there," said Roy.

"You're right, Roy, that's smart," said Ed Carter. "D'you really read that *Dionestics* book by that Hummer guy?"

"Carter, what the *hell* are you talking about?"

"Aw, jus forgit it, Roy. I think Bob was messin' with me again.

Chapter Fifty

Melanie rode with *Phodan* to the Walker farm to catch up with Carla and maybe talk her out of another drink. When Carla agreed, she learned that Carla had decided to stay off alcohol until the baby came. "That's so cool, Carla. I'm so happy for you and Cap'. Is this your first?"

"Yes, believe it or not. You'd think at my age I'd have a whole slew of kids, but Cap' and I just never got around to it until now."

"Well, I think it's wonderful. Never too late to start a family. I think that *Phodan* is leaning that way finally also."

"You're kidding? Phodan? A father?"

"Sure. Why should you guys have all the fun?"

"I think that would be great, but I just never thought of him bouncing a little tyke on his knee. Bouncing a space ship off the moons of Saturn maybe." Both of them began to laugh at the thought of that.

"I see they're building a fence around the whole lake," said Melanie.

"That was someone else's idea, not ours, but we'll enjoy the privacy. I think it has something to do with the ship that Cap' will moor under the lake. I guess you two are going to *Preculis* from the way station and not by ship."

"That's what *Phodan* says, but I'm going to try to get him to stay here for a while."

"Good. I hope you can stay for a long time. I know the sirens will be here soon, but I don't know any of them personally."

"From what I understand, you'll be fast friends. They're really very nice. Shelly Simon is one of them. I have fond memories of a day sitting in the garden of the Church with her. She's pregnant, too. You might end up sharing baby-sitters."

"That would be nice. As Cap' says, it will be nice to have some young blood around here."

"But you're young, Carla."

"Trust me. I'm not as young as I look. Ask *Phodan* about it."

~

Christos Somah sent out a mental message for *Phodan* that there was an urgent situation back on Siren that required his attention. A young girl was missing, and it is believed she was last seen walking up the hill to the Church. It was feared that she may have gotten caught in a *space/time exchange chamber* by mistake. When *Phodan* received the message, he knew that his presence would be required on the way station. He told Melanie that she could stay with Carla while he and Cap' took the ship back up.

"What's the problem, *Phodan*?" asked Cap'.

"Stow away."

"Seriously, to the station?"

"Yes, I believe so. It is a girl who was brought to me for healing. She had a blood disease and has gotten relief from the *Prayers of the Church.*"

"That seems like some powerful stuff," said Cap'.

"You have no idea, Cap'. No idea at all," said *Phodan*.

~

The Situation Room
Of The White house

"The logistics are terrible, Mr. President. It's a farm. There is no effective cover for a mile in each direction. We can't guarantee your safety there."

"Find a way," he said.

"There is no way."

"I am *The President*, Mr. Conroy. You work for me. When I tell you to find a way for me to get safely on that farm, I expect you to follow my orders. I don't care if I have to ride down the road in a God-damned tank. Do I make myself clear?"

"Sir, with all respect, you aren't really interested in the resting place of the ship. It's just a lake. Perhaps you could persuade the pilot to land in a hanger at Patrick Air Force Base. It's only a stone throw away."

The president thought that over for a minute and then said, "Very well. Set it up. Your contact is Walter Purness out of St. John's Island. Get the number from logistics, and I'll be in my office. Contact *Marine One* and arrange a flight to Patrick."

"Very well, sir." Bill Conlan was the current head of the president's personal secret service staff. It was days like this that he rolled his eyes to the heavens and muttered, "I hate this job."

~

When Walter Purness got the call from Bill Conlan, he was not surprised. It's not everyday of the week that the lead operative of the president's personal secret service detail contacts you on the phone, but then again, Walter Purness is not your average man. Presidents in the past have "borrowed the use of his yachts and planes" all in the interest of National Security, of course. Mr. Purness had been semi-retired for the last twenty years and during that time, he had never once dropped lower than the teens on the Fortune Five-Hundred List.

He said to his wife, Edith, "I got the call. The one we were expecting."

"Where does he want to meet the ship?"

"Patrick. 10:00 A.M. tomorrow."

"That's pretty close to the fallout zone."

"They say it's safe. Patrick is still open."

"Do we get to go?" she asked.

"Edith, I think that after the last meeting you had with the president, you can do anything you damned well please."

"You don't have to say damned, Walt."

"Damn you're a remarkable woman, Edith."

"Except when you say that."

"Call the space man, Edith. Tell him that the president wants Cap' to give him a ride."

Walter and Edith knew that any communication about the operation of the ship based in Alligator Lake was extremely sensitive. It would never be discussed over a phone line or radio waves. The only communication about the workings of the ship had to be relayed by word of mouth personally or through a mind link with *Phodan*. Since Edith had a prior link to *Phodan*, she was able to contact him on the way station.

When *Phodan* heard Edith's mind calling his, he stopped his conversation with Julianah Mantah in midsentence. "Excuse me, Julianah, someone has to talk to me from the planet below."

Phodan heard Edith say that President Amalah wanted a ride in the ship and would like to board it at Patrick Air Force Base in Satellite Beach, Florida, the next morning at 10:00 A.M. *Phodan* didn't see a problem with that, but it would be much more advisable to employ the ship's photo-reflective properties, so it would be invisible. That problem was that the Pegasus Mane was running dangerously low on nuclear fuel. *Phodan* made a mental note to ask the president for some enriched plutonium to be used in the ship's plus-light drive. That would free up the supply of *Xerium* for the stealth properties.

~

Isabelle drank a cosmopolitan along with Melanie, and Carla had a diet Coke. The three of them had a very peaceful time watching the sunset over the lake. It shined through the stained glass windows of the Church across the lake, and when it dipped below the horizon, the sky was a vibrant purple and red awaiting the stars that would shortly creep over the eastern horizon.

"I'd like to settle here, Carla," said Melanie.

"We'd like to have you, dear," said Carla.

"Rooof!" agreed Isabelle. *We love you, Melanie.*

"But I think the stumbling block there is the word settle," she said. *Phodan* is the Master of the Universe for God's sake. How can I ask him to settle in one place and raise a family?"

"You can ask, and he has the right to say no," said Carla.

"Rooof!" *But he won't.*

~

Chapter Fifty-one

Capt. Walker piloted the ship to Patrick Air Force Base at 10:00 A.M. the next morning from the way station in Earth orbit. The trip took about four minutes. Cap' was amazed that the gravitational forces from massive acceleration were absorbed by the ship. He could go as fast as he pleased and stop short in an instant and the relative G-forces within the cockpit were negated somehow. He eased the ship into an open hanger at the Air Force base and shut down the engine. He waited until there was a procession of airmen approaching the ship to open the ramp on the side of the ship. Cap' remained isolated in the cabin of the ship and communicated with the passenger hold through an audio device. "Welcome, Mr. President. Please make your way up the ramp and find a comfortable seat to your liking. We will be at the station in Earth orbit within ten minutes. I look forward to meeting you then."

That was the extent of the message Cap' had for the president. *Phodan* was aboard as well, but had nothing to say either. Both men were aware of the double-edged sword that the United States government could sometimes be. It was not from personal experience and a situation both of them were interested in perpetuating.

Bill Conlan was with the president and made one last attempt to talk him out of the risky prospect of traveling to an unknown space station aboard a mysterious spacecraft.

"Have you thought this through, Sir?" Conlan asked, perspiring heavily in the Florida heat, but most of the reason was the dicey situation that was unfolding around him. He was leery of the safety factors regarding the unprecedented action by the president. He thought it was a foolish action by a foolish man.

After Conlan met Walter and Edith Purness who were waiting in the hanger, his fears were somewhat allayed and he settled down and was almost as calm as the president.

"Yes, Mr. Conlan, I have thought this through to answer your question. I have every confidence in this technology and the peaceful intentions of all parties involved. Think about this for a moment: Before us we have technology hundreds of years in advance of our own. The ability to travel from one star to another as this ship had done requires plus-light speed. The nearest star to ours is four light-years. This ship didn't spend four years in space traveling to Earth. Why would anyone bother with such a waste of time. I would venture a guess that the trip can be made in less than a week."

"Less than that, Mr. President," said Edith.

"Think about it," continued the president to Conlan. "Aren't you the least bit curious to see what the future holds?"

"Yes, Sir. I suppose if you put it like that, then I am."

"I thought so. And as far as our safety goes, I'm sure that a people this advanced would never risk their own safety if they didn't have to. We will be safer aboard this ship than any airplane and that includes *Air Force One.*"

"I'm just puzzled why you have so much faith in these people, Sir."

"Because I've met them, and so have you, but that information remains highly classified, do I make myself clear?"

Conlan looked at Walter and Edith in a different light all of a sudden. *Could these kindly old people really be alien?* he wondered.

The president continued, "I know of their benign nature and good intentions. Believe me, if they had any ill will or hostility toward humanity, they could easily destroy this planet never having left their own. It all boils down to faith, Mr. Conlan. Have a little faith."

The president started up the gangway steps and entered the ship with Bill Conlan in tow. Walter and Edith Purness followed them and the cabin that could hold over twenty passengers held only four. There were no other members of a secret security detail. None were necessary. This flight to the way station was merely a courtesy by Phodan and Cap' Walker to show the president where the sirens were placed prior to their being shuttled to the Alligator Lake Port Housing Area, or *ALPHA* complex. When they took their seats, Conlan said, "Why don't they show themselves? This just seems to strange to me."

"When you board an airliner, does the pilot come out and show himself to you?"

"Not usually, no."

"Well, there you have it. Think about it like that. You are on an airliner, but the airport you are traveling to is one-hundred ninety miles above sea level in Earth's orbit."

~

Roy Becker met with Bob Ellis and Ed Carter after their second reconnaissance mission looking for Mexicans at Alligator Lake. He asked them, "How'd it go?"

"No Mexicans, Roy," said Bob Ellis.

"Not a single one," chimed in Ed Carter.

"Something doesn't add up, boys. If Billy Ray and Joey got tangled up with them and then got killed, why would they take off? Where would they go? Back to Mexico?"

"I don't know, Roy," said Bob.

"There sure is plenty of work around there for em'," said Ed.

"What do you mean, Ed?" asked Becker.

"With the construction going on."

"They're building something out there at Alligator Lake?"

"Looks like a wall to me," said Bob.

"A wall? What the hell are you talking about, Bob? Where are they building this wall?"

"From the looks of it, all around the whole lake. You know, now that I think about it, it sure is strange. You know how there's always Mexicans at a job site shovelin' sand and mixin' mortar. Well we musta' seen over twenty cement mixers and not one Mexican."

"What did you say?" asked Becker incredulously. "Do you mean to tell me that you saw over twenty cement mixing trucks and didn't think anything about it?"

"Like I said, I thought they was building a wall. Big one, too, from the looks of it."

"And that didn't strike you as strange?"

"Not particularly. Some people like their privacy, I guess."

"The alligators for Christ's sake? Make sense, Bob. What are you an idiot or something?"

"Now there's no cause to be rude, Roy. We done what you asked. We looked for Mexicans like you said and didn't see any."

"No but you saw a big construction project and neglected to mention it."

"You didn't ask us to look for no construction project, Roy."

"Oh, forget it," he said hotly. "Morons," he muttered to himself.

~

Chapter Fifty-two

When Cap' docked the ship with the way station, he left the cockpit and traveled back to the passenger compartment to meet his passengers. Just a few minutes before, *Phodan* had left the ship by the forward stairwell that descended from the cockpit. He didn't feel like showing his presence just yet. When Cap' reached the cabin, he reached out his hand in greeting and said, "Pleased to meet you, Mr. President. I'm Nigel Walker, captain of the Pegasus Mane."

"Nice to meet you, too, Captain Walker. This is my head of security, Bill Conlan," said the president making the introductions, "and these fine people are Walter and Edith Purness."

"Pleased to meet you," said Cap' to Walter and Edith. "I'm told that we have you to thank for arranging our utility needs at ALPHA."

"ALPHA," asked the president. "Do you mean the space station?"

"Not that Alpha, Sir. The housing complex at Alligator Lake is called the Port Housing Area, hence A.L.P.H.A."

"Ahh, I see. Well that makes it easy to remember. We go to ALPHA to get to Alpha, which is the International Space Station."

"The docking ports are identical, Mr. President. It should be a simple matter to shuttle your astronauts to the space station once my present task is completed."

"And just what is your present task, if I may ask?"

"I am shuttling some people back to Earth. I was told you were informed of the situation by Mrs. Purness," said Cap' looking over at Edith.

"Yes, I got the gist of it, but not the particulars."

"There will be over three hundred souls here on this way station soon, and they need a lift to the ALPHA complex. We're just waiting for the infrastructure to be completed so they can be accommodated. The wall construction is under way, and I'm told the utilities will be online shortly."

"I'll see to it personally, Captain Walker," said the president.

"Nice to have friends in high places," said Cap'.

"You can't get much higher than this," said the president chuckling.

Roy Becker was not going to send Bob Ellis and Ed Carter on any more reconnaissance assignments. He was pretty sure that they couldn't find their own asses with both hands. But his curiosity was piqued by the mention of the huge wall project. *What were they hiding out at Alligator Lake?* he wondered. It sure wasn't Mexicans. In fact, now Roy was considering the fact that Mexicans may not have been involved in his son's death at all. But it had something to do with Alligator Lake, of that he was sure.

He decided to take a drive out there and take a look for himself. When he parked on the road at the end of Cap' Walker's driveway, he noticed the cement trucks. They were driving on a recently cleared path just outside the perimeter of the large wall that was under construction. He could see across the lake that there was a church with another building close by. He saw that there was a newly paved road that led up to the church, but didn't see any parking lot. That was strange. He didn't think that the church members walked to church, but he supposed it was possible. He made a mental note to try to get a look behind the church to look for the parking lot. After seeing the curious looking wall under construction and the Walker farm and the church across the lake, Roy decided that he had seen enough to the time being. He was getting some stares from the truck drivers that passed him sitting in the car out by the road. Finally, he drove back to the clubhouse to consider his options.

~

Walter and Edith had learned that Durbah and Alex had already arrived at the way station and were anxious to see them. Edith asked Cap', "If you don't mind, we haven't seen our daughter Durbah in almost two years. We've talked to her, of course, but we haven't met in the flesh for all of that time.

We are very anxious to see her. Can you take us to where the sirens are staying, please?"

"Certainly, Mrs. Purness. Come with me and I'll show you the staterooms. You can find which viewport they are using by the directory or just asking a very nice man named *Zo*."

Cap' led Walter and Edith to the hallway leading to the living quarters. When they rounded a bulkhead, he said, "There he is now. Greetings, *Zo*. Nice to see you."

"Greetings, Captain Walker. It is nice to see you as well."

"I'd like to introduce you to my friends here. This is Walter and Edith Purness," he said motioning to the older couple, "and this is President Amalah of The United States of America and with him is his security advisor, Bill Conlan."

"It is a pleasure to meet you all," said *Zo*. I am *Zophan*, but please feel free to call me *Zo*. I am the caretaker of the way station, and I will assist you in any way that I can."

"Thank you, *Zo*," said Edith. "We would very much like to see our daughter who is in one of your staterooms here on the station. Her name is Durbah Purness."

"Yes, of course, Mrs. Purness. Please come with me," *Zophan* led Walter and Edith down a long corridor and came upon a stateroom called, Crab Nebula. "Here we are," said *Zophan*. "This suite is one of my favorites. I will leave you to your reunion with your daughter."

"Thank you, *Zo*." Edith knocked on the door to the Crab Nebula Suite. The door opened and standing before her was a man she didn't recognize at first. Then it dawned on her, "Alex?" she asked tilting her head, wrinkling her brow.

"I don't blame you for your reaction, Edith. Yes, it's me," he said.

"You've lost a considerable amount of weight," she said.

"Yes, I'm afraid I have. I was caught up in an addiction on Siren."

"They have drug problems there?"

"Worse than drugs, Edith. It's a long story. Come and see Durbah, she's in the next room."

Walter and Edith entered the solarium where the viewport showed the Crab Nebula. It was beautiful, but the thing that was more beautiful was the sight of their only daughter. Durbah rose from a sofa and crossed the room to her father. "Daddy, I've missed you so much. You look wonderful."

"You do, too, dear. We've missed you very much, but now you're coming home. We are so pleased."

Durbah broke away from Walter's embrace and turned to face Edith. She reached out and hugged her as well, "Hello, mother, I'm so glad to see you," she said. At first Edith didn't have anything to say, and then finally offered, "Yes, dear, I'm glad to see you, too." Then she whispered in Durbah's ear, "A siren knows her daughter. Can you tell me where mine is?"

Durbah whispered back, "Later, Edith, please don't give me away to Alex or Walter."

"I'll play along for now," she whispered back.

Chapter Fifty-three

Durbah missed her mother and father very much. It pained her to remain on Siren when she had the chance to return to Earth with the other Earth sirens, but she had a strong attraction to Christos Somah and a dream to become a very powerful force on Siren.

She had invited Christos Somah to join her for dinner at her apartment in a luxury complex at the peak of Creston. The walls were made of glass and the panoramic views were spectacular. To the east was the monopole valley where the sun would creep over the horizon each day and light up the valley with a sheet of glistening diamonds on the river. On the opposite wall facing west was the steep slope down from the Sirenian Mountain peaks to the Sea. The sunsets were more beautiful than anything she had ever witnessed on Earth. One added advantage to Siren was each sunset featured the elusive green flash that is rarely seen on Earth. It happens at the precise moment when the sun disappears over the horizon. The sky pulses with a soft green light from north to south across the whole sky in an instant. Christos Somah and Durbah had just witnessed the flash.

"Spectacular," said Durbah. "It never fails to amaze me."

"Yes, it's very nice," said Christos Somah, but there was little emotion behind the comment.

Durbah asked him, "How about an appetizer? Do you like oxala clams? I have some fresh ones from Alantis."

"Yes, that would be very nice, Durbah."

When she came back with the plate of clams and two glasses of wine, Christos Somah asked her, "You chose not to return with the other Church members to Earth. Why is that, Durbah?"

"I see you get right to the point," she said.

"I simply asked a question. You don't have to answer if it makes you uncomfortable."

"I'm not uncomfortable at all," she told him. "I just wanted to stay here on Siren for the time being. I wanted to get to know you better. Is that a crime?"

"Not that I know of."

"How do you feel about me, Christos Somah?"

"I like you. I liked sharing the monopole valley with you. The strange tribal people were interesting, and I was interested in the posi-grains as well. Did you know that I have studied the valley tribes in school?"

"Yes, I think you mentioned it. But you have never gone into the valley before have you?"

"No."

"How come?"

"I have always been told it is not safe."

"But you went with me. Actually, you took me there. That was very brave of you, Christos Somah, considering what you have always been told about the dangers."

"I suppose most of it was only rumors. It didn't seem very dangerous to me. It was rather uneventful if you want to know how I really feel about it."

"Yes, I do want to know, Christos Somah. That's why you're here. It's why I invited you to dinner. I want to know just how you feel about your experience in the valley."

"It was a bit dull. The pagan dance rites are interesting, but the climate and the scenery were boring."

"What if I told you that you had an exciting adventure in the valley?"

"I don't know what you mean."

"What if I told you that you rescued a young girl from a condor's nest and had to fight off the mother bird to do it. And then what if I told you that you went into the valley and killed a valley cat, encountered a large viper, flying fish and rescued a downed flier from another condor's nest? What would you say if I told you that?"

"I would say that you must be dreaming."

"No, Christos Somah, this is the dream. Soon I will wake you from it."

"What are you talking about, Durbah?"

"I'm talking about this," she said releasing her powerful pheromones on him. Her eyes began to light up with the gold and silver flecks of electrum, and she motioned for Christos Somah to come forward and embrace her. She whispered in his ear, "Now I will give you back your experiences in the valley. You have gone where no sirens have gone for thousands of years. You have gone into your heart, and you have had feelings for me. I held them in check for a while, but now I no longer care to do so. I want to let you love me." She broke away from his embrace and held his eyes with hers. She could see he was helpless to refuse her anything. She began to undress and said to him, "Now it is your desire to please me. For now, it is your only desire. You can think of nothing else. You will give me your body and then, you will give me your heart."

She was right. He did.

~

Chapter Fifty-four

When Alex's Durbah got a chance to speak to Edith alone, she said, "I knew you would see that I am not your daughter, but you may want to know that in a way, I am."

"A mother knows her daughter. Especially a siren. I'm surprised that Walter doesn't suspect anything. I suppose he is getting older."

"His love for his daughter is in his eyes. That may be why he doesn't see clearly."

"I don't think it would be fair to disappoint him again. It took him a while to get over Durbah leaving Earth."

"Then please don't take me from him again."

"You sound like you are actually Durbah. Do you have feelings for Walter and me?"

"I have fond memories, yes. I have all of Durbah's memories, and I know every inch of how good you were as parents. I feel she is very lucky, and so I feel that I am very lucky to also have those memories."

"But you don't have her emotions."

"No, I'm afraid that I don't yet."

"But you expect to, in time?"

"I don't see why not. Every minute I spend with you brings up good memories, and naturally I want to have them.

I'm not sure how all this will pan out, and I'm not even sure that Master *Phodan* knows either.

"I've never met the man," said Edith.

"When you do, you will love him, simple as that."

"What makes you say that?"

"He has been a great friend of the sirens, both from Earth and on Siren. He is from *Preculis* and has been our benefactor for hundreds of years."

"Of course, I've heard of *Preculis* and *Phodan* as well," said Edith. "He is the one responsible for the transfer of the Church to Florida."

"And the transfer of all the Church members as well," said Durbah.

"I have asked the president to intervene on your behalf. He is supporting the ALPHA complex and building a secure wall around the lake to insure your privacy."

"That is very nice of you, mother, er . . . Edith."

"Well, you're not going to call Walter by his first name, so you might as well call me mother."

Durbah hugged Edith with genuine warmth. That was something that Edith could tell also. She knew that the woman standing before her was not her original daughter, but she also knew that she was something more than a mere facsimile. Edith hugged her back. "Okay, Durbah, it sounds so strange asking this, but where is Durbah?"

"She's back on Siren," said her daughter's replica.

"Does she intend on returning to Earth?" asked Edith.

"Possibly. I would say probably in due time, but she has an agenda within the political circles there on Siren. She's your daughter, Edith, so you know that if she feels she can make a difference, then she has to try."

"Try what? What difference does she think she can make?"

"I'm not entirely sure, but I think it must be something positive. Perhaps, it is as simple as love."

"She intends to teach an entire planet to love each other?" asked Edith.

"Not the entire planet, just the native sirens."

"I don't follow."

"When I was your daughter, before my creation by Master *Phodan*, I traveled to a place called the Monopole Valley where I met a very spiritual group of people who live there. They are called the *Valegatos*. They openly love each other and pray to the Creator and give Him thanks for their lives. The native sirens regard them as savages. Sirens don't have love or religion. I think that Durbah feels the need to change all that."

"No small task from what I'm hearing."

"I think if anyone can make a difference, it's Durbah. She must use her powers of persuasion to bring about a change in their society. Although I have her brains and beauty, I don't have her powers. My eyes will never display the electrum, and my pheromones are never going to be as powerful as hers."

"You are still a remarkable beauty, dear."

"I suppose I have you and Walter to thank for that."

Edith hugged her once again and said, "That's a very nice thing for you to say, Durbah. You are very much like the original." When she let her go, she asked, "What on Earth happened to Alex?"

"It wasn't on Earth, mother." Both women laughed at that.

~

Christos Somah's father, Christos, was paid a visit by the very influential medicine man called Mantah. His young girl had been spirited away by accident to the way station in Earth orbit. He was very concerned and wanted to know what Christos planned to do about it.

"I assure you, Mantah, as soon as *Phodan* becomes aware of the situation, your samah will be returned on the next transfer."

"How could this have happened? Don't you have any safeguards in place to prevent this kind of thing?"

"I am not coordinating the transfers, Mantah."

"Well, perhaps you should be. Remember, my wife and I voted for you, and there is another election in the near future."

"Please, Mantah, give me some time to correct this unfortunate accident. I am assured that your samah, Julianah, is well and enjoying her stay on the way station."

"How many more transfers are going to take place?" asked Mantah.

"About five."

"So there are still about one hundred Church members on Siren?"

"Yes, about a hundred, but not all of them are Church members. Some of them are just Earth sirens."

"I don't mind telling you that I'll rest easier when they are all gone."

"They're not all going, Mantah. A few are remaining on Siren."

"Will they be registered?"

"I'm not sure what you mean?"

"Well, for the sake of your position with regard to the next election, you had better figure out what I mean."

"You're talking about profiling. That is something we have never done."

"No, because all the savages were isolated in the valley. Now we have savages in Creston and probably Baseton, too. I wouldn't be surprised if Alantis were next."

"I would hardly call them savages, Mantah."

"You haven't lost a child to them."

"You haven't either, Mantah. Please give me a chance to return her to you."

"You will have your chance. I expect to see my daughter on the next transfer back from the way station."

Chapter Fifty-five

Roy Becker was addressing *The Sons of Destiny* at a clubhouse meeting. "There's something going on out there at Alligator Lake that stinks."

"Probably gator poop," said Ed Carter through the missing teeth in front of his mouth. He laughed at his own joke.

"Very funny," said Roy, but he didn't really think it was. Roy had lost his son to some pretty strange circumstances, and he wanted answers. "No, it ain't gator poop that stinks, it's the situation with that big wall going up. There's only one reason to build a wall around something and that's to hide it."

"What do you think they're trying to hide?" asked Bob Ellis.

"There's nothing to hide. At least not yet. All that's out there is a farm with two old people and a dog on it and a church on the other side of the lake. They're not trying to hide those things. There must be something else. Something that's coming that they don't want anyone else to see."

"You got any clues?" asked Ed Carter.

"No, but it feels like the government."

"What would the government want with Alligator Lake?" asked Ellis.

"I don't know, Ed, but when we find out, we'll find out why my Joey had to die."

~

Carla was teaching Melanie how to catch bluegills on the lake. They had rowed out to the center and were holding their fishing poles over the side of the boat resting them on the freeboard. Isabelle sat on the rear seat and watched the ducks and cormorants longingly. Occasionally she would stand up and prepare to leap over the side when her good sense would take over and she would say, "Rooof!" *Oh, yes, now I remember. Alligators.*

Melanie said to Carla, "Cap' is a good man, Carla. I'm sure he'll be a good father."

"Rooof!" agreed Isabelle. *Yes he will.*

"Thank you Melanie. I think he will, too."

"Why didn't you have any kids before this?"

"I'm not really sure, to tell you the truth. We dated a long time before we got married, and I always took the pill. Then after about ten years, we got married and did some traveling to Europe when Nigel could get away from work. He always traveled a lot with the cruise line when there wasn't a ship to moor out of Canaveral. You have to go where the work is. So with Nigel traveling, we just never got around to having kids. Hell, I was forty-five when we got married. Then I went off the pill because I figured I'd go through menopause pretty soon and bingo, a cake in the oven."

"A female cake, right?"

"How did you know?"

"Dan mentioned it."

"We thought of naming her *Phodana*.

"Dan would be so proud."

"What do you think of the Church?" asked Carla.

"It looks the same. I've seen it on Siren. Dan reproduced it down to the fountain in the garden with the benches. I think it's beautiful."

"Do you go to church?"

"No, never had. But I'm starting to pray."

"I'm sure you would be welcome there."

"I'm sure you would, too, Carla."

"That's good because I plan to go every Sunday."

"What do you think about the miracles?"

"What miracles?" asked Carla.

"There was some talk on Siren about how the prayers of the Church were answered. A young girl was cured of some kind of disease."

"I think that's all *Phodan* if you ask me. I think he just lets the Church think that they are the ones doing the healing."

"Why do you think he would do that?" asked Melanie.

"Maybe because if the Church members do it long enough, they might get it right."

"Now wouldn't that be something special."

"Rooof!" *Be careful what you wish for.*

~

Phodan found Julianah on the solarium overlooking Jupiter's moon Io. She was watching a volcano shooting red and green gases into the atmosphere. Then they would burst into flame and rise up into the sky like an upside-down contrail of a huge rocket. When she saw Phodan enter the room she ran to him, "*Phodan*, I'm so glad to see you. Have you heard the news? I'm cured."

"Yes, Julianah, I have heard. I told you that you would be well again."

"It was you who cured me, wasn't it?"

"It was the Creator."

"Then I should be grateful to the Creator, shouldn't I?"

"That's up to you."

"I think it will be hard for me back on Siren. I'm not sure that I belong there after my second chance at life."

"You have to return to Siren, samah. Many people are counting on it."

"My parents don't really care about me. They just like to make trouble."

"Nonsense, your Jomah cares for you very much. Shelly said she came to her in tears when you were ill."

"Well, all she ever does is yell at me."

"I think that most samahs feel the same way about their Jomahs."

"Wait until she sees me praying to the Creator. Then she's really going to yell."

"Maybe that is something you should keep to yourself for awhile," advised *Phodan*.

"I am not ashamed to pray."

"No, and you should not be."

"There is also something else that I am not ashamed to do."

"What is that, Julianah?"

"Now, I am not afraid to love."

"Give me your hands, Julianah," said *Phodan*, "I need you to open your heart and trust me."

"What do you intend to do?"

"I intend to grant your wish."

"What wish is that?"

"To love and pray without having to hide it."

"How?"

"By making you appear to be two places at the same time."

"I don't understand."

"Give me your hands. Trust me. You will."

Phodan took the young girls hands in his and implanted her memories into the synaptic connections of the stem cells he had collected when he was first asked to heal her. They would be used to make another Julianah to take her place once someone came to retrieve her as he knew they would. Unfortunately, the cells he collected were taken before she was cured of the blood disease. It was a secret *Phodan* would share only with Julianah and otherwise take to the grave.

~

Chapter Fifty-six

Christos had never had a lover like Durbah Purness. He didn't know it was possible to feel the things that she made him feel. The world looked more beautiful, and the sounds of the birds in flight sounded more cheerful, and the prospect of Durbah staying behind on Siren to be with him was glorious. He told her, "Why didn't you do that a year ago?"

"You know why."

"You hadn't yet given up on the flier. You thought you could get him back."

"Something like that."

"I'll tell you one thing: if you did to him what you just did to me, you would have got him back for sure. He would have forgotten about flying over the valley in a heartbeat."

"So you sent him on alone."

"Not exactly."

"What do you mean?"

"As far as he knows, I'm still with him."

"What are you talking about? You're here with me."

"This Durbah is here with you. Another Durbah is with Alex on the way station soon to depart for Earth."

"You really are a sorceress."

"Not me, Phodan."

"So that old wizard is still up to his tricks, eh?"

"I don't think he'd like hearing himself referred to as a wizard."

"Yes, perhaps that was unfair. You won't tell him, will you?"

"Now I've got you where I want you, Christos Somah. You have to be my love slave."

"It's a dirty job, but somebody has to do it."

"Oh, shut up and make love to me."

The next *space/time exchange* transfer took place and Julianah was still not at the Church site on the top of the hill in Creston. It would just be a matter of time before Mantah got the news. Some of the sirens were monitoring the progress of the departure of the newcomers. They would report to Mantah, and he would have words to say to the Regent of Creston. When Durbah and Christos Somah went to the Church site to say farewell to the next group of sirens, there was talk of the young girl's accidental departure. Durbah asked Alankha's uncle Zaphi, "What happened? Why didn't the girl make the exchange?"

"Perhaps she is caught up in a wonderful experience on the way station. She is probably seeing things she knows she will never see again. It can be hard to drag yourself away from such wonders."

"But her place is here, correct?"

"It is not my place to say. They say the girl is sixteen-years old. On this planet, that is the age when most people begin to make their own decisions."

"You think she may be having second thoughts about returning?"

"I know that she came to the Church to thank the members for their prayers. That is a powerful emotion, wouldn't you say?"

"Yes, of course."

"Now, consider that the young girl has never had a strong emotion in her life. Think of how she might react."

"Like opening a floodgate."

"Precisely."

"This could be a very bad thing for newcomers like me who plan to stay here on Siren. I could be caught up in a civil conflict."

"Then perhaps it is in your best interest to retrieve the girl."

"I can't do that Zaphi."

"Why not?"

"Because I already appear to be *on* the way station. My alter ego so to speak is already there. It would look kind of suspicious if I showed up again."

"Ahh, Master *Phodan* strikes again," he said knowingly.

"Yes, he gets around," said Durbah.

~

Just then, *Phodan* was confronting the young girl named Julianah. "You know it is your duty to return to Siren."

"I know no such thing, Master Phodan. I am grateful to you for my life, but it is my life. I am sixteen-years old. I have electrum in my eyes. Would you like to see it?"

"Please, samah, you know I am helpless to the charms of the Earth sirens. Now, you claim to have the same charms as they?"

"Yes."

"How can that be?"

"I don't know. I know that my people don't have the fire in their eyes, but I have seen it in mine."

"Have you tried to charm anyone?"

"No, Master *Phodan*. That wouldn't be appropriate. But I believe I could if I wanted to."

"This is a very strange development," said *Phodan*. "Perhaps if you had spent a long time with the *Valegatos* or one of the other tribes I could understand. But there simply should be no electrum in your eyes."

"Perhaps it is more than the prayers that were said for me."

"What do you mean?"

"Now, I feel it is my place to pray. And I also feel it is my place to love those around me. Do you think I will fit in with my people back on Siren?"

"No, I don't."

"And you think I should return and be eventually banished to the valley to live with the cats and condors and the vipers?"

"No, I do not."

"Then you agree with my decision to stay with the members of the Church on Earth?"

"I was not aware you had made such a decision."

"Neither was I until just this minute. There is no other place for me now."

"Perhaps you are right, samah. But soon there will be two of you. When I asked you to hold my hands and open your heart, I gathered the seeds of your existence and will soon make another of you. She will be an exact copy with one exception: your emotions belong to you. She will have to make her own. I think she will return to Siren in your place when the time comes."

"How can you be sure?"

"Because she doesn't have the need to love or pray as you do. She will choose to have the wealth and privilege that you enjoyed on Siren. Those things are no longer important to you, but they will always be important to her when she is created."

"That sounds so strange. When exactly will she be created?"

"As soon as I can arrange the cells properly for incubation. Probably back on Earth within the church complex. I can do it in about four days. But there is something that you must know."

"What, Grand Master?" asked the girl.

"I have collected your blueprint for life in the form of stem cells. They are life given by the Creator and must be developed in accordance with Her will. Life is precious and can never be discarded for any reason. That is why I went ahead and placed your memories into the cells."

"So what is the problem?" asked the girl.

"I collected the cells *before* you were cured."

The girl was quiet for a moment trying to digest what *Phodan* had told her. A tear came to her eye and she said, "I will pray for her."

"I hope that your prayers are answered, child," said *Phodan*.

"Do you think they will be?" she asked.

"That is *Her* will, Julianah, but I know *She* listens to our prayers."

"Thank you, Grand Master. I owe you so much. How can I ever repay you for your kindness?"

"Call me, *Phodan*."

~

Mantah stormed into Christos's office. I warned you that you are walking a thin line, Christos."

"I have no idea why your daughter did not return in the last transfer, Mantah. Perhaps she was away from the chamber when the turn-around occurred. I'm told that the timing is critical."

"I'll tell you what is critical, Christos. Your career is in critical condition right now."

"Please remain calm, Mantah. I'm sure that your samah will be in the next transfer."

"If she isn't, you might as well join the savages off-world. There won't be any use for you here."

"Listen to yourself, Mantah. Our people haven't spoken to each other in those tones for thousands of years. What is wrong with us?"

Mantah thought over Christos's words for a minute and then said, "I don't know. Of course, you are right. We are acting with a vitriol not seen in millennia. It both saddens me and worries me very greatly, Christos. What use is it to gain whatever we want if we lose our own soul in the bargain."

"What use indeed, my friend. Let us just wait and hope for the best. Perhaps your samah will be on the next transfer."

"I wish I was better at hope," said Mantah.

Chapter Fifty-seven

Roy Becker was again parked at the end of Cap' Walker's driveway. He had been sitting there for over an hour when Carla and Melanie walked by his car to the mailbox. Carla retrieved the mail and when she walked by the open window of Roy's truck she asked, "See any Mexicans?" Melanie couldn't help giggling slightly.

"Excuse me?" asked Roy. "What did you ask?"

"Mexicans," said Carla. "A couple days ago, there was a truck much like yours parked here. When I came to get the mail, a man told me he was supposed to meet his friend out here by Alligator Lake."

"What's that got to do with any Mexicans?" asked Roy.

"I'm glad you asked me that," said Carla, "and I'll tell you. The man said his friend was a Mexican. He said he thought his name was Juan. Naturally, I asked him, 'you think your friend's name is Juan, but you're not sure?' "

Morons, thought Roy. *Why do I surround myself with morons?* "I was just looking around, ma'am. I'm trying to find some work and this is the kind of thing I do. I have a masonry company and that is one big wall that they're putting up."

"You might want to go over to the next entrance off the highway there. I think there's a trailer where you can talk to the foreman."

"Thank you, ma'am. I just might do that."

"Good luck," said Carla. When she and Melanie were halfway back to the house, Carla said, "Good luck finding Mexicans," under her breath. They both got a good laugh about that. The two women had no idea why the man in the truck was parked at the end of their driveway, but there was one thing they knew for sure: he wasn't looking for work. Carla made a mental note to discuss it with Cap' when he came back from the way station.

~

When John Poole, Jr. met Julianah on the solarium deck of the way station, she was watching Io's gaseous light show and sipping on a tall pink lemonade. He didn't wait to be introduced and walked right up to her extending his hand, "I'm John. Who are you?"

"My name is Julianah," she said.

"I haven't noticed you in the Church before, but then again I haven't really been there much myself lately. I was in the Monopole Valley."

"Seriously?" she asked. "You actually went into the valley?"

"I lived there among the *Valegatos*."

"That's so cool," she said. "That's something that I could never do. My parents have always told me they are savages."

"Not true. They're very nice."

"It wouldn't be the first time my parents were wrong," said the girl. "Obviously, you are one of the newcomers, right?"

"That's right," he said.

"What did you think of Siren?"

"I liked it in the valley. I thought that Creston was kind of cold."

"The temperature is regulated, John."

"Not that kind of cold."

"Oh. I think I know what you mean. I have had some interesting thoughts lately. A week ago I might not have known what you meant, but now . . ."

"Now what?" asked John.

"I guess you could say that I'm not the same girl I was a week ago."

"What happened?"

"I was healed. I was dying, and I got my life back. Master *Phodan* said that the prayers of the Church brought me back, but I think he did it himself."

"I would believe in *Phodan*. I don't think he ever says things that aren't true."

"He is kind of a special person. They say he re-located your Church on Earth. It will be all ready for you when you get there. There will also be housing units for all of you to live in."

"Yes, I've heard that as well," said John.

"We're all very grateful for *Phodan* aren't we."

"Are you going back to Siren?" asked John.

"I haven't really made up my mind," she said coyly even though she had.

"I think you are very nice looking. I hope that you decide to join us on Earth. We can always use more young people."

"I must say that you are making my decision easier, John."

"Are they going to be mad at you if you don't return?"

"I suppose so, but from one-hundred eighty million miles away, I might not even hear them."

~

Roy Becker got back to the clubhouse and looked for Bob Ellis and Ed Carter. When he found them shooting pool, he said, "You *think* his name is Juan? Jesus H. Christ!"

"What?" asked Ed Carter. "Jesus's name was Juan?"

Bob Ellis knew what Roy was talking about. He didn't say a thing.

~

Chapter Fifty-eight

President Amalah and Bill Conlan took a tour of the way station, guided by *Phodan*. When he directed them to the solarium, both men were speechless. The telescopic nature of the viewports was beyond anything they had ever experienced. When they focused on the Russian space complex at Star City, they could see the finest details of the Soyuz rocket sitting on the launch pad. Amalah inquired about the weapons system aboard *The Pegasus Mane* and was told by *Phodan* that certain information must remain beyond the reach of political factions. The people of *Preculis* have been duty bound to aid Siren and make amends for contaminating the emotional state of mankind; however, *Phodan* made it clear that he would not allow the ship to be used as a weapon. Amalah then told him, "I'm just curious as to the strength of the weapons. I'm not asking to use them."

"In the wrong hands, this ship could lay your entire planet to waste in a matter of hours. Is that strong enough for you?" said *Phodan*.

"All I can say is, I'm glad you're on our side," said the president.

"As a *Preculian*, I am on no one's side, President Amalah."

"I think I can understand your position," said Amalah. "It would seem that your people are as far advanced from us as

humanity is to the insects of our world. I would imagine that it
will be thousands of years before we catch up to your species."

"I don't mean to be rude, Mr. President, but I can assure
you *there will be no catching up* by your species. Time is the
issue, and let's just say that we have had quite a long head
start."

"How old is *Preculis*?" asked President Amalah.

"Roughly the same age as your planet, but we as a
species, have been evolving for nearly fifty thousand years. The
greatest lesson we have learned is that the lesson still goes on.
All of our technology couldn't avoid the mistakes made by our
lack of wisdom. Rest assured that we will never expose you to
the same fate."

"But what about furnishing my country transportation
to the International Space Station? Is that offer still on the
table?"

"Yes, Mr. President, but it is on the table for all
countries, not just yours. When Edith Purness made the offer,
she said nothing of exclusivity. The offer must be for
everyone."

After the president and Bill Conlan had become
exhausted by trying to digest so much information in such a
short period of time, they asked Cap' to shuttle them down to
the Air Force Base. The president thanked Cap' for the trip to
the way station and thanked *Phodan* for the tour.

Phodan told the president that the transfer of the
Church members would be completed in a few days, and then
the ship would be at his planet's disposal for the time being. He

made no promises about providing the ship and Cap's services in perpetuity, but he intimated that he would not leave the United States in a position of depending completely on the Russians for transportation to the I.S.S. Alpha. At the same time, he reiterated that he would not give any one country an unfair advantage over any other one.

The wall completely surrounding Alligator Lake was completed in a little over three weeks. The utility company was online to the ALPHA complex as were the Orange County water and sewer facilities. Everything was in place for the Church members and all that was needed to complete the community was for Cap' to shuttle the members down. President Amalah arranged for some enriched plutonium rods to be placed in the plus-light drive of *The Pegasus Mane*, so Cap' was free to engage the photo-reflective side panels to render the ship invisible. When they arrived back at Cap's farm, Carla and Melanie were waiting with them at the water's edge with some ice-cold beers. Isabelle came up to the two men and said, "Rooof!" *Next trip, I get to go.*

"That's up to Cap', Belle," said *Phodan*.

"Ok, Belle, you can come on the next trip," said Cap'. He felt like he was beginning to speak dog. Carla took Cap' aside and gave him a big kiss on the lips. "What was that for?" he asked.

"I just like doing it," she said.

"You'll hear no complaints from me."

"I missed you. How was meeting the president?"

"He seemed like an okay guy. His security guy was a little bit of a spook."

"They call them spooks, Nigel."

"I thought they called them *suits*."

"Yeah, that, too. Speaking of spooks, there's something that I think you should know."

"What's that?"

"There were a couple of guys hanging around the end of the driveway kind of snooping around. Then they asked me if I had seen this Mexican guy who they claimed was their friend."

"What's so strange about that?" he asked.

"The guy said he *thinks* his name is Juan."

"You're kidding?"

"Nope."

"What a goofball thing to say. The guy's not sure what his *friend's* name is? I think that one of the sirens needs to have a talk to those boys."

"I think that's what they're looking for. They're suspicious about the wall going up around the lake."

"It does look suspicious. It will all calm down when the military shows their presence. I don't think anybody wants to mess with them. The problem is now they aren't yet visible. When they are, believe me, all the goofballs will disappear into the woodwork."

"Yeah, you're probably right. I just thought I should mention it."

"You were right. I'll ask *Phodan* to talk to Isabelle. She probably noticed more than you did."

"Have you talked to *Phodan* about dog speak?"

"I haven't had a chance. There was an issue on the way station."

"Oh?"

"A stow away. I think the girl wants to come here and wants asylum."

"Uh-oh."

"You said it."

~

When Julianah wasn't on the next transfer, Christos knew there were only three left, and he was quickly running out of time. Mantah would soon storm through his door and continue to make threats. He decided to head him off. Christos went to the home of Mantah and told him that Julianah was not on the next transfer. He suggested that Mantah and his wife make the transfer to the way station themselves and confront their daughter. Christos told them that it may be possible the girl is choosing to join the Church on Earth.

Mantah Jomah was very upset. She knew it wasn't Christos's fault, but she needed to strike out at someone. She said, "Alright, we'll make the next transfer. And I suggest that you make the transfer as well."

"I have no authority there, Mantah Jomah."

"I know that, but it may make an impression on Julianah."

"I'll do whatever I can," he said. *Dammit!* he thought.

The three of them went up the hill to the Church site and asked to join the next group in the *space/time exchange chamber*. Zaphi Hannas, who was coordinating the departing groups of Church members, was happy to grant their request. When they arrived on the way station, they learned that Julianah was no longer there and she had taken one of the first shuttles down with Cap' Walker to the ALPHA complex. Christos was contemplating his political future on Siren. It didn't look promising.

~

Chapter Fifty-nine

President Amalah received a phone call from the Soviet Embassy in Washington, DC. The Ambassador was requesting a meeting to discuss a change in the pay schedule for the upcoming launches from Star City. The president met with him the next morning in the Oval Office. "Alexi, it is nice to see you again."

"And you as well, Hussain."

"I trust your family is well?"

"Very well, thank you. My wife is presently at Disney World in Orlando. It is fortunate that the fallout from your recent . . . accident didn't reach that far. It would have been a terrible loss."

"Yes, as it is, we have only lost our space port, which is the only way we would have to launch heavy lift vehicles to service the space station and further space missions to the moon and Mars."

"You have no intention to going to Mars, Hussain. You canceled your shuttle program, which is a mere drop in the bucket compared to the cost of a Mars mission."

"You have become a bean counter, Alexi."

"Perhaps. I just marvel at numbers, Hussain. I always have. One of your journalists has recently pointed out that you have spent one-hundred-fifty-nine billion dollars fighting Afghanistan, a country that has no natural resources for you to acquire, and yet you have only spent nineteen billion dollars on your now defunct shuttle fleet. I hope you got your money's worth."

"Time will tell, Alexi. You may find the terrorists don't like Russian capitalism any more than they like American capitalism. We feel it is money well spent. I pray you do not learn the hard way that your frugality will be your undoing where your Pakistani border is concerned. But if history serves to tell us anything, you will find the attempt to find a warm-water port through Pakistan a fruitless endeavor. You have never even made it through Afghanistan."

"Thank you for your advice, Hussain. But that is not the reason we are here today. I regret to inform you that we will be unable to fulfill our earlier agreement with regard to the delivery of your personnel to the space station."

"Have you run out of rockets, Alexi?"

"I applaud your American sense of humor. No, we have plenty of rockets. Unfortunately, there has been a period of unrest in the surrounding countryside of Star City, and we had to employ considerable assets to contain the threat to the facility. These costs must be passed down to our customers as well."

"A deal's a deal, Alexi. We contracted for ten passages over the next three years at sixty-million apiece."

"Well, now it seems that figure will make us fall short of our operating expenses."

"Let's get to the bottom line, shall we Alexi? How much?"

"My government has authorized me to contract ten passages for eighty-million apiece over the next three years."

President Amalah didn't say anything at first. He rose from his chair and walked to the window overlooking the huge expanse of lawn where *Marine One* often landed. He folded his hands together in front of his chest, appearing to be in deep thought. Finally he said, "And this agreement that we compose today is written in stone as opposed to our earlier agreement?"

"It is what I have to offer you today, Hussain."

"I will take your proposition under advisement. I am thankful that the space station is well equipped for the next six months. Some decisions are kind enough to allow us some grace time to consider our options."

"As far as manning and outfitting the space station, Hussain, you are running out of options," said the Russian.

"There are always options, Alexi."

"Golf again on Sunday, my friend?"

"Sure, why not. You'll give me two shots a side?"

"Negotiation never sleeps."

Chapter Sixty

When all of the Earth sirens were relocated to the ALPHA complex from the way station, the first thing they did was set up a community of worship within the church. The building was situated right on Alligator Lake, and when weather permitted, they brought the service outside and set up chairs along the shore. They all faced the lake, and the members could see the clouds reflected in the surface that was like a sheet of glass showing a window to Heaven. Some of the Earth sirens had not chosen to join the church, but they were welcomed to attend the services as well. Shelly Simon assumed the position of Acting-Priestess until the members could elect a permanent one. Some of them favored Durbah Purness for the position; however, she seemed to be taking less of an interest in the church than she had in the past. She often traveled to John's Island, a wealthy beachside community near Vero Beach, to visit her mother and father. Edith and Walter Purness had been recently appointed to The President's Council of Space Exploration and frequently had to travel to Patrick Air Force Base to board *Marine One* for the trip to The White House. Alex and Durbah often would house-sit their ten-thousand-square-foot mansion on the Intra-Coastal Waterway when they were away. The First Church of Siren just chose to carry-on without her on those occasions.

Shelly held church services on Tuesdays, Thursdays and Sundays for the ALPHA community, but the general public was not encouraged to attend. They knew it would be a simple matter to absorb the general public into the fold with the use of their considerable powers, but they sought privacy for the time being to discuss their *Mission to Earth*. Shelly began the service, "Good morning."

"Good morning," answered the congregation.

"She continued, "We are gathered here in the eyes of God, but not *beneath* the eyes of God who drives our hearts in the *Mission to Earth*. Together we stand shoulder to shoulder with a daunting task set before us. We are charged with the mission to heal a world that we helped to set on a path of ill-will and destruction. That decision was not ours to make as we were merely tools directed by our sensors, who were in turn directed by the political machine on Siren. We were the instigators for thousands of years, but now our mission is to be the healers. We will bring love and true worship to this planet with every tool at our disposal. Can I hear an Amen?"

"Amen," shouted the congregation.

Shelly continued, "As High Priestess, I vow to uncover every weakness in the spiritual body of this planet and set forth a plan to recover the peace and goodwill that is afforded to us by love. As an apostle once wrote in a letter to the Romans, 'benevolence without love is empty. Worship itself without love is empty.' Love is the fuel of our God and will carry us through this seemingly endless mission to a fruitful completion. The fruit of our labors will be a world as the Creator intended it to be. It will become free of petty jealousness, greed, avarice and cruelty. This world will be allowed to heal from the harmful actions of its inhabitants and once again grow into a living, breathing mother to all of us."

"Amen," shouted the congregation.

"The people of this planet will learn to stand up and embrace each other's differences and recognize that we are all valuable in the eyes of our Creator. They will concede that there are many roads to Heaven and no one religious group holds the patent to eternal life."

"Amen," said the congregation.

"Now, before we begin our prayer, are there any special needs that you would like to bring to the attention of this body and our God?"

The sirens began to raise their hands and speak aloud any concerns they had for their friends and families. In time, those spoken concerns would extend to specific needs of the general public as well, and The Church of Siren would grow to be a force for goodness and love and healing for all the people of the world. As more and more people are healed, the powers of the sirens would expand to the humans as well. More people would exhibit the electrum in their eyes and the Godliness in their hearts. The world will heal itself with the help of the sirens. They would undo the wrongs they had done in the past. The world was finally on the right track again.

When all the concerns of the congregation were spoken aloud, Shelly said to them, "Our Creator hears our needs and

wants to deliver us from our adversities. It shall come to pass.
Let us pray."

Epilogue

John Poole held the hand of Julianah when they descended the steps leading down to the back lawn of Cap' Walker's farm. He said to her, "Welcome to your new home, Julianah."

"Thank you, John. You make me feel welcome. This was once your home, so it is very familiar to you, but I have never been here before."

"You will like it. There are many beautiful things to see. Tonight I will show you the moon."

Julianah squeezed the hand of John Poole, Jr., and cried.

~

When Councilman Christos returned to Siren, he summoned his son to his home. Christos Somah didn't bring Durbah along only because she had the good sense to urge him to proceed into their relationship gently. His father was matter-of-fact about his expectations: "You will begin training next week to become a pilot. We are building you a special ship that will be able to operate in orbit around Siren or Earth. It will be very maneuverable and will be able to land on the surface of either planet. You will have weapons at your disposal, but we hope that they will never have to be used. Your task is to go to Earth and find the girl Julianah and persuade her to come back to Siren.

The *Preculians* are building us a *space/time exchange chamber* especially designed to transfer the ship to Earth orbit. It is the least they can do since they interfered with the young girl in the first place. Do this for me Somah, and my political career may be salvaged. If you fail, I fail, and we all know what that means for our future."

"How many seats are in the cockpit of the ship, father?"

"Four."

"That's good because I will bring an Earth siren guide with me. Her name is Durbah, and she will be a great asset."

"Whatever it takes, Christos Somah. Whatever it takes."

~

When *Phodan* was finished with training Christos Somah for his journey to Earth with Durbah, he took Melanie with him to the way station and summoned Cap' to shuttle them down to the ALPHA community. The Earth sirens warmly welcomed them to live amongst them, but they chose to live with Cap' and Carla for the time being. For the next nine months, Carla and Melanie could share something wonderful that they never experienced before. *Phodan* and Melanie had conceived a child as well. When communications to *Preculis* were established, *Phodan* arranged to take a leave of absence from the Great Council, handing over his position of Grand Master to Councilshama *Oshiana*. She accepted the position with the understanding that it may be surrendered at any time of his return. Her first ruling as Grand Master was that *Phodan* should enjoy a peaceful existence in his new home and not be troubled by any scrutiny regarding the use of his artifacts. The two ships of plus-light ion drive systems are his property as is the robe-shield and the belt-shield. *Phodan* has always demonstrated a cool head and poses no threat whatsoever to the planet *Preculis*. *Lojahn* tried to object, but was quickly stifled, and his argument died on the table.

~

Roy Becker called a new meeting of *The Sons of Destiny*. They had a new agenda. The blacks and the Mexicans were an issue to be dealt with at another time. Right now, it seemed that the civilian population was at war with the U.S. Military. The first casualties were his son, Joey, and Billy Ray Shockley. Their names wouldn't be inscribed on any wall, but they would not be forgotten. They would not be left behind. *The Sons of Destiny* took care of their own, and now they had a target in place on which to exact their revenge. Alligator Lake was as good a place to start as any. May God help any who stand in their way.

The End

www.ingramcontent.com/pod-product-compliance
Lightning Source LLC
Chambersburg PA
CBHW070837260626
47170CB00007B/2403